BEYOND
THE
BLUE
BORDER

BEYOND THE BLUE BORDER

Dorit Linke

Translated by
Elisabeth Lauffer

CHARLESBRIDGE
TEEN

Copyright © 2014. First published as *Jenseits der blauen Grenze*, by Magellan GmbH & Co., Bamberg, Germany

English translation © 2021 Elisabeth Lauffer
First English edition published by Charlesbridge in 2021
Cover illustration copyright © 2021 by Levente Szabo
Map credit: United States Central Intelligence Agency. West Germany. 8-69. 1969. 1:1,625,000 scale, 57 x 41 cm. Library of Congress Geography and Map Division, Washington, D.C. https://www.loc.gov/item/gm70003216/.

Published by Charlesbridge
9 Galen Street, Watertown, MA 02472
(617) 926-0329 • www.charlesbridge.com

Library of Congress Cataloging-in-Publication Data
Names: Linke, Dorit, 1971– author. | Lauffer, Elisabeth, translator.
Title: Beyond the blue border / by Dorit Linke; [translated by Elisabeth Lauffer].
Other titles: Jenseits der blauen Grenze. English
Description: Watertown, MA: Charlesbridge, [2021] | Audience: Ages 12. Summary: Expelled from their secondary school in East Germany because of their rebellious attitudes, Hanna and Andreas plan to escape by swimming across the cold and choppy waters of the Baltic Sea in a harrowing twenty-five-hour journey to freedom in West Germany—Hanna is an accomplished distance swimmer, Andreas is not, and the danger of being caught, drowning, or dying of exhaustion is very real, but the two teenagers are desperate to escape their lives in the East.
Identifiers: LCCN 2020000985 (print) | LCCN 2020000986 (ebook) | ISBN 9781623541774 (hardcover) | ISBN 9781632899699 (ebook)
Subjects: LCSH: Teenagers—Germany (East)—Juvenile fiction. | Long distance swimming—Juvenile fiction. | Escapes—Juvenile fiction. | Germany (East)—History—Juvenile fiction. | Germany (East)—Juvenile fiction. | Baltic Sea—Juvenile fiction. | CYAC: Long distance swimming—Fiction. | Swimming—Fiction. | Escapes—Fiction. | Germany (East)—History—20th century—Fiction. | Baltic Sea—Fiction. | LCGFT: Historical fiction.
Classification: LCC PZ7.1.L562 Be 2021 (print) | LCC PZ7.1.L562 (ebook) DDC 833.92 [Fic]—dc23
LC record available at https://lccn.loc.gov/2020000985
LC ebook record available at https://lccn.loc.gov/2020000986
Printed in the United States of America
(hc) 10 9 8 7 6 5 4 3 2 1

Display type set in Blauth by Sofia Mohr
Text type set in Adobe Caslon by Adobe Systems Incorporated
Printed by Berryville Graphics in Berryville, Virginia, USA
Production supervision by Jennifer Most Delaney
Designed by Diane M. Earley

The German Divide

International boundary
State (Land) boundary
National capital
Köln State (Land) capital
Railroad
Autobahn
Other road
Airfield
Principal port
Secondary port

Populated places
Over 1,000,000
350,000 to 1,000,000
20,000 to 100,000
Under 20,000

Scale 1:4,625,000

The next time we see Saxony Jensie, it'll be on Kurfürstendamm, and he'll still have that stupid preppy haircut. And his BMW will be old and junky, but he won't care. Neither will we. We'll all be insanely happy and so incredibly proud of one another.

Our bags are buried under a wild rosebush. Anyone finds them and we're screwed. I strapped the canteen to my body with Mom's belt, the one with the gold buckle. It's so heinous, she'll never miss it.

Later on, at just the right moment, the plan is to take off and start crawling, like we practiced in Young Pioneer drills.

It's just that we can't wind up in the beam of the searchlights, which roam for kilometers across the beach. The spot we found is good, far away from the border watchtower.

There's NVA—National People's Army—presence all around us. Right behind us is a sign:

Restricted Area. No Trespassing.

Grandpa told me to be on the lookout for patrols. They'll walk past us; plus, there will be patrol cars driving around, headlights blazing. He also told me that the searchlights have to be turned off every hour to cool. That's the moment we'll use to run down to the Baltic Sea.

There's a boulder by the water we can hide behind. We'll get down there in no time. The beach here isn't as wide as the one in Warnemünde. Later, once we're in the Baltic, we'll just dive underwater whenever the searchlights come near.

I put a note for Mom under the bedspread. I don't want her to worry—which she will anyway. She'll never suspect I'm in Kühlungsborn but will be waiting for me at the Neptune Indoor Pool. I almost gave myself away yesterday, because I shooshed her during the weather report. I'm not usually interested in it.

Over thirty kilometers to Fehmarn. That's really far to swim.

If the water current cooperates, we'll make it there in twenty-five hours. There's an offshore wind now. Hopefully it stays that way. Once it gets dark, we'll start swimming, so we'll already be a good distance from shore by daybreak when the boats start searching for refugees. If a patrol comes along, we'll dive and breathe through our snorkels, which I lengthened with plastic hoses in the basement yesterday. When our neighbor Frau Lewandowski saw me messing around with them, she asked why. I told her I wanted to observe the carp in Lake Dobbertiner.

Water temp's around sixty-five, so that's good. It will be colder farther out. This is going to be hard. It's impossible even to train enough. But we'll make it. It's finally happening! I'm agitated and calm at the same time, focused on our plan.

Andreas looks pale. I'm glad he's here—I couldn't do it without him. He just gives me a smile.

He's scared. I am too, but we're not allowed to think about it.

Andreas is holding a copy of "The Black Felucca." It's for Saxony Jensie, wrapped to be watertight. The only issue of *Mosaik* missing from his collection, released in November of 1982. He can't get it in the West, so we have to bring it for him. We promised.

Pirates on the cover, fishing boats, surging waves, fire beacons, and men in turbans. Andreas studies the image, which is blue as the twilight surrounding us. I'm sure he wants to page through it, but he can't because of the shrink-wrap.

I put a note inside the comic book with my parents' phone number. In case anything happens and someone finds it, they'll know where to call.

What would Saxony Jensie say if he could see us here in the dunes, waiting, our eyes trained on the Baltic? All this excitement gives me a warm feeling in my belly! It's nice. I'm glad we're leaving. I feel light again for the first time in months, almost carefree. I close my eyes and breathe in deeply. The air smells of salt water and algae.

I open my eyes again. Rose hips dangle from the bush, between me and the glassy water, and there's beach grass growing a few meters off.

Saxony Jensie would try to stop us because he's a wuss. I smile. During math once, years ago, I sprinkled wild rose seeds into his collar and rubbed them around. He freaked out, scratching his skin so bad that Frau Bauermeister kicked him out of class.

Andreas unzips his wet suit and slides the issue of *Mosaik* in with his documents: ID card, birth certificate, tenth-grade diploma. I stuffed my packet of documentation in between my wet suit and my bathing suit. We'll need to prove who we are in the West, after all.

Andreas must have felt me watching. He unzips and pulls out "The Black Felucca."

"You take it," he says quietly. "You're the better swimmer."

That's true. The thought terrifies me, and I can't lift my hand.

"Come on," he insists.

Our fingers touch as I take the comic. I swallow hard. I can't look at him, and I squint at the water instead.

"We're going to make it," I say.

We have to keep telling ourselves that; it's really important. It will be hard. But we have to believe. Otherwise we'll never last.

We'll start swimming at nine, as soon as the moon sets. You can hardly see it—it might as well still be new.

4

The thin crescent is visible through the treetops. It gives off very little light, but still, it's better to wait till it's gone down. Says Grandpa.

A gentle breeze from the southeast . . . perfect.

It was a nice day—hot, the air heavy. We got here early. We didn't want to look suspicious by arriving at dusk. After swimming, we got soft serve on the boardwalk, surrounded by vacationing FDGB organization members. I felt like a fraud. To everyone else it was a regular old day at the beach, but not to us. We stared out at the blue water, knowing what would happen tonight. At one point, though, I completely forgot about it as I ate my ice cream and watched a kid play with his beach ball, as I soaked in the sun and breathed in the smell of summer. For a moment, I was happy. Then I remembered again and got butterflies in my stomach, like when you ride a carousel.

We tried to get some sleep on the beach in the afternoon, because we wouldn't exactly get around to it tonight. It didn't work, though—we were way too jumpy. I only dozed off for a second, while Andreas poked around in the dunes beside me and couldn't settle down.

At the restaurant later, we ordered pasta with tomato sauce as a solid fuel base. Athletes always eat pasta. We drank a lot too because we can't take much water with us.

Andreas taps my arm.

Two lights, down on the beach. They're coming!

I hunker down deeper under the bush, Andreas close beside me. I can tell he's holding his breath, and I freeze too, ducking my head, barely daring to peer where the men's voices are approaching. They're border guards who constantly comb the beach looking for anything suspicious. If they have a dog, they'll find us, and this whole thing will be over before it starts.

The men talk quietly, and I can't hear what they're saying. An unsteady, flickering light flits through the branches in our direction. They're inspecting the brush along the beach with flashlights. Andreas presses up against me. The light beam dances before our eyes, nearly grazes us.

Then it goes out again. The men don't move. No dog, luckily.

I hear one of them clear his throat. Why aren't they moving? My heart is beating so hard, I'm worried they might hear it. Like in the Edgar Allan Poe story.

There's a glimmer of light, part of a face in the weak glow, then a second flare. Cigarettes. The smell of smoke, but it's faint. The two patrol guards slowly continue down the beach.

"Oh man," Andreas whispers next to me. "That was close."

The wind is chilly, and I'm already cold. What'll it be like in the water? We covered ourselves in Vaseline earlier and went through more than ten tubes. It was Ulrich's tip, to slather on as much as possible. The body loses heat four times faster in water than in open air. We have to swim fast, in order to keep warm. We must maintain the balance between heat production and heat loss, our physics teacher, Herr Kowalski, would say.

I bought the Vaseline at the drugstore, never more than two at a time, so as not to attract attention. The last time I went, though, the sales lady gave me such a weird look that I got scared. I didn't go back again.

The Vaseline will trap the heat in our bodies. You can't layer much under a wet suit, because it's so tight. I put on my swimsuit, a cropped shirt, and nylons. They've already got runs in them, so Mom won't be mad that I took them from her dresser.

What would Ulrich say if he could see me now? I hope he didn't rat on us.

The empty Vaseline tubes are now buried with our bags and clothes. At some point, someone will find them and sound the alarm, but not tonight. And by this time tomorrow, we might already be on Fehmarn.

The searchlights continue to move past us and bathe the shoreline in bright light. Everything goes dark in between passes, the moon now nowhere in sight.

Andreas rustles beside me. He's checking one last time that everything is well stowed. He brought along a bag that he straps to his body. Four Block chocolate bars—Saxony Jensie would definitely be jealous. He'd be less interested in the little canister of painkillers, not to mention the waterproof adhesive tape. And he wouldn't have the faintest clue what the nylon string was for.

"Wrap the bag tighter around the chocolate and tape," I say quietly. We can't let any salt water get in, or everything will be destroyed.

7

"Yeah, of course," Andreas murmurs as he zips up the bag. He touches the collar and black hood of his wet suit, under which his blond curls have disappeared. He puts on the weight belt. His goggles hang around his neck, and he holds his snorkel and flippers in one hand. He looks creepy—dark and determined, like in a James Bond movie.

Except for my dark-blue swim cap, which I put on now, I don't look much different. My wet suit doesn't have a hood, which is why I need the cap. It reduces water resistance and protects against the cold. I borrowed the suit from Frank. He lent me his compass too, which I've tied to my left wrist.

"Make sure your ears are completely covered," I say softly.

Andreas knows that, but it doesn't hurt to say again. Getting water in your ears can have serious consequences. "And cover your forehead down to your goggles. It's very sensitive to cold."

I slip on a pair of black gloves, to make sure my hands are dark and unnoticeable while I'm swimming. Then I grab my snorkel and flippers. We'll wait till we're in the water to put them on, over our socks. Ulrich says that socks help against chafing. And that black gloves will prevent my hands from being seen in the water.

The glaring searchlight wanders across the beach, and we wait for them to finally turn it off.

"Let's hope your grandpa was right," Andreas whispers. With the swim cap on, I can barely hear what he's saying.

Grandpa helped me find this spot. He thought nothing of it when I asked where he would launch an escape through the Baltic if he still could. Topics like that are totally normal to him. He loved the question and talked about finding a sand beach that wasn't too wide or too narrow, about thick brush along the coast, and about boulders near the water. Then we all took the bus to Kühlungsborn and walked the beach, Grandpa wandering among vacationers, waving his cane about and yelling, "This exact spot! And don't even think about going out to the point farther west. It's crawling with NVA!"

What would Grandpa say if he were here now? Would he encourage me? Would he have any other tips?

I watch the retreating light and in a flash of memory see Grandpa tramping around down there on the beach with his cane. That was less than six weeks ago.

Suddenly everything goes black, the spotlight extinguished. The time has come. Now's our chance.

"Grandpa was right," I say quietly.

Andreas clears his throat. "How'd he know?"

From comrade Johnson, officer in the Coastal Border Brigade. Grandpa goes candlepin bowling with him once a month, where he gets Johnson drunk on Goldbrand cut brandy and pumps him for details on seaside border security. In other words, we've got firsthand information, provided that Grandpa didn't get carried away and invent some of his own facts. Which he probably did since, unfortunately, he gets carried away with lots of things.

"Hanna." Andreas touches my forearm.

He wants to go.

I crouch in the sand, ready to lunge, Andreas right beside me.

"Remember not to crawl with your arms," I say. "Gentle flutter kick and breaststroke."

We cannot attract attention to ourselves, which also means making as little noise as possible swimming near the border.

Hopefully Andreas manages okay with the extra buoyancy. It's his first time swimming in a wet suit; his West German relatives couldn't smuggle it over the border till two weeks ago, along with the weight belt.

I got my weight belt from Ulrich.

A blackbird sings up in the trees. Its call pierces the darkness and accompanies the rustle of leaves. At times, the melody cracks and swells, then quiets again. The bird will sing here again tomorrow.

I look at the water, see the velvety blackness of rippling waves, and hear the quiet surf.

"Now," whispers Andreas.

I sprint through the sand in my socks. At the top of the dunes, I sink up to my ankles and almost fall. Andreas is right behind and accidentally bumps into me. He gets snagged on something too and has to push it off. As I run, sand flies into my eyes.

We finally reach the boulder and hide behind it. We hold still, listening to the night, breathing heavily. I feel the edge of a shell under my knee and smell seaweed. The wind is stronger down here, and the sounds have changed too. A rushing sound surrounds us, although there are barely any waves.

I imagine I can still hear the blackbird singing.

My heart is pounding like crazy, although I haven't swum an inch.

We could still turn back. We still haven't been spotted.

"Let's go."

We wade through the water. It's warmer than the air, which cooled down a lot after sunset. We walk slightly hunched. Despite the tension, I can't help but laugh. If they shine a light out here, they'll see us, whether we're hunched or not. Luckily, everything stays dark.

When the water reaches my hips, I stop wading. Andreas stops too. I take off my gloves, use my teeth to hold them, and pull on the flippers. It's not easy—I can't get them on over my heels. It probably would've been better to do this on land, but they would have made it harder to wade. I fall backward into the water to help me get at my feet. Cold water immediately rushes into my wet suit, filling the spaces between my clothes and the rubberized fabric. It's really uncomfortable. But the water will soon warm up to body temperature and then serve as insulation.

I finally manage to get the flippers on and stand back up. Even through the rubber, I can feel how rippled the seabed is from the current.

I put on my swim goggles and thread the end of the snorkel under the goggle strap, to hold it in place.

Andreas takes out the nylon string and hands it to me. I tie the string around his left wrist and pull the knot tight. The other end goes around my right wrist. This way, we won't lose each other in the water and we can use the string to send signals.

I'm still holding the gloves with my teeth. The wool makes my lips itch. I put them on, my hands trembling with excitement.

It's almost time.

I position the snorkel mouthpiece between my teeth, and it presses into my gums, but that's normal and the sensation will pass in a while—at least, it always did in training. That said, the longest I ever swam with the snorkel was eight hours.

"I'm ready," Andreas whispers.

I adjust the canteen. Mom's belt holds it in place, tight against my belly. Hopefully it won't get in the way too much while I'm swimming. I couldn't wear it to practice, either at the pool or in the Baltic. If someone had seen me with it, I'd have been arrested on the spot.

I look back toward land.

In what will be the last time for a long time, I have solid ground beneath my feet.

I kick off the seabed and start swimming. After a few meters, cold salt water finds its way into my goggles. I swear under my breath. These things never hold a seal.

I have to fix them, and so I search for the ground below. I can just barely touch the sand with the tips of my flippers, which gives me a little support.

"My bag is loose," Andreas mutters. He has to sort himself out after these first few strokes too.

I pull off the goggles and dump out the water, then press my fingers against the lenses to force out the air and create a vacuum. It hurts my eyes a little, but at least it means no more salt water will get in. That would do more damage.

I slowly move my legs, the flippers tight on my feet, then increase my kick amplitude, but not too much so I don't break through the surface of the water. The canteen slows my movement a little, but it's not too bad.

I can hear the gentle waves, overlaid by the sound of my breath. Since I'm using a snorkel, everything seems louder than usual.

I start swimming the breaststroke with my arms, which isn't easy when you're doing the crawl with your legs. I gradually find my pace and feel the water resistance with my hands. Because of its higher salt content, seawater is much denser than the pool water.

The waterline keeps appearing right before my eyes. It's the border between air and water. I dip under the line with every stroke, breathe out, let the water carry me forward, then come back up to the surface.

Andreas's flippers slap the water. He notices and corrects his form. We can't make any loud noise out here.

I breathe through the snorkel so I can keep my head underwater and don't need to turn it. Every last move requires energy.

After only a few meters, I sense something I've known for a long time. Everything out here is completely different than in the pool. There's no Ulrich, no one calling out instructions. We're on our own.

All I hear is the gurgle of waves that break on my body. Bubbles rise from the dark depths.

We quietly swim into the Baltic Sea, headed north.

"Just how many records you trying to break?"

Ulrich winked at me from the side of the pool. He wore his orange tracksuit and red plastic slides.

I pried the goggles off my head. "That's enough for today."

"I bet. Three hours. Did you count your laps?"

"A hundred seventy-nine."

Ulrich screwed up his eyes. "One seventy-nine times fifty meters equals 8,950 meters. Holy smokes! You. Out. Shower."

I pulled myself out of the cold water. My neck and right shoulder hurt. It cracked weird when I moved them.

"Frank and I are going to play a round of rummy at Konsum-Klause. Care to join?"

That was the local pub. I nodded and grabbed my

towel. As always, there was a strong draft in the hallway to the showers. I let the hot water stream over me for several minutes, then dried off quickly and got dressed. I hurried out.

A few other athletes stood chatting outside the public pool building.

"See ya!" I shouted to them, then took a right and walked the short distance to the pub.

Ulrich and Frank sat at one of the tables, cards out already.

Ulrich turned toward the bar. "Coupla colas for the kiddos here, and a pils for me," he called to the bartender. Then he started dealing, before I'd even sat down.

The air was stuffy, thick with cigarette smoke. Three men sat in one corner, probably playing skat, and there was a woman Mom's age at the bar, drinking a large glass of beer. She had big teased hair and wore heavy makeup. She was checking Ulrich out, but he didn't notice.

Playing faintly in the background was "The Power of Love," by Jennifer Rush.

"You didn't dry your hair," Ulrich chided me.

"But it's warm in here."

He shook his head. "You'll all catch your death. The same goes for you, Frank!" Frank hadn't blow-dried his hair either and shrank down in his seat to hide behind his cards.

My hand looked good. King of clubs, jack of clubs, ten of clubs.

"How come you're training so much anyway?" Frank

15

peered out from behind the cards. He was a little walleyed and gazed slightly past me.

"I dunno."

"Isn't it boring to just swim back and forth the whole time, for no reason?"

I needed the queen of clubs in order to show my cards. I discarded a seven of hearts.

"I just think about something else."

The bartender brought us our drinks. He wore an ASV jacket and didn't say a word.

Ulrich winked at me over the top of his cards. "What about?"

Frank discarded. Queen of clubs. I lunged across the table, but Ulrich was faster and grinned wickedly as he took the card.

"About a poem," I said distractedly. "Or a book."

"Mm-hmm." Frank scratched his head thoughtfully, tousling his ash-blond hair.

Ulrich rearranged his cards. "Probably better than thinking about can openers, huh?"

Frank looked awkwardly at the table. It was an uncomfortable topic for him because he'd been allowed to take the *Abitur*, unlike me.

I leaned back and lowered my voice ceremoniously, like the announcer at May Day demonstrations. "Each and every day, I achieve my quota. Should I remain this diligent, I may start an apprenticeship in industrial design. Perhaps two years from now."

Frank laid all of his cards on the table at once. "Gin!"

We stared at his hand.

Frank chugged his entire cola, got up, and went to the bathroom.

"Cheater!" Ulrich called after him. The bartender set down another beer for the lady at the bar. Foam spilled over the edge of the glass.

Ulrich shuffled the cards again and didn't look up. "You know, Hanna, you keep swimming like that, you really would make it to Gedser."

I picked up each card as he tossed it to me, one by one. "It'd be worth a shot."

Ulrich lifted his beer glass and took a sip. His eye twitched strangely. "And one shot is all you'd get," he said quietly.

Frank came back from the bathroom and sat down. "I just thought of something. If you ever want to do long-distance training in the Warnow River, instead of laps, you can use my wet suit. I'll lend it to you."

Ulrich paused in sorting the cards and looked at me.

"Yeah." I glanced back and forth between them. "I'd love to swim up and down the Warnow sometime."

"Up and down the Warnow," Ulrich repeated.

"I'll just bring it on Friday," Frank decided, picking up his cards.

He won that round too. None of us felt like playing after that, and we left the pub.

It was pouring out. Frank bolted toward the bus that

had just rounded the corner. I was about to make a run for it too, but Ulrich grabbed my arm.

"Wait, I'll drive you home."

"Are you kidding? That's way out of your way!"

But he dragged me to his ancient Škoda, which was practically falling apart. I bumped my head as I got in, I was so exhausted from practice. It smelled of gasoline inside.

We drove slowly through the rain. The wipers chattered across the windshield, and red rear lights shimmered through the wet glass.

Friedrich Engels Strasse was deserted and dark because, as usual, several streetlights had gone out. Ulrich stopped at our house and switched off the engine. The silence was almost spooky.

"How's your dad doing?"

I looked at him in amazement. No one usually asked. "Good. He's been reading his books himself lately."

I reached for the door handle. Ulrich turned to me. "Cover yourself in Vaseline. Slather on as much as you can. Because of the cold. And wear socks inside your flippers; otherwise you'll tear up your feet."

He sat forward and fumbled with the rearview mirror. "And take chocolate, for an energy boost."

"Okay." I opened the door and climbed out.

"Wait!" Ulrich leaned over the passenger seat. Cold rain pelted my back as I bent toward him.

"Wear black gloves."

I knew what he meant by that and nodded.

He studied me for a long time, which made me a little uncomfortable.

"Hanna, why?"

I didn't know what to say. How could I explain it? There was just no way I could let Andreas swim by himself.

"Is it really that bad?"

I took a deep breath, looked him in the eyes, and nodded. It was the best I could do.

Ulrich grabbed the handle and slammed the door shut. The engine didn't turn till the third try. The Škoda rattled so loudly that our neighbor Frau Lewandowski pulled back the blinds and peered warily out the window.

And with that, I had a wet suit.

I had to let Andreas know. The tips from Ulrich were huge for us too. I approached the front door, stopped again to watch Ulrich go.

I was suddenly scared he would inform on me. Not out of ill will but because he was worried.

Turns out a thought I just had was wrong—we do end up on solid ground again. I was swimming along and totally freaked out when my knees bumped into it. I instantly pictured an animal—the great white shark, which is obviously ridiculous. You start imagining some pretty crazy stuff when you're swimming at night through black water and can't see a thing.

"Did we somehow wind up back on the beach?" Andreas asks in the darkness.

"No, it's just a sandbar."

I turn onto my back, sit down, and look at the sky. It's nice, letting go for a second, feeling the ground, although we haven't been in the water long and don't need the rest. I try to make out the horizon, but it's still too dark. The sea glistens in the starlight.

Andreas comes over, lies down beside me, and whispers, "A sandbar halfway would be a lot more useful."

I look at the sky, hear the splash of the waves. Strange situation. We're venturing into the unknown, the way sailors used to. No map, destination unknown, and with only the stars to help. Although we at least have a compass and a destination—the West. I'm not even scared right now. It's all so clear. . . .

"Easy as ever to spot," Andreas says precociously. "The Big Dipper. See the two outer stars that form the bowl? Extend the line connecting them by five."

Might as well be in geography class. I arrive at another very bright star.

"The North Star," Andreas says, pleased. "That's the direction we need to go in."

I nod in the dark. "Then let's go."

One last time, I touch the seabed with my flippers.

This time it's for real.

We start swimming and get tangled in the string after just a few meters. We have to find the same pace. We start again, slower this time and more deliberate.

One stroke, then another. I'm careful to stay next to Andreas as I plunge underwater and swim through the eerie darkness. I have trouble keeping my balance—I don't have any focal points, and I have to concentrate on pulling evenly with both my right arm and my left. Sometimes we collide, slam an elbow into each other's ribs. Without the string, we'd lose each other at sea. If it stretches tight between us for too long, it means we're drifting apart, or if it jerks a few times, then I know Andreas is pulling on it because he needs help.

I keep getting water in my snorkel. It's annoying. I inhale and choke on it, the salt water burning my throat. I blow it out with bursts of air that waste energy. Using a snorkel in the pool is easier because the water is calmer.

Suddenly there's light.

Andreas tugs on the string. I look around.

The spotlight shines over the Baltic Sea again from the border watchtower in Kühlungsborn. They're looking for refugees. For us.

The light glides toward us. We've got to get the timing right, cannot get caught in the beam.

Now.

We dive and stay underwater for several seconds.

When we resurface, the beam is far away.

But it will return.

I flip onto my back, keep swimming, and train my eye on the beam. It's simple, really. I can see it and avoid it. They can't catch us this way.

The light beam comes back, and I jerk the string three times.

We dive down again.

Andreas starts coughing afterward. He probably got water in his snorkel. Diving is new to him, something he didn't practice. He still has issues with swim technique—his kick is irregular, which I can tell from his flippers splashing. He has to get used to the wet suit and adjust his movements to counteract the increased buoyancy so that he doesn't roll onto his back the whole time. I outlined the theory for him in the dunes, and it's up to him to apply the knowledge.

He's certainly got time to practice now.

I glide through the water on my back, moving the flippers evenly. They're tight and will really start to hurt at some point.

The beam is now even farther away. I turn back onto my stomach. The water beneath me is black, a dark, endless universe. Little green dots sometimes light up before me—phosphorescent microorganisms—and I hear bubbles float up from the depths and pop at the surface.

Now we're free to swim wherever we want—we're totally free.

We don't need to go back anymore, don't need to stay in the lane, don't need to flip turn at the concrete wall, and don't need to follow the black line at the bottom of the pool. The air is fresh and doesn't smell of chlorine.

The string tightens. Andreas can't keep up. I wait, gazing toward the dark strip of land behind us. Just four weeks ago, I was swimming parallel to the coast, but today I'm headed out into the Baltic.

I've never been this far north.

Suddenly, light. Square in the face. I didn't see it coming, hastily dive down, yank on the string. I try to plow into the water but can't, because the wet suit keeps pulling me back up.

I choke, cough, rip the mouthpiece out of my mouth. Have to surface, can't breathe.

The light blinds me as badly as if someone were holding a flashlight in my face.

I was just looking at the coast, though, and didn't see anything.

I turn my back to the beam, cough out the water in my lungs, and spot Andreas's silhouette amid the blazing light.

"What is that?" I yell. I swallow water as I speak and start coughing again.

"It's not coming from land," Andreas calls out beside me. "It's coming from the water."

The waves toss his body against mine, and he tries to back off, then drifts away. The string tears at my wrist.

It's probably light from a coastal defense boat. The beam doesn't move on but remains trained on us.

"Shit," Andreas yells. "They see us!"

23

"Dive," I roar. "Back south!"

The snorkel mouthpiece hangs down by my voice box, and I can't get it in my mouth. Luckily, the snorkel is attached to the strap of my goggles.

I go under. Which direction? I can't see anything. What's south, what's up, what's down? My flippers thrash through nothingness—I'm still stuck at the surface, can't get down deep enough.

Andreas kicks back up, the string tightens, and I have to follow and break through the surface of the water.

I emerge smack in the middle of the beam. Burning light in my eyes.

"Keep going," Andreas bellows and flails his arms about in the water. He's trying to dive straight back down.

I grab his shoulder. "Wait! We have to dive slowly, swim underwater for a minute, and try to keep on course. Then we'll come back up. If the light is still there, we'll do it again. Till it's gone!"

I can't see his reaction, as a million little lights dance before my eyes.

"They can't keep track of us out on the open water forever. Our chances are better than theirs."

Andreas lowers his head. Was that a nod?

"All right, let's go."

We dive down and move quietly and intently through the water. This time, we're deep enough.

When we surface, the beam is several meters away, swooping across the sea.

But it comes dangerously close again.

"Come on, a little farther!"

We both tear off in the direction we think is right.

When we come back up, the light is far away.

"We got lucky," Andreas says. He lifts his goggles and water pours out.

I exhale with relief. "Listen. You keep swimming normally, and I'm going to turn on my back and watch out for the light. We'll switch every ten minutes. Keep your head underwater and breathe through the snorkel. We're going to give them as little a target as possible."

"Sounds good." He doesn't move, just treads water and looks back at the coast. "But they did see us, didn't they?"

"I think so."

"So what are they doing now?"

I cough to conceal my fear. "Nothing. We're a needle in a haystack. Come on, let's go."

We start swimming. In the distance the searchlight swings across the Baltic, still looking for us, but the danger has passed.

Darkness surrounds us.

After a while, I can no longer see the light and roll back onto my front to swim faster.

Thanks to the phosphorescent microorganisms, I can read the compass and point us north.

Andreas has found his pace and swims quickly and evenly. One, two, one, two. I'm sure he's counting his strokes.

If we maintain our speed and no one gets in our way, eventually we'll reach international waters. But it'll be a while.

Right now we're here.

They'll be searching for us, because they saw us. The light wouldn't have hovered there for so long otherwise. That was no coincidence.

Damn it. At this very moment, they're probably sounding the alarm on the coast; maybe even comrade Johnson from the Coastal Border Brigade is making the call. Grandpa's drinking buddy. They'll search the beach with dogs and find our clothes.

And then they'll have two important coordinates: our starting point and our position in the Baltic. The direction we're swimming should be pretty obvious. To find us, all they have to do is extend the line, maybe even taking the water current into account, something they know more about than we do.

I'm really scared. Does Andreas realize that? I'd rather not say anything, just let him focus on swimming.

There's not much we can do.

Diving under, that's it. As long as it's nighttime, we've got a chance, because they can't see anything. If they're smart, they won't search for us till dawn.

Unfortunately, they are smart.

My flippers are chafing. Don't think about it—focus on something else. But what? There's nothing out here.

Just water and night.

Fortunately, Saxony Jensie isn't involved in this whole ordeal. He couldn't swim an inch before starting to howl with fear, like on his first day at school. He was the new kid, which really sucked for him. New kids never have it easy, much less when they're from a backwater place like Saxony.

He drove us insane with his crying. We all thought he was a wuss, but he's not. He just has weird reflexes. Some people scratch their head when they're upset. Saxony Jensie cries.

"Now really, there's no reason to cry!"

Our heavy homeroom teacher, Frau Thiel, laid a hand on the kid's shoulder. The boy bowed forward under the weight. "We've got a new student at Friedrich Engels Secondary School. Jens Blum. I've already told you about him."

"What a crybaby!" Andreas shouted. "And what's with those stupid freckles?"

Frau Thiel shook her blond perm. "Now please remind us of your full name and where you're from."

"Jens Blum from Dresden," he whispered in a thick Saxon accent. It sounded like "Jens Pluum from Dräsdn."

"What was that?" Christian squawked from the corner.

"Jens Pluum, Dräsdn," he screamed.

"A Saxon. Oh no!"

Everyone in class groaned.

"Quiet, all of you," Frau Thiel snapped.

She pointed at me. "Sit next to Hanna. She'll help you with your homework."

That was the last thing I wanted to do.

"Hey, Saxon, say something about Angola!" We couldn't wait to hear the kid's accent make mincemeat of the pronunciation.

Enormous Boxer-brand jeans slid down the new kid's skinny butt. He had to hold on to the waistband as he shuffled toward me.

"I could drink myself to death *on cola*," Andreas screamed, and everyone laughed because that's how Jens would have pronounced Angola.

Jens slid into the seat next to me and pulled his Russian textbook from his brown schoolbag, which was emblazoned with an enormous Donald Duck sticker.

"I'm not a very good student," he whispered. "Especially not in Russian. You definitely have to help me there!"

His Saxon dialect was atrocious. And his red T-shirt was way too big for him.

Annoyingly, we also had the same way home. Jens wore a jacket covered in brown fringe that made him look like a scruffy little bear.

"Here's the corner store where Andreas and I always buy candy, and over there is Novak's Bakery, the dermatology clinic, Timm's Butcher Shop, and Gerloff's Bakery."

We crossed the street to Gerloff's and bought a jelly

doughnut. Jens took a bite. Jelly ran down his chin, making him look like a vampire. With his mouth full, he said, "You can just call me Jensie!"

The saleslady stared at him.

I was so embarrassed to be walking around with a Saxon. Still, I took him to visit Grandpa.

"What a coincidence!" Jens exclaimed happily as we climbed the rotted staircase. "I live on this street too!"

"His apartment is probably a total pigsty," I warned.

I knocked on the door. Three short, three long, three short. Our code.

"Save our souls!" Jensie looked up at me triumphantly. He wasn't so dumb after all, even if he was almost a foot shorter than me. I knocked a second time because, as usual, Grandpa hadn't heard.

"Three short, three long, three short," Jensie recited as I knocked. "SOS!"

He got on my nerves.

There was a creak behind the door. Grandpa opened it a crack and peered through. His face was ashen.

"Open up, it's me."

"Who?"

"Me. Not the Gestapo."

"And who's that creature next to you?"

"Jensie from Dresden. He sits next to me at school now."

Grandpa let us in. He wore his brown wool cardigan with the leather patches at the elbows, which Mom replaced every year. He hadn't combed his white hair.

He studied Jensie as he took off his fake bear fur.

"Is that all the rage at the clothing *Kombinat* these days?"

"You know it," Jensie said meekly.

Grandpa went into the living room. There were torn-up newspapers all over the place. It was very cold in the apartment, and as always, it smelled like wet glue.

"*Ostsee–Zeitung, Neues Deutschland, Norddeutsche Neueste Nachrichten,*" Jensie read the names of the papers out loud.

"Grandpa Franz clips and collects the articles, then compares them. Why are you sitting around in the cold again? Why don't you make a fire?"

Grandpa turned around. "If everyone squanders coal, then it won't take the GDR ten years to go broke—it'll get there in three."

Jensie squeaked.

Grandpa gave him a stern look. "What's the matter with you?"

"You sound like my dad."

"*And* he's a Saxon," Grandpa crowed.

I rolled my eyes. "I told you, he's from Dresden!"

Grandpa clapped his hands. "Say something about Angola!"

Jensie shook his head. "No!"

"Turn on the TV. Someone already told that joke at school."

Grandpa erratically punched a few buttons. We flopped

down on the couch and wrapped ourselves up in a wool blanket. The springs poked out of the cushions in a few spots, but it was still really cozy. I liked visiting Grandpa because he usually said funny stuff and fell asleep at some point. Then I could watch TV in peace without anyone bugging me.

"*There's the Music*," Grandpa announced enthusiastically. It was a musical variety show and one of his favorites.

We opened our math books.

"I hate math," Jensie stated.

"We do not learn for school but for life," Grandpa cried out, staring at the television.

"Yeah, yeah," Jensie whispered. "Nice saying."

I elbowed him in the side and read the word problem aloud. "On May Day, rows of 12 are formed for the parade. How many rows do the workers from one factory form if 48 of the factory's 1,176 workers cannot participate?"

"You can count me out too," Grandpa said. "I'm not going. So make it forty-nine."

"Ninety-four rows of workers," I said. "Even if Grandpa doesn't go."

Jensie giggled.

"Don't you have swim practice?" Grandpa asked. He was on the verge of nodding off.

"Nope, never on Wednesdays."

"We usually have Young Pioneer sessions on Wednesdays," Jensie bragged. "So, how often do you practice?"

"Four times a week. I might even get into the sports academy."

His eyes widened. "Wow! I bet you'll win gold at the Olympics!"

Grandpa snored in his armchair. His cuckoo clock went off, but not even that woke him.

"Let's get out of here," I said.

It was snowing out.

We bumped into Andreas on Paul Strasse. His blond hair was covered in snowflakes. "Man, I've been looking all over for you!" He pulled me aside. "Should we take the Saxon to the Stasi high-rise?"

Jensie stopped in his tracks. "Why?"

Andreas pointed out the white twenty-four-story building, which could be seen from anywhere.

"That's where the State Security Service for all of Rostock lives!"

"I doubt that." Jensie sneered. "Wouldn't be much of a secret then."

Andreas boxed him in the back. "We're going there right now and spitting off the roof!"

We ran down Augusten Strasse and took a right before Novak's Bakery, into the narrow alley that led to the high-rise.

But the entrance was locked.

"They obviously don't let just anyone in," Andreas said. "Much less a Saxon."

He rang the doorbell to the Müller family's apartment.

Sabine Müller was the teacher's pet in our class. "Hello?"

"It's Andreas," he brayed into the intercom. "Can you help me in math? I don't know how many workers are attending May Day celebrations."

Nothing happened at first, then she buzzed us in. We plowed through the doorway.

"Man, is she stupid."

We got into the elevator, and Andreas punched the button for the twenty-third floor. It smelled like stale cigarette smoke. Jensie watched the flashing lights. "Why not take it all the way up to twenty-four?"

"'Cause they keep that door locked so no one goes out and jumps. Which is kinda dumb, since you can go outside on any other floor."

Jensie grinned stupidly. "Seems the twenty-third floor would do the trick too."

The elevator stopped. We got out and walked down the hall, opened the door to go outside, and leaned against the railing.

"There's the park around the old city ramparts where we hang out!" Andreas hopped up to get a better look.

"And Saint Mary's Church!" Jensie added.

"All right, where's the Stasi at? Let's spit on their heads!" Andreas shouted.

I got dizzy looking down. Andreas missed his first target, a woman with a red shopping bag. "It's so cold, your spit freezes on the way and changes direction."

Two People's Police officers walked past the building.

Jensie hocked up a bunch of snot. "You guys ever hear this one? What are the four hardest years of a policeman's life?"

"That's an old one," Andreas and I said at the same time. "First grade."

Jensie's spit splotched against the wall a few meters below us.

"I'm cold." I opened the door to the hallway, and we went back to the elevator.

While we waited, Andreas leaned against the wall and stuck his hands into his jeans. "All right, Saxon, guess how many people jump here every year."

Jensie stared at the gleaming floor and thought it over. "About five."

"Wrong! At least seven. Whenever someone from the Stasi blows his cover, like if everyone at his day job finds out he's Stasi, then he has to kill himself. It's his duty. He signed a contract. Then he comes here and jumps."

The elevator door opened, and we got in.

"I don't believe you," Jensie murmured. "You all seem to think I'm an idiot, just 'cause I'm new here!"

The elevator stopped at the nineteenth floor. A man with a gray goatee got in. He clearly wasn't suicidal because he was headed down too. The moment the elevator started, he shrieked at us, "What are you doing here? You don't live here!"

His breath was horrendous.

I leaned back. "We're here to work on math with Sabine Müller."

"Yeah!" Jensie exclaimed. "They gave us this tricky word problem about May Day and the workers."

"Sabine Müller lives on the sixth floor," the Goatee snapped. "So what are you doing up here? Names? School?"

Andreas plugged his nose and pressed the six. He pointed at Jensie and mumbled, "He hit the wrong button. He's from Saxony and wanted to take a ride in the elevator."

Jensie nodded. "'Cause we don't have elevators in Saxony."

"School?"

"Rosa Luxemburg," I lied.

The Goatee studied us darkly. Finally, the elevator stopped and we got out.

"Man, did he stink!" I said. "Like he was rotting on the inside."

"That moron's gonna have fun staking out the wrong school," Andreas gloated.

"So whatta we do now, here on the sixth floor?" Jensie asked.

"Nothing. We're taking the stairs down," Andreas replied and took off.

We should have given ourselves more time. The Goatee was lurking by the front door. When we rounded the corner, he grabbed Jensie by the ear and Andreas by his blond curls.

"Ow," they both howled.

"You're liars too, I see! Never show your faces here again."

Outside, the Goatee shoved them so hard, they almost fell.

He hit me in the back as I passed. "That goes for you too, missy!"

Jensie watched him leave and rubbed his ear. "So what now?"

Andreas buttoned up his jacket. "We're going to the Reifer."

"What the heck is that?" Jensie asked.

"A playground."

We walked through the driving snow. There was almost no one at the Reifer because it was so cold. We scrambled around the covered stern of the wooden boat. We could see our breath.

"Do you guys know the *Sons of Great Bear* series?" Jensie rubbed his hands together. "They're my favorite books! I have the entire set!"

"Of course we do. I read some to my dad the other day, but all he wants to hear is Jack London."

Jensie looked at me in surprise. "Why do you read out loud to him? Can't he do it himself?"

"He's got a bit of a screw loose," Andreas said, but I gave him such a dirty look that he shut up.

"We could become blood brothers," Jensie said. "Like Harka. Harka's name changes later to Tokei-ihto!"

I looked him in the freckled face. "But we hardly know you."

Andreas tapped his temple at him. "Plus you're from

Saxony! What the hell are you thinking? No way we're becoming blood brothers."

"But I want to. I need a group to belong to here."

He stretched out his scrawny legs, folded his furry arms, and stared at the sand.

Andreas dug around in his parka and gestured at me. I didn't understand what he wanted.

Jensie looked up. "What's going on?"

Andreas pulled out a razor blade.

"Oh my goodness!" Jensie screamed.

I grinned at him. "Didn't see that coming, huh?"

"Gimme your arm, Saxon!" Andreas hollered.

Jensie bristled. "No way."

"I thought you wanted to. You just said so!"

Jensie didn't move.

"Come on, ya Saxon sissy!"

Jensie held out his arm in slow motion and closed his eyes. Andreas pushed back the bear fur and placed the razor blade. Jensie immediately screamed and jerked his arm back. The blade sliced his skin. He jumped up and slammed his head into the wooden roof.

"Ow! Shit!"

He crumpled back into the sand and held up his arm. "I'm bleeding!"

Andreas slid over. "Let's see!"

Red blood dripped into the whitish sand. It was more than just a scratch.

"Looks pretty bad," Andreas said.

Jensie started bawling.

"You have to go to the *Poliklinik*! Quick!" I yanked him up.

The doctor at the clinic told us off because Saxony Jensie had cut an artery. He cried all the way home because he was afraid of what his parents would do. I'm sure he had pictured his first day of school a little differently.

Even though he was from Saxony, we became friends. Andreas always called him Saxony Jensie. After his wound healed, we took him to the ramparts and raced down the steep, icy hill on our snowskates. We realized then what a show-off Saxony Jensie was. After every run, he would claim that the mountains in Saxony were a hundred times bigger than our hill. Not that those towering peaks had done his snowskating any good—he fell constantly.

We hear rumbling. Growing louder.

I pull on the string. Andreas stops swimming and turns to face me. The waves pitch us toward each other. He braces his hand against my shoulder to provide a buffer. Everything is dark, and we can't see a thing.

Swelling engine noise. "A boat," Andreas says.

One driving around without lights. They're searching for us, maybe even found our clothes already.

I grab Andreas's arm. "They can't see us! We just have to keep quiet."

38

"So what do we do now?"

"Nothing. We keep quiet. If a light appears, we dive down."

"And if they start spraying bullets?"

"Come off it. This isn't the Wild West!"

"How would you know?"

I don't.

The engine noise gets louder. Still no light.

It's unclear where the sound is coming from.

I turn in the water, listening, but the sound comes from all sides. What do we do?

At any moment, their spotlight could find us, then we're done for. At this range, they really could catch us.

I dive, and the sound is much louder, but even underwater, I can't locate the source. It's coming from all directions. I swim back up.

They must be really close. I lie rigidly in the water, not moving.

Andreas grasps my shoulder. "Oh shit."

I also feel something big approaching.

They're going to run us over.

Engine noise envelops me. I hold my breath.

Suddenly the sound changes. It isn't any quieter, but it seems less threatening. Its frequency changes. The boat is moving away.

"Christ, they drove right past us!" Andreas coughs and spits out water.

A huge wave slams me in the face, steals my breath,

then another follows. I turn away until the waves recede. We ride the swell, up and down, as the engine noise fades.

"What a scene. They are absolutely batshit." He coughs again. "I gotta take five."

He lies on his back and doesn't say another word.

I have stomach cramps from swallowing salt water. And from the fear.

Grandpa's stories. Would be nice if he'd spared me some of them, especially the ones about commando frogmen. Stationed in Kühlungsborn, more than a hundred strong. They jump out of boats or helicopters and swim for kilometers, even in winter. They train in the Baltic Sea, sometimes swimming all the way to the Danish border.

If they just jumped off that boat to hunt for us, we might as well pack it in. They could simply pull us underwater, and no one would ever know.

They're going to find us!

I look at the sky and try to breathe evenly. A few stars give off a hazy glow through the clouds. I can't hear the boat anymore, and everything around us is quiet. But that doesn't mean a thing. Frogmen swim silently.

I can't let myself think that way.

"We have to start swimming now, but really quietly," I whisper.

Andreas turns over in the water, back onto his front. "What?"

"Quiet," I say.

"Why? The boat's long gone."

"Doesn't matter. It's better if we don't make any noise."

"Okay."

Andreas is going along with things, which isn't his style. But he knows that when it comes to the Baltic, I'm better informed, and besides, in the bus earlier today, I told him he needed to listen to me, especially if things got dicey. Grandpa gave me so many details, I don't want to share them all with Andreas. He would just get scared, and we can't have that. Things are bad enough as it is.

We continue swimming, carefully and quietly.

Then a dark shadow appears on my left.

What is that?

Now the shadow's on the right.

Frogmen!

They're beside us in the water, surrounding us, closing in on us.

Everywhere, the shadows are everywhere!

How can Andreas not notice?

We've got to get away from them. I plunge my arms into the water, swim faster, can barely breathe, haul on the string. Andreas is way too slow. The string cuts into my wrist. I wanna go!

But the string holds me back too much. It's impossible.

I stop swimming and try to catch my breath through the snorkel, which is full of water. It makes a rattling, gurgling sound in the silence.

"What's wrong?" Andreas asks. He's close behind me. "Why are you swimming like a psycho?"

The shadows are gone. Water rushes in my ears, but otherwise things are quiet. There's no one here. We're alone.

I take the snorkel out of my mouth, and my gums ache.

All in my imagination.

Which I won't admit. Andreas knows my dad is crazy. I don't want him thinking it rubbed off on me.

"You know I'm not as fast as you are," Andreas snaps at me.

"I'm sorry, it wasn't on purpose."

And we swim on. I pay attention to my pace, to my breathing. Sometimes I see a shadow, an illusion drawn by my fear. Like in the "Erlkönig." The child in that poem isn't in danger at all. He dies because he's afraid.

Something grazes my arm. I recoil and stop moving.

In front of me is Andreas. "Look, the coast."

I turn in the water and look back.

Spotlights still sweep over the Baltic. The beams can't reach us now. We're too far out.

They're no longer a threat. On the contrary, the lights can help us orient ourselves. As long as they're behind us, we know we're swimming in the right direction.

We're hardly in the clear, though. They're looking for us, that much is certain.

"Think we've reached the three-mile limit yet?"

"I don't know," I murmur. How could I? It's my first

42

time out here. I got water in my ear, which is uncomfortable and actually really bad, because it can throw off your sense of balance.

Grandpa told me that the three-mile limit isn't marked and that you can only tell you've passed it by the increase in shipping traffic.

I'm thirsty, but it's way too soon for that. We don't have much water with us.

"We might have," Andreas continues. "We've been swimming for a while now."

I should boost him up. "We definitely would have gone that distance by now in the pool."

"I can easily swim about six kilometers in a couple hours," Andreas says. "So there's a chance we're already out that far. We should probably turn west then, huh?"

Funny, the word *turn*. As if we were driving down Lange Strasse in a Trabbi.

"Better not quite yet. We need to be positive we're outside the border zone. Otherwise we might get caught in a current and wind up back onshore."

I drift along for a moment and look at the sky. Grandpa told me that international waters aren't actually safer. There's more activity there, more ships going by. That's good. Sooner or later, someone will see us. Just depends who. If we're unlucky, it'll be Eastern European ships. They'll report our location to authorities, who will then send out boats to catch us, even if we are beyond the three-mile limit. Grandpa says it's all happened before.

They even captured someone just a few hundred meters shy of the Danish coast and brought him back to the GDR.

"Do you feel kinda queasy out here too?" Andreas asks.

It's so weird to hear Andreas but not see him. "No."

"Lucky. I never knew I got seasick. Never happened to me in the wave pool. I hope I don't puke."

And the swell's not even that heavy.

"Over there's Warnemünde," Andreas says.

I look back toward where I figure Hotel Neptun should be. I can't make it out, but I can picture it—I've seen it often enough. "Remember at the Intershop that time? That West German lady Saxony Jensie was so into?"

"What a stud," Andreas says, laughing. "He can't tell that story to anyone in the West. It's way too embarrassing."

Andreas starts swimming, and the string between us tightens.

"Guys, you smell that?"

Saxony Jensie stretched the word *that* out long, with his thick Saxon accent. He raced around the Intershop, his hair disheveled. "It smells so different than in our stores. More like flowers and less like Wofasept disinfectant. The heating is better too!"

He stopped and stared at the Matchbox cars inside the display case with his mouth open. The glass immediately fogged up. Besides us, the only other person in the Intershop was a woman with blond hair. She had a deep tan and wore stylish white slacks and a gold wristwatch.

Andreas looked up at the records. Paul Young, Nena, Michael Jackson, and David Bowie were on display. "I want *Let's Dance* so bad!"

Saxony Jensie touched everything he could get his grubby hands on. "Man, it smells good in here!"

The store clerk's heavily made-up eyelids twitched. She smoothed down her pink cardigan in agitation.

"What would you buy if you had ten West German marks?"

Andreas furrowed his pimply brow. "That won't get you a record."

"But you could get Nutella! And licorice wheels and ice cream treats!" Saxony Jensie exclaimed.

"Mars and Raider bars," I said.

"Gummy bears."

"Duplo bars."

The woman in the fancy clothes was next in line.

"She's from the West," Andreas whispered in my ear.

She bought a bottle of Jack Daniel's and lots of candy.

"For a bottle of Jack Daniel's, you could get twenty-five bags of licorice wheels, sixty packs of Duplo, forty Mars bars, or fifteen jars of Nutella," Saxony Jensie hissed. All of a sudden he was good at math.

The salesclerk didn't let us out of her sight. Her bright pink lips pursed. "And what will you be buying?"

"We're just looking," Andreas replied.

"She's so high and mighty, just 'cause she gets to work at an Intershop and doesn't have to go to the fish *Kombinat* every morning," I whispered.

"Like your mom." Saxony Jensie bounced lightly in his sneakers and stared at the bacon in the meat case. Spit collected in the corners of his mouth and then sprayed across the glass as he continued, "Have you guys heard the one about the policeman who jumped over the counter at an Intershop and applied for political asylum?"

"Ha ha ha, what an idiot!" Andreas exploded.

The West German woman smiled nicely.

"How about this one? A guy walks into a store. 'Do you have any underwear?' he asks. Shopkeeper says, 'Nope, next door sells no underwear. We just sell no sheets.'"

The salesclerk cleared her throat. The West German woman was still smiling nicely.

"A guy comes home. He bursts into the apartment, finds his old lady in bed with another man, and screams, 'Here you two're screwing around, while down at the store, they just got a shipment of oranges!'"

"That's enough; go tell your jokes somewhere else," the salesclerk yelled angrily at us.

The West German woman grinned and took her bags. On the way out, she gave us a wink. Saxony Jensie almost fainted and latched on to me. "She should take me with her! In her BMW," he whimpered.

"Get out. You've done enough looking! Beat it!"

"Why can't we look?" Andreas asked.

"Because there's nothing you can buy."

"How would you know?"

She pointed at the door. "Out!"

"I'll be back tomorrow with my twenty Forum checks, then you'll see!" Saxony Jensie stuck out his tongue at her. We bolted. I buttoned up my quilted jacket on the red carpet outside the store. It was cold and dark.

"Think that fancy lady could tell we're from the GDR?"

"You are such an idiot, dude. Listen to yourself speak! Man, just look at you!" Andreas pointed at Saxony Jensie's Germina sneakers and baggy Boxer jeans. "And then there's that heinous brown bear fur!"

Saxony Jensie looked at us pathetically. "My relatives in Hanover haven't been that active sending packages lately. You guys are obviously having better luck with your West German family."

I was wearing my blue-and-white Pumas, and Andreas was in his Levi's, which by now were highwaters. His mother kept sewing material to the bottom hems, so they wouldn't look stupid.

We walked toward the lighthouse.

"James Bond is on West German TV tonight!" Saxony Jensie hopped up and down because he was so cold. "Have you guys heard this one? What does the TV network ARD actually stand for? Access Restricted in Dresden."

No one laughed. That joke was ancient.

"Hey there! Hey! Wait a second!"

We turned around. It was the West German woman. She was racing after us like a maniac. She abruptly stopped and stared at us. Her blond hair blew in the wind.

"What, are you fleeing from the KGB or something?" Andreas asked.

She looked around fearfully. Then she reached out her arm. "This is for you."

I took the bag.

"Take care!"

She ran back to Hotel Neptun and didn't turn around again. We watched her leave, staring after her like idiots.

Saxony Jensie was the first to move. He tore the bag out of my hand and took off down the street. Andreas and I caught up with him, and everyone tugged at the bag.

I held it high above my head. "We're splitting it fairly!"

We sat down under a streetlight.

"Did you notice how good she smelled?" I asked.

"Duh," Andreas said. "Western perfume."

Three Raider bars, three Mars bars, three packs of Maoam, three Duplos, and three bars of that chocolate with air bubbles in it. One bag of licorice wheels, one of gummy bears. One jar of Nutella. Splitting the licorice went quick, but counting out the gummy bears and dividing them by color took forever. I traded Saxony Jensie my licorice for his Mars bar. Andreas got to keep the bag.

At the end, we all stared at the jar of Nutella. "So, what do we do with this?"

"Split it between containers," Andreas suggested.

"But how?"

"I know, I know!" Saxony Jensie's hand shot up, like in school. "I'll take it home, and you come by every morning for breakfast."

Andreas shrugged. "Why not? But don't hog it all!"

"No way. Never." He grinned happily. He would obviously dip into it.

We walked to the city train station.

"How could you ask such a stupid question?" Saxony Jensie griped. "Whether she was fleeing from the KGB."

Andreas tossed up a gummy bear and caught it in his mouth. "I couldn't think of anything else. What would you have asked?"

"Like, maybe if she would take us in the trunk of her BMW. To Kurfürstendamm!"

"Why the hell you wanna go there?"

"No reason. Just to look."

"Lame," Andreas replied. "My dad says that Kurfürstendamm is no different from Lange Strasse. It's not exactly must-see."

Saxony Jensie's gummy bear landed on the sidewalk because, as always, he was too clumsy. He picked it up and popped it into his mouth. "They don't check every car at the border. It could have worked."

"But there's no way she could fit all three of us in the trunk," I said. "Even a BMW doesn't have *that* much room."

The train was already waiting at the platform. We sat

49

down in a four-person section. Andreas propped up his feet on the seats.

"Man, it reeks of piss in here!"

"She was really nice!" Saxony Jensie pulled out the licorice wheels. "Should we go back tomorrow? Maybe we'll bump into her again."

"Dude, stop fidgeting so much. Besides, the whole thing is embarrassing."

"What is?"

"Well, we never should have accepted," Andreas said.

Saxony Jensie knit his bushy brows together. "Why the heck not?"

"Well, 'cause she looks down on us!"

"Bullshit!" I took a bite of my Mars bar.

"The way she looked at us when she said, 'Take care.' Like we were headed for a concentration camp or something."

Saxony Jensie's face turned white, down to his freckles. "Are you crazy or something?"

Andreas nibbled on a Raider. "She'll probably tell her rich West German friends at tennis all about the poor, poor GDR kids she helped."

"Who cares?" Saxony Jensie uncoiled a licorice wheel. "What's wrong with that? Imagine you were in Africa and could buy lots of bread. Wouldn't you give some to the children?"

"You can't compare the two."

"Yeah you can!"

"I thought she was arrogant," Andreas argued.

"Well, I thought she was really nice!"

The train stopped in Lütten Klein. Andreas kept ragging on the woman. At some point Saxony Jensie got fed up. "Well, if that's your opinion, then you don't get to eat the candy. Give it to us!"

He spoke with his mouth full, the end of the licorice dangling like an earthworm.

"No!" Andreas scowled at him.

"Then shut your trap!"

I had never heard Saxony Jensie talk that way. Andreas was surprised too. He ate the second Raider bar in silence.

He couldn't keep his own trap shut back at school, though, and told everyone what an exciting thing had happened to us. Someone snitched, probably Sabine. We were doing exercises with our SR1 calculators in math when someone knocked at the door.

The smell of lavender streamed into the room. "Now then, everyone set aside your calculators!"

Frau Thiel scanned the rows. "Hanna, Andreas, and Jens."

As if on command, we all looked down at our desks.

"You should be very, very ashamed of yourselves!"

I peeked up at her. She leaned on the teacher's desk, fuming. Her golden medallion bobbed between her breasts like a buoy in the Baltic Sea.

"What you three did is reprehensible. And despicable!"

Behind us, someone snickered.

Frau Thiel looked up. "And why is that? Ronny, what do you think?"

"I dunno," he muttered.

"Hm, I see."

She went down the rows. "Should they have accepted something from an enemy of the state? Christian!"

"No," he answered.

"Hm, I see. And why do you say that?"

"Because it's despicable to take something from an enemy of the state. And reprehensible."

"Exactly! These three are very, very bad examples and should be very, very ashamed of themselves."

Instead of just letting her talk, Andreas snapped his fingers. "But it wasn't an enemy of the state, it was this gorgeous blond lady."

Someone else giggled.

Frau Thiel turned bright red. "That makes no difference! Enemies of the state have many faces!"

Saxony Jensie raised his hand and started spouting some nonsense about starving kids in Africa. It was the last thing Frau Thiel wanted to hear about.

"Jens Blum—out! This goes beyond the pale! To equate the African people's struggle for freedom with your greed for Western sweets! Get out this instant!"

He shuffled out, his jeans slipping down his butt, like always.

"And you, Hanna Klein. I would have expected you to take a different stance," she screamed at me.

I looked down at my desk again.

"Answer me, at the very least!"

But she hadn't even asked anything.

"Answer!"

"Answer what?"

"Sabine, could you please answer the question!"

Sabine rattled off, like a machine gun, "Hanna should have said that the children of the GDR are not reliant on gifts from imperialist foreign nations."

Frau Thiel nodded in time to Sabine's response.

"The gifts aren't from a foreign nation, though. They can be bought at a store in the GDR."

"I beg your pardon?" Frau Thiel glared at Andreas in disbelief.

"You just need the right kind of money."

"Are you implying that the currency of the GDR—that is, the currency of a Comecon member nation—isn't real money?"

Andreas stared at his desk. His blond curls hid his face.

"We're all ears!"

"It's so light," he said defiantly.

I thought of Grandpa, who always complained about the lightweight aluminum coins. "Play money for play people" was one of his favorite lines when we went shopping.

"'So light'?!"

"Like play money when you play store," I said, to deflect the focus from Andreas.

That was the final straw. "Out. Both of you! And go to the principal's office after this period! This is absolutely outrageous!"

Principal Schneider hobbled back and forth and gave us a long-winded speech about socialist achievements and how horrible it was that we allowed ourselves to be debased by an enemy of the people. We had to stand at his desk and watch as he sharpened all his pencils, broke the tips, then sharpened them again.

When it was over, we walked out with bold red disciplinary notes in our homework planners.

Everything around us is dark.

Again and again, boats narrowly pass by. They won't give up, are determined to find us. Engine noise swells in the darkness, grows louder and louder. Can't see a thing in front of me, and surrounding me is nothing but black water.

I swim blindly, cloaked in noise—I can't even hear my breath. Then things get quieter and the waves come. I take a deep breath, spread out my arms in the water, and drift along. No use fighting. You'll always lose.

Wave crest, wave trough, wave crest.

The waves wash in from the right this time, 'cause that's where the boat was. In a second, they'll come in from the front, to the left.

They're circling us. Maybe it's multiple boats; maybe it's always the same one.

Strange. Hunting us without light. Almost running us over without realizing.

Andreas swims beside me, and I rarely feel the string pull. He's keeping up, only occasionally falling behind a little. Amazing he's even able to swim that fast after such a brief training period. I never would have thought it possible.

The tug on my wrist is a good feeling, as if it were keeping me safe. Although I can't see Andreas, I know he is there.

I have no sense of distance, no idea how far I've swum.

It's easy at practice. You just count laps. Eighty, one hundred, a hundred twenty laps. Four thousand, five thousand, six thousand meters. The last few times, I swam at least a hundred fifty laps: seven thousand, five hundred meters.

Everything out here is different, much harder. No breaks, no edge of the pool.

Just the current, wind, and waves. And water pouring into my snorkel.

My right calf hurts. I'm getting a cramp. And there's not a thing I can do about it. If I rest my right leg and favor the left, we'll veer off course and have to correct for it later. That's a waste of energy.

All of a sudden, millions of green dots dance around me in the black water, swirling before and beneath me. It's beautiful. As if I were dreaming.

Sea sparkle. We learned about it in Bio. When disturbed, microorganisms in the water emit light, and the sea appears to glow.

I duck underwater and look back. Stretching out behind us is a bright, glittering trail through the darkness. Greenish dots glow around Andreas's flippers. It's as if the starry skies extended into the sea, as if we were creating our own Milky Way down here.

A tug on the string. I have to keep moving, and I put in a few powerful strokes to catch up. Thanks to the glow, I can see the compass.

The needle is pointing north.

If we're lucky, we're already beyond the three-mile limit. As soon as it's light out, we'll be able to spot passing ships. Hopefully they won't be border patrol.

It's already getting hard to lift my arms out of the water. I can't crawl as much as I'd like but end up swimming the breaststroke, which slows me down. Andreas is doing well keeping up. I hope he's pacing himself. I should point that out to him, but he's swimming so steadily right now, I don't want to interrupt. It's good to be in the flow, not thinking about anything, just swimming. But it's important to remember that this phase won't last forever.

We can do it. Just need to tough it out, like at practice, and not focus on our weakness. Look straight ahead! One lap, then another! Think of it in stages, Ulrich always said. Never approach the full 10K all at once, but take the first hundred meters, then the next. And so on. Till you've already got the first half behind you. Then it gets easier.

I mean, if someone had told me a year ago that I would swim from Wilhelmshöhe to Tower 3 in Warnemünde one day, I never would've believed them. Let alone from Kühlungsborn to Warnemünde! That was only four weeks ago. More than nineteen kilometers. Totally different from this, though, can't even compare, the coast always within reach. Andreas was sick and couldn't join. Grandpa dropped me off in Kühlungsborn, then went to Warnemünde, where he waited at Tower 3 with my clothes.

Ever since that day, I've known how bad cramps can get when you can't grab the side of the pool, when you need to stay in the cold water, when you can't take any breaks.

I ended up puking from the exertion, so nasty. And my bathing suit chafed around my neck.

Wonder what Grandpa's doing right now? He's probably asleep, but not for much longer. He'll get up soon, before dawn, and do crossword puzzles.

Hopefully Andreas can keep up. He's an inexperienced swimmer but makes up for it in courage. The courage of desperation. After last winter, he couldn't take it anymore. It's no wonder.

They just wouldn't get off his back. It wasn't a good spot for us, the diesel engine plant. Everyone knew where we came from. Kids of the elite class winding up in production, that was a real novelty. The workers thought we were conceited and arrogant, but we weren't—we were

57

trying to figure things out. Several remembered us from the times we had visited as part of our Productive Work class when we'd spent hours filing little metal plates. We had to make an appearance there every fourteen days, but not without cracking lots of loud jokes whenever we did, which I'm sure annoyed the regular workers. Socialist production requires student support; otherwise workers would never meet the quotas.

We paid for our cockiness a year later when we were transferred to the factory for disciplinary reasons and had to show up every day. All the other workers ignored us or cussed us out, accusing us of doing our work wrong. I complained once to our manager. All he said was, "You've only got yourself to blame. Quit bitching. There's a reason they transferred you here."

Andreas always sat alone at lunch. No one talked to him. It sucked, but at least he got a little breathing space.

Not me. Every day, my coworker Hannes asked me back to his place after our shift. Those who overheard just laughed. He sometimes followed me home after work, all the way to my front door. I was terrified of him and yearned to be back at my new high school, something I never would have expected, considering how lame I thought it was the first day. I didn't know a soul there. Thomas was the only other person from our old class allowed to continue on to extended secondary school after tenth grade, in preparation for the *Abitur*, but he was in a parallel class. They split students up on purpose, so we wouldn't form groups. Everyone was afraid of screwing up their educational opportunity and tried to avoid making any mistakes. There was no more goofing off.

And the teachers lectured us about how our serious adult lives had now begun. We sat stock-still in our seats and didn't make a peep. At recess, we ran laps around the schoolyard, like they do in prison.

Still, it was better than working at the diesel engine plant, way better than dealing with stupid Hannes. I didn't tell Mom about him—she was worried enough as it was, after my transfer. Of course Dad was completely oblivious. New medication. All he wanted was to be left alone, didn't want to hear any Jack London stories, just kicked me out of the room.

If they catch us now, we won't be sent back to the plant—we'll go straight to jail. Things would be even worse.

There's a stabbing in my lung. The cold air hurts. What can I do? I have to breathe. I remember this from practice at the outdoor pool. Sometimes we swam there into November, but then it was only the air that was cool, while the water was heated.

Everything is cold out here. I'm freezing, even though I'm moving.

Is Andreas feeling what I'm feeling? He probably didn't really know what to expect. I did warn him about the cold. I could barely believe it when he proposed this crazy idea last winter. He was serious, wasn't just saying it.

Crossing the Baltic to the other side? Unreal.

Then he started training like a beast.

I still refused to accept it.

But at some point, it became clear that I would be joining him. I couldn't leave him alone. He needs me, after all. I need him too.

I couldn't imagine a single day at the plant without him, so I had to go too. We didn't have much time. Training in winter, spring, and summer, then leaving in late summer. Swimming across the Baltic! At first, it sounded totally crazy, absolutely absurd. But over time, it became more tangible, more real. Within a few weeks, we had a coherent plan—it's not like we had an alternative.

Why shouldn't we give it a shot?

"No more waiting around for a miracle," Andreas always said. "We're taking matters into our own hands."

When I finally told him I wanted to come, he was beside himself. I couldn't change my mind after that; I couldn't rob him of that joy. I felt uneasy at times and wanted to call the whole thing off, but there was no way. Andreas was counting on me. I'm all he's got. He had to escape. No one stuck by him, not even his parents. He couldn't stay.

Besides, I have to look out for him, because we know he's not a perfect swimmer.

Hopefully it'll be light soon.

Hopefully they don't find us.

Crazy that they even know where we're swimming.

They make our lives hell, then don't even let us leave.

Idiotic.

The water is getting colder and colder. I can barely feel my toes; they're numb.

The gloves get in the way of my swimming and don't even help keep me warm. At this point, they're completely useless.

I peel them off and drop them in the water, and wonder where they'll end up.

Eventually, the sun will rise and warm the air.

I have to look straight ahead. It'll be easier during the day. And we have a goal.

That was already a big help last winter when we were planning to leave. Everything looks different when you have a goal. Stuff like the factory doesn't bother you as much then because you know it won't be like that forever.

After we made our decision, Andreas turned into his lively old self again. For the first time in weeks, he cracked me up with his jokes, like when we were little. He used to play so many pranks. This one time, while the teacher was out of the classroom, he pushed a table up to the wall and climbed on top. I can still see his blue-and-white checkered shirt and blond curls as he stood right in front of the picture of General Secretary Erich Honecker, our country's leader. And his devilish grin as he spit out his gum and stuck it onto Honecker's nose. He earned himself a disciplinary note in his homework planner for that.

61

I remember that we bummed around after school that day. Andreas regretted getting in trouble again and didn't want to go home because he was scared of his dad.

We wandered over to the ramparts and played in the bushes, then dug a hole to hide his planner with the damaging entry. Andreas was going to tell his dad that he'd lost it.

While digging, we unearthed a soldier's helmet with part of the skull still in it as well as the jawbone with seven teeth attached.

We took our find to Grandpa's house on Paul Strasse. He opened a new bottle of Goldbrand, gave us a speech about the Nazi armed forces, and examined the jawbone with his dessert fork. He said the soldier had drunk too much Vita Cola, which had made his teeth fall out. It was another one of his stupid jokes—I doubt that soldiers were drinking Vita Cola during the war. Grandpa told us he'd had a helmet just like this one in Stalingrad, before the Soviet army had caught him.

To this day Grandpa keeps the helmet on a wardrobe hook in the front hallway. He puts it away whenever sensitive guests come by, like Aunt Erna, who lost her husband in the war. She can't bear the sight of it.

On his birthday once, Grandpa wore the helmet and ate his pound cake in silence as we all sat around the coffee table. When Mom complained about it, he said he was an important witness of the past.

"Great, he fell asleep again, even though he's on duty."

Herr Behrens sat slumped over on the low stone wall. We crossed the schoolyard to Karl Strasse.

"They can collect recyclables and contribute to world peace on their own today!" Saxony Jensie was trying to catch his breath and hung back a few meters. "It's so stupid, ringing at everyone's door and asking, 'Do you have any recyclables, do you have any recyclables; paper or glass, glass or paper?'" He wheezed loudly. "Grandma Wulff will say she needs her jars for jam, like she always does. And old man Schröder on Augusten Strasse will give everyone a peppermint. Yuck. Did you guys like those?"

"No, because we don't shove everything in our mouth, the way you do," Andreas scoffed, turning back to face him. "Now come on, you slowpoke."

We fought our way through the underbrush on the ramparts, down to the Teufelskuhle, a deep pit filled with water at the western end of the parkland. The path was very steep.

Sitting under a willow tree by the water, Andreas pulled a book out of his schoolbag. "I borrowed this from the children's library on Barnstorfer Weg."

It was a book about the Teufelskuhle.

We looked at the pictures. The walls used to be less steep, and there were far more swans in the water.

Shortly before twelve, Andreas told us what he had

read in the book. "A long time ago, there was a castle that sank into the pondwaters of the Teufelskuhle. You know that bronze statue of a lady at the entrance to the park? Well, she was once a princess, who is now damned to drink water for all eternity. That is, unless someone saves her. There's only one day a year she can be saved, though, and that's at noon on Saint John's Day, when a silver bowl rises up from the bottom of the pond. You need to fill that with water, then go up the Teufelsberg and dump the water over your left shoulder. That breaks the curse."

"Whoa!" Saxony Jensie exclaimed.

"The book also says that the Teufelskuhle is bottomless and connects to the Baltic Sea."

"What?"

"But the Baltic is so far away!"

I reached for a willow branch. "Grandpa once told me that there are lots of bunkers and tunnels under the Teufelskuhle. They're all full of water because a bomb exploded there during the war."

"A bomb?" Saxony Jensie started to fidget. "Whoa. Does it say anything about that in the book?"

Andreas shook his head. "My dad once told me that there's a shaft dug into the ramparts with train tracks at the bottom. And that the bunker at the top of the ramparts is connected to the Teufelskuhle."

We sat by the water for more than an hour but didn't see any enchanted bowls come floating up to the surface. All we saw was a duck swim by and give us a weird look.

When one thirty rolled around, Andreas angrily chucked a few rocks into the pond.

"Whatever! Let's just go to the bunker and hang out there!" Saxony Jensie trudged up the steep hillside.

The entrance to the bunker was hidden behind lots of scrub. I crawled into the hole and turned on the flashlight we had hidden under a brick in the corner. It smelled musty and damp inside. I touched something slimy.

"Should we search for the passageway to the Teufelskuhle?"

"No," Saxony Jensie wailed.

"Hell yeah!" Andreas slunk in behind me.

"There might still be bombs and stuff lying around," Saxony Jensie said. "I'll guard the entrance. For your safety!"

"Wuss," Andreas said. The light darted across bricks, rotted boards, a shoe, and a beer bottle.

"Do you see anything?"

"Quiet back there!"

The air got cooler the deeper we went. We finally reached a steel door, whose rusted handle was half broken off. I held the flashlight while Andreas jiggled the handle. It wouldn't open. Some plaster fell from the ceiling.

"Damn!" Andreas was disappointed. "It won't work. We need a tool."

"What are you guys doing in there?"

Andreas turned around. "Hey, Saxon, we found a dead body in a fascist uniform."

"What?"

Saxony Jensie's scream reverberated so loudly in the bunker, we had to cover our ears.

"We're bringing it out for you to see!" I yelled.

"No!" Saxony Jensie's shaggy hair stood on end. He stared at us wide eyed.

I held the flashlight at an angle under my face. "Ooooaah!"

"Stop it!" Saxony Jensie screamed.

Andreas groaned loudly. "Man, is he heavy! For someone who's been lying here for forty years, he's kept pretty well."

I could barely crawl, I was laughing so hard. Saxony Jensie ducked and took a few steps back.

"You can still see the skull patch on his collar!"

"You guys are psycho!" He ran away from the entrance.

We climbed out of the bunker. It was really warm outside. There was something green stuck to my hand. It smelled funky. My shirt was covered in grime.

"Ew, I think I'm gonna puke," Andreas gagged. He was filthy too.

There was a rustle in a wild rose bush a few meters off. Saxony Jensie had hidden.

"Ready or not, here I come!" Andreas shouted.

I knelt and tied my shoe.

"You can come out now, Saxon!"

A few branches moved.

"We were just kidding, dude!"

Saxony Jensie threw a rose hip out of the bush. It landed several meters away from me.

"So you don't have a skeleton with you?"

"Nope."

He crept out of the bushes. One of the buttons on his Saxon-style lederhosen was undone. He was so scared, he'd had to pee.

"You're a real champ, you know that?" Andreas brushed off his jeans. His curls were full of dust.

Saxony Jensie exhaled sharply into his enormous handkerchief. "You guys can be really scary!"

"I have to go home," I said. "Reading."

"Just 'cause I'm not from here, you always give me such a hard time. It's so mean!"

"What's today's selection?" Andreas asked as we scrambled up to the path.

"*The Road.* Jack London rides the train across America. Sometimes on the roof, sometimes underneath the boxcars."

"I swear, I'll go straight back to Dresden, *then* you'll see, you stupid northern fish-heads!"

"He always has to hide so they don't kick him off the train. My dad likes the story."

"Your dad's mental too!"

I turned around and slapped him. "Don't you dare say that!"

Saxony Jensie clutched his cheek and started bawling. He tried to kick me but lost his balance and tumbled

67

back down the hill. Andreas and I laughed ourselves half to death.

⁓

The starry sky still stretches out above me. I have a stitch in my side and can barely breathe.

When will it finally be light out? It's so hard to swim in the dark. I'm tired and wish I could sleep.

Just keep swimming. It's all I can do.

Andreas is swimming the front crawl beside me, slower now. We need to be careful, can't afford to let our guard down. The border patrol boats will be back at dawn.

Things have been quiet for a while, no one circling us anymore. It's not like the boats can be everywhere at once either. The sea's a big place.

All of a sudden, I feel bad for smacking Saxony Jensie back then on the ramparts. He sulked about it for a long time and barely acknowledged me. Him and his stupid comments. He didn't understand why I read aloud to Dad.

It was just because then I could spend time with him. He usually kicked everyone out of his room immediately. He liked Jack London best. When he'd had enough, he pulled the blanket over his head, and I knew it was time to go.

I couldn't stand it when people made fun of Dad. I was well aware that he wasn't normal—Saxony Jensie didn't have to rub it in.

The day after I'd slapped Saxony Jensie, there was trouble with Dad. He totally flipped out, almost as if he'd heard what the Saxon said. Tried to run away, headed for the bank in his pajamas, passbook in hand. I just happened to see him, as Andreas and I were walking through the public rose garden. We followed him to the bank and brought him back out. He made a huge scene. Everyone was staring. Not that he would have gotten any cash in that getup anyway. We dragged him home, him yelling the entire way back that he wanted to catch the ferry to Gedser, in Denmark. He stopped in his tracks outside the Stasi building and waved at the guard, who fortunately didn't react. Two kids with schoolbags and a man in pajamas were not his concern. We tugged on Dad to keep moving, but he wouldn't stop waving. Some grandma waved back, to his delight. Back in his room, he lay down in bed.

"At least I tried," he said, as I gave him his pill and pulled up the blanket.

I can't believe that he used to be normal and go to work like everyone else. When Mom first met him, everything was fine, she once told me. Dad taught Marxism-Leninism at the University of Rostock.

Grandpa always said that was why he went crazy, but that's ridiculous. It might be a boring subject, but it definitely won't drive you insane.

Jellyfish, in my path, and lots of them.

They glow in the water. I can see them easily, graze one with my hand and flinch. The feeling is unpleasant. I stop doing the crawl stroke and just paddle with my legs to pass through the swarm without a lot of arm movement. I always thought jellyfish were gross whenever we pelted each other with them at the beach. They move majestically through the water now, their forms rounding, then stretching long, then rounding again, shimmering blue shapes in the dark. Ninety-eight percent water. Hard to believe. They're so beautiful. Bet they're not cold.

They'd be better off avoiding the beaches, where they're at the mercy of playing kids, who imprison them in their sandcastles. Stay on the open water, like us.

Dad was sometimes like a jellyfish. Whenever he had an attack, he lay motionless on the wood floor, and everything went limp. His hand fell heavily when you let it go.

He wouldn't understand me and would look at me weird, like he didn't know who I was. He just lay there. Sometimes it went on for hours and Mom would call the ambulance. They then took Dad to Gehlsdorf, on the other side of the Warnow.

He would stay there for weeks. At some point, we'd go pick him up in our blue Trabbi. He usually came home with less hair and would just stare silently at the wall. Following every stay, he'd have more pills to take than before.

I jerk back, my heart racing.

What is that?

Something dark, right in front of me!

My hand!

Suddenly I can see it in the murky, black water.

70

There's only one thing that can mean.

It's getting light out. Finally.

I lift my head out of the water. Andreas feels the string twitch and stops swimming. It's very quiet.

I gaze toward the east. The sky is dark—the sun hasn't risen yet, but blanketing the water is a soft pink gleam that concentrates at the horizon.

"It's morning." Andreas's voice is hoarse.

We paddle on.

The Baltic Sea slowly changes color. It becomes lighter, less dense. I swim through fog and can only see a few inches ahead, but it's a start. Things will be easier during the day.

We'll see where we're swimming.

Most importantly, we'll see each other. No more fear of getting separated in the dark, should the string come undone.

Horrifying thought.

The water is charcoal gray now.

We can finally be spotted by others—just need to be careful they're the ones we want. Soon we'll be in international waters, then our chances will improve. We can't give up but have to take breaks once in a while and be careful not to stray off course. Maybe a West German ferry will see us.

A glimmer permeates the water.

When I extend my arm in the water, I can see all the way to my fingertips. I stop swimming and lift my head.

It's dawn!

I yank off my goggles and snorkel and take a deep breath. Nice not to feel the pressure of the goggles for a moment.

Andreas moves his arms through the water beside me to stay in place. I see him for the first time since last night. He blinks at me through the plexiglass of his goggles and slowly takes them off. His eyes are dark and serious, his skin very pale. He looks haggard. It's from the strain and fatigue.

"You look beat," he says.

I try to smile. I look past him toward the horizon.

The silver waves of the Baltic and its infinite expanse lie before me, at once terrifying and beautiful. The sky is still dark in the east, the clouds dark red.

The sun is nowhere to be seen, not yet.

I'm practically standing in the water, slowly moving my flippers. Can't look away. It's almost time.

Andreas's gaze is also fixed toward the east.

A glitter on the horizon. It intensifies, transforms into an intense gleam, a semicircle of light that spreads across the water.

I squint—the light blinds me, and the salt water is burning my eyes.

The sun rises, a blazing red ball climbing slowly through the gray clouds. Beams of light break through and the sky begins to glow. Orange and pink and yellow and red.

It's finally daytime. And not a boat in sight.

My swim cap shifted, so I pull it back into place over my forehead and put on my goggles. Andreas nods at me.

We swim on.

Grandpa stood in the hallway in his dark-green wool suit. He had combed his wispy white hair straight across his head, with glimpses of pink scalp shining through.

Mom rolled her eyes when she saw him. "You wore that suit to our wedding!"

"That's right!"

"I want to stay here," Dad said.

He had just returned from Gehlsdorf and spent all his time sleeping.

"No. You have to come," Mom said. She tossed his black leather shoes onto the bed. "Come on, get up! We're taking a trip in the car."

Dad threw off the blanket and got dressed. He loved trips. Mom wore a black dress and a pearl necklace. She looked like a sad princess.

Dad and I crawled into the back of the Trabbi. Grandpa settled into the front passenger seat. He got to sit up front because he was so ancient.

I had brought my language arts textbook because I had to memorize "The Cranes of Ibycus" by next class.

The Trabbi sounded funny as it started.

"Where is Corinth's isthmus?" I asked. The poem opened with that.

"Siberia. Unfavorable strategic position," Grandpa responded.

"Nonsense," Mom snapped. "Somewhere in Greece, honey."

Dad was always happy when we drove the car around Rostock. He pointed out the window. "There's the sport and convention center. I go there to watch handball tournaments. Go, SC Empor Rostock!"

"Baloney," Grandpa snorted. He was right. Dad had never been to a single handball match.

The Trabbi was making really weird noises. "That's socialist-quality production for you," Grandpa complained. "Are we picking up Liselotte?"

Mom nodded.

"And where's Acrocorinth?" I asked.

"Also Greece. The whole poem is set there."

I kept reading, while Dad rattled off the names of places we passed. "Hundertmänner Bridge. Saarplatz."

"And what's a prytanis?"

"The boss," Dad said. "And that's Klement Gottwald Train Station."

"Enough!" Mom shouted, annoyed.

"And what's a rostrum?"

"Come on, kid, you should be able to work that one out," Grandpa said. "It's where the people sit, gawk like fools, and wave, just like at May Day celebrations."

We pulled over on Lenin Allee. Aunt Lilo was already waiting outside her door and trembling so badly, her crutch wobbled. She had gotten dolled up as if headed for the boardwalk in Warnemünde—there was a bright-red curler still stuck in her white hair. I giggled when I saw it.

Grandpa got out, held the door for her, and roared, "So, we do our hair today?"

She flinched and squeezed in between Dad and me, which didn't work very well. She was very fat, and her crutch was always in the way.

"May I?" Mom reached back and pulled out the red curler.

"Thank you, my dear child!" Aunt Lilo tossed it into her purse and plucked at my blouse.

"And what's that you're reading, child?"

"Schiller."

She plucked some more at my blouse. It tickled.

"Baltic Sea Stadium! Neptune Indoor Pool!" Dad shouted.

"That's where I always go for practice," I said. "And where is Theseus's town?"

"For God's sake! In Greece!" Mom hit the gas and the Trabbi lurched forward.

Aunt Lilo's chin, which was streaked with tiny red veins, had a long black hair growing out of it.

She pointed at my book. "Schiller is very romantic. Read us something."

She must have been confusing him with Goethe, but I

went ahead and started reading from stanza fourteen, which I had just reached:

> *"With loins in mantle black concealed,*
> *Within their fleshless hands they wield*
> *The torch, that with a dull red glows,*
> *While in their cheek no life–blood flows."*

I looked up. Aunt Lilo was watching me in bewilderment.

> *"And where the hair is floating wide*
> *And loving, round a mortal brow,*
> *Here snakes and adders are descried,*
> *Whose bellies swell with poison now."*

Aunt Lilo shook her head furiously.

"Real romantic," murmured Grandpa.

Mom braked. "We're here."

We were at the cemetery.

Aunt Lilo started to cry.

"There, there." Grandpa reached through the space between the seats and patted Aunt Lilo's knee. Now I realized where we were going. To the cemetery, to Uncle Max's funeral—Lilo's husband.

Dad never would have come had he known beforehand. He couldn't stand Uncle Max because Max had supposedly spied on him. But Aunt Lilo couldn't help that.

I suddenly felt really bad for reading this disturbing stanza out loud and not looking for a more romantic one.

"I'm sorry," I said. "Next time, I'll read 'Welcome and Farewell' by Goethe." Lilo nodded sadly at me.

After we all got out of the car, Mom pulled a little package from her purse. It was time for Dad's white pill. He happily put it in his mouth, and his Adam's apple bobbed up and down.

Dad and I took Aunt Lilo by the hand, Mom walked ahead, and Grandpa dawdled behind. Aunt Lilo refused to walk properly. We had to pull her across the street to the cemetery. When we reached the wrought iron gate, she began to cry again. We lugged her down the gravel path.

Behind us Grandpa complained about the ugly flower beds and grumbled that under socialism, even death was a burden.

Outside the chapel, Dad stopped, looked at Aunt Lilo, and opened his hand. Lying there was the pill. He hadn't taken it after all. "It will help. You take it," he said to her. "It will make things easier."

She opened her mouth and stuck out her tongue. Dad placed the pill there.

Inside, we were greeted by friends who immediately tended to Aunt Lilo. Everyone else was quiet and composed.

We all sat in a row. Grandpa threaded his cane between Herr and Frau Hagen and pointed it at the coffin on a platform at the front.

"Max. Lilo's husband."

The minister gave a speech, which I could barely follow, because Dad went on the whole time about how Max was in the Stasi, and Grandpa kept yelling, "Quiet!" Aunt Lilo fell asleep during the sermon and started snoring. We couldn't wake her. She sat in her chair and didn't move, just slept through everything. No one knew what to do. Since the next funeral was about to start, a group of relatives finally carried her from the hall and set her on a bench outside.

In the commotion no one was watching Dad. Outside, he took my hand and pointed at the sky, which was cloudless and blue. "Let's skedaddle."

We ran to our Trabbi. Dad pulled the key from his pocket. Evidently, he'd stolen it from Mom's bag.

I sat down in the front passenger seat. Dad looked at me solemnly. "And now, we're driving to the sea."

"But what about Mom? And Grandpa?"

He grinned. "They'll have to take the train home today."

And with that, he took off. I didn't like the fact that Mom didn't know what we were doing, but I couldn't do anything about it.

Dad sped through Rostock like a madman, taking the Schutower Ring and passing by the new housing developments on the way to Warnemünde.

At Hotel Neptun, we almost crashed into a fat West German guy who was just standing in the middle of the street, not moving. Dad slammed on the brakes. The Trabbi came to a stop only a few meters away from the man.

This jerk then threw his arms in the air and started hollering, even though it wasn't our fault.

Dad rolled down the window. "Make room, zoom zoom!"

The man stared at us stupidly as we passed.

We parked behind the hotel and ran down to the beach. It was actually way too cold for swimming, but Dad didn't notice things like that. He took off his clothes and sprang through the surf in his underwear. I followed him, although the water couldn't have been more than sixty degrees. Still, it was fun doing something with Dad. I scrabbled into his arms, and he flung me into the waves. I didn't know what was up and what was down. When I surfaced, I heard gulls screeching above my head as the white foam of the waves danced around me.

I feel strong, erratic tugging on the string. I look up.

Andreas has flung an arm out of the water. "A ship!"

My heart pounds with excitement. I kick my flippers to hoist myself out of the water a little so I can see better. Through my goggles, I detect something dark hulking on the horizon, probably a tanker. Water keeps splashing into my field of vision. "It's kilometers away. But still, it's a good sign."

The shipping route isn't far off now.

Andreas lies on his back and slowly moves his flippers for balance. The bag is on his stomach, and he opens it carefully so nothing falls in the water. He pulls out the plastic baggie of chocolate.

"Where's your snorkel?" I ask.

"In my bag. It cuts into my gums, so I'd rather breathe normally, even if I sometimes swallow water."

He hands me the small packet.

Our precious Block chocolate.

"Saxony Jensie would freak and wolf it all down." Andreas grins.

With numb fingers, I break the bar in the middle and hand him half. "You have to eat really slowly. It's best to suck on it; otherwise it'll come straight back up."

I painstakingly peel off the wrapper and contemplate it. "Where do I put this?"

Stupid question, really.

Andreas smiles again. "Take it to the West. They'll be thrilled."

I let the wrapper float off. Andreas nibbles on his piece of chocolate. I need to be careful not to choke as I eat. Without meaning to, I dunk my chocolate underwater. I carefully take a bite, and it's salty, but then the sweetness overpowers it.

The sugar hits the spot. I can feel the way it moves through my veins and into my cells. The headache I've had for a while fades, and my field of vision expands.

I watch the orange-and-brown wrapper meander toward the south.

"We're leaving a trace," Andreas points out.

"More importantly, we're swimming against a current. We can't hang out here much longer. We have to continue."

"Hm." Andreas looks at the sky and seems lost in thought, as though he hadn't been listening. But then he starts kicking his legs harder. I check the compass.

We paddle slowly northward on our backs, sucking on chocolate. There are blue skies and a good number of clouds above us. They're cumulus clouds, fat and white, some tinged with gray.

I pause to take a swig from the canteen. Andreas is thirsty too. We have to ration the water carefully.

The sun has grown stronger, and steam rises from the water—you can see the gentle movements of the waves. The wind has picked up too, and it blows keenly across the water.

"I gotta pee," Andreas says, breaking the silence.

It's so disgusting; we would have to pee in our wet suits. You can't take off your suit in the water because it's impossible to get the thing back on. You need resistance and solid ground beneath your feet. I only learned this recently myself. Besides, we can't just pee.

"Remember what Grandpa said."

"Yeah," Andreas mutters. "Great trick. Another one from his drinking buddy in the Coastal Border Brigade?"

"Don't think so. War experience."

"Or hearsay."

"As long as your bladder is full and you have to fight to hold it in, you won't fall asleep. Grandpa's friend fell asleep and died after swimming for hours on end."

"And how did your grandpa know his friend had peed?"

"How should I know? Maybe none of the survivors did."

Andreas falls silent for a while, unconvinced. "I can't imagine them talking about stuff like that during the war."

We keep swimming on our backs, looking at the sky. The sun shines on my belly and warms it up. It feels nice.

"Then again, we're talking about peeing," Andreas says, more to himself than to me. "This is similar to the war, what with boats chasing us."

Tune everything out and keep swimming, that's best. Don't think and don't pee.

The sunlight changes the color of the water. It turns dark blue, then lightens. In the distance, some layers of water appear to move more than others—maybe the current is stronger there.

We have to concentrate on swimming. That's the most important thing right now.

"By the way, the sun blinds me when I crawl," Andreas says. "The light hits on the right, exactly where I breathe."

"Same here." The goggles intensify the effect, but we can't take them off.

"Can you breathe on the other side?" I ask.

82

"Nope, it throws off my rhythm. Crazy, all the things you need to consider when fleeing. Who'd a thunk it?"

Ulrich wanted me to learn to breathe on both sides, to improve my form. You always swim more powerfully on your breathing side, but if you breathe every three strokes, it balances out your crawl. I never did figure it out.

I'm about to turn onto my front when I notice these poles behind me, sticking out of the Baltic in a line that runs parallel to the coast.

I jiggle Andreas's arm and point. "What are those?"

Andreas studies the poles for several seconds, then looks at me through his goggles. I can read the surprise in his expression. "Is it the border?"

"I don't know."

"Is the border marked?"

I don't think so, but how should I know?

According to Grandpa, international waters just start, without any kind of special sign. That's what comrade Johnson, from the Coastal Border Brigade, whispered to him, but whether Johnson always tells the truth when he's drunk is uncertain.

Grandpa. Comrade Johnson. Our sources aren't exactly reliable.

"Let's crawl again. It's quickest."

I roll onto my front and look north. We see it at the same time.

"Another ship," Andreas cries excitedly. "A tanker! More than one, actually!"

There are at least three ships in the distance, out of our reach. A glimmer of hope, nonetheless. Just hang in there a few more hours, and our chance will come.

"By tonight, we'll be in Hamburg," Andreas says.

The chocolate gave us energy. Besides, it's finally light out, and we can see where we're swimming. I never would've thought that would make such a difference.

I'm not tired anymore, and Andreas is acting very lively too. I read the compass. "We're going to keep swimming north, to get as far away from the GDR as possible. Once we've put in a few hours, we'll correct toward the northwest."

"Spoken like a true sea dog," Andreas murmurs.

I just think that's the way to do it. I hope I'm right. "We have to be careful not to drift too far east."

"Even if we do, we'll still arrive in Fehmarn or Gedser. Either would be fine."

Andreas starts to crawl. I feel the pull of the string and follow him.

It's not that simple. The Baltic Sea is full of currents you don't even notice. We could theoretically swim north the entire time and still wind up in the East.

But I won't hold him back.

We swim side by side, evenly and without tripping each other up. The string doesn't even tighten anymore—we've found our pace. Sometimes Andreas twitches the string, probably to check whether I'm still there. I respond by sending him the same signal.

I don't know how long I've been swimming. I lose all sense of time.

There's water everywhere. It flows through my fingers, past my face, always yielding, never providing support. It's there but impossible to grasp.

I yearn for something solid to brace myself against, something that won't fall back. But that doesn't exist in the sea. No bottom, no wall, no side of the pool. This far out, there won't be any more sandbars sneaking up on us.

The boat from that TV show *The Dream Ship* won't suddenly appear either.

I almost burst out laughing, remembering Saxony Jensie. When the GDR bought *The Dream Ship* from the ZDF network, he was proud as a peacock, actually believed he might go on a cruise sometime as a regular FDGB vacationer. But the ship was only intended for big wigs. And its name wasn't *Astor* anymore but *Arkona*, like the town on Rügen, the northernmost point in the GDR.

Grandpa said that the new name had to start with *A*, because there was a big *A* engraved in the fancy silverware that came with the ship. That way, they wouldn't have to replace all of the knives, forks, and spoons. Which would have bankrupted the GDR, he said.

The water no longer glows the way it did at sunrise, or maybe my eyes have adjusted. There doesn't seem to be anything out here, no life. The Baltic is murky, and there are no fish here, not even jellyfish.

The swimming has changed too. It's more predictable, the sea now less choppy than it was near the coast. Back there, the waves would break and we had to dive under to maintain our pace. The rhythm is more regular out here—the waves approach slowly and retreat slowly, lift us up and let us back down, rolling on. Sometimes it feels like I'm flying, hovering over things.

The profound emptiness below scares me.

What if I fall and can't hold on? If I stop swimming, I'll sink. There's no fighting it.

Think about something else!

You're in the pool!

Ulrich—he's standing by the edge of the pool. He looks down at you, then up at the big clock. He's not impressed—you're too slow.

The orange life buoy hangs on the wall. In a second, you'll have to turn. The black stripe on the bottom of the pool, the big *T* at the end of the lane that announces the approaching wall.

One, two, boom, turn. Now back again! Swim faster!

Ulrich runs the length of the pool, establishing the pace. I have to keep up with him, just have to keep swimming. He's got the whistle in his mouth and is running way too fast, then whistles several times in a row, setting the rhythm for my strokes.

He holds up the stopwatch, the sign that I'm too slow.

I just have to keep swimming.

He'll be disappointed if I don't stick it out.

Fifty meters in thirty strokes, remember to follow through.
Faster. Pull and glide, pull and glide.
Think of a poem. It'll distract you.
Pull and glide.
See, they come,—and come flooding, those waters all!
No, not that poem, a different one.
One that's set on land.
Before his lion-court, to see the griesly sport, sate the King.
Pull and glide. *Beside him group'd his princely peers.*
One poem after the other, whatever pops into your head.
That will get you through a few more kilometers.

And the poems will lead to other thoughts to distract you. Just don't think about the water.

It isn't easy to focus on a poem and swim at the same time. Every poem has its own rhythm that you need to align with your movements without slowing them down or speeding them up. Some poems work well with the breaststroke, while others are better for the crawl.

I can only recite "The Diver" while doing the breaststroke—I get the words mixed up when swimming the crawl. And you have to think the stanzas through to the end. It's not enough to just have them in your mind. But my thoughts run wild while I'm swimming; I can barely contain them, have to concentrate on every last line. Like in language arts class with Frau Kröger.

Of all our teachers, I liked her best. In our class, she started out as a sub for old man Behrens, who was always sick. But on the first day of eighth grade, she came and told us that she was now our official language arts teacher. The boys started fidgeting and got all excited, probably because she was a lot prettier than Herr Behrens.

~~

"Let's start off the first day of school nice and easy."

Frau Kröger placed *The Iliad* on the table and reached for the class roster. She wore a blue dress.

She ran her finger down the list of our names, then looked over the top of her glasses. "Which of you is Jens Blum?"

A few people snickered. Everyone knew what was coming.

Saxony Jensie obediently raised his hand.

"Please come to the front and read out loud for us."

Saxony Jensie stood up. "I'm not very good at that, though!"

He shuffled to the teacher's desk. As always, his Boxer-brand jeans were practically falling off him.

"His Saxon accent is always worse after vacation," Andreas commented.

"All those weeks in enemy territory," Ronny hooted.

"Well, you all reek of fish and don't even notice," Saxony Jensie screamed back.

"Quiet, now, all of you!" Frau Kröger took off her glasses.

Saxony Jensie sat down and opened the book. He flipped pages back and forth for ages, looked up, bounced his legs, then turned more pages.

"The red slip of paper," Frau Kröger said patiently.

He finally found it and stared at the page. "I can't read this."

"Just give it a try."

Saxony Jensie leaned over the book. He groaned. Then he began, haltingly: "'Sing, O goddess, the anger of Achilles son of Peleus, that brought countless ills upon the Achaeans. Many a brave soul did it send hurrying down to Hades, and many a hero did it yield a prey to dogs and vultures, for so were the counsels of Jove fulfilled.'"

Some people giggled, presumably because the text sounded even stupider in a Saxon accent.

He helplessly looked around the class. "What the heck is this?"

Frau Kröger turned toward the window, so we couldn't see her face. "This is Homer. Please continue."

Saxony Jensie kept losing his place and had to start over from the beginning. It got old quick. No one understood a word.

Eventually, Frau Kröger saved us. "Thank you, Jens. You may return to your seat."

"Those are some really weird words. I didn't understand a thing." He got up, shaking his head.

"And who here can read better than Jens Blum?"

Andreas whacked the table with his ruler. "Hanna! She reads to her father every day because he's laid up in bed!"

I punched him in the back.

"Ow!" he cried.

Frau Kröger gave me a nasty look. "What's gotten into you, Hanna?"

I stared at the floor and walked up to the teacher's desk. I didn't make the same mistake I had in the past and tell the whole class about my dad. When I was little, I once wrote a story about taking the ferry to Gehlsdorf in response to the prompt "My Favorite Vacation." Mom and I rode the ferry across the Warnow to visit Dad in the mental hospital. Everyone in class teased me afterward and spread the news that my dad was bonkers. Frau Pinnow gave me an A on the essay and advised me not to write about my everyday life in the future but to think up something nice instead. I thought that was stupid—after all, Jack London was my role model, and he didn't just think things up. He had experienced everything himself.

I sat down at the teacher's desk, opened *The Iliad*, and read for the rest of the period. Jack London is definitely an easier read. When the bell rang for recess, I hung back. I was alone in the room when I suddenly heard Grandpa bellowing.

"On toward dawn, comrades in arms!"

I ran to the window and opened it. He was standing under a chestnut tree by the schoolyard fence, brandishing his cane.

"Let's go to Barnstorfer Wald! Go on the swing ride, eat some cotton candy!"

I dashed into the hallway but didn't get far. Someone caught me by my schoolbag. I recognized her by the scent of lavender.

"Where do you think you're going, young lady?"

"To Grandpa."

"Out of the question!"

Frau Thiel couldn't stand him. He once called her a fat wench at a solidarity bazaar for Nicaragua, because she ate three pieces of cake.

She dragged me back into the classroom. "Sit. You should be ashamed of yourself!"

She fished her keys out of her purse, and she simply locked me in.

I ran back to the window and looked out. It was way too high to jump.

"I'm locked in!"

"What's that?" Grandpa cupped a hand behind his ear.

"I'm locked in!" I screamed even louder.

"What?"

"I can't get out!"

He hoisted up his cane in agitation and held it like a rifle as he ran across the schoolyard. His tie flapped in the wind, and his hair went every which way. Students anxiously scurried aside as he passed.

In the hallway, he thundered, "I wish to speak to the director of this educational institution immediately!"

"That's out of the question, Herr Klein. Your grand-daughter has classes to attend!"

"Well, well, well, if it isn't the fat wench!"

There was a loud crack in the hall. Grandpa's cane. "I want to see my granddaughter!"

A few students had gathered and were laughing.

"All right, everyone back to class. Chop-chop!" Frau Thiel yelled.

"Chop-chop," Grandpa mimicked her.

Apparently Frau Thiel got a bit rough because Melanie Paul started shrieking. She shrieked whenever she got the chance.

There was another crack. "So that's what socialist education looks like! Goodness gracious me. Reminds me of my time in the labor camp."

"Would you shut your mouth!"

Party Secretary Karlow.

Now I was scared. The worst of the worst. She spit when she talked because she was always so worked up about imperialists. She would often barge into class to complain about NATO, Ronald Reagan, or West German television, glaring at us the whole time, as if it were some-how our fault. Sabine, who sat at the front, always got showered in Karlow's spit, but she deserved it. She was a dirty snitch.

"Well, well, well. Where there's a comrade, there's the Party!" Grandpa exclaimed down the hallway.

Then he began to sing, cracking his cane down on the

tile floor to the beat. "For he who fights for what's right, is always in the right . . ."

"There will be consequences," Party Secretary Karlow hissed.

"He called me a fat wench!" Frau Thiel cried.

I pounded against the inside of the door. "Grandpa, stop it and go home!"

"You can hear for yourself," Party Secretary Karlow seethed. "Leave now to stop making things even worse for your granddaughter!"

Grandpa blew his nose. "Tell me, comrade Karlow, what is it you teach anyhow?"

He knew very well that Party Secretary Karlow didn't teach, but agitated.

I hammered against the door again. That seemed to bring Grandpa to his senses. "I'll go now, to prevent matters from escalating unnecessarily and to allow you to focus entirely on the education of our glorious youth."

He shuffled down the hall, dragging his cane behind.

"Your granddaughter can be thankful for a grandfather like you," Party Secretary Karlow snapped.

I ran back to the window. The bell rang for class.

Grandpa's checkered handkerchief hung from his pants pocket. His head was bowed as he crossed the schoolyard. He was so exhausted, he didn't even look up at me.

Then I heard the key. *The fat wench*, I thought, and hid behind the curtain. Someone entered the room, humming

"Jenseits von Eden," by Nino de Angelo. I inhaled deeply. No hint of lavender. I cautiously peeked past the curtain and saw Frau Kröger setting down a few books on the teacher's desk.

I stepped out. "Hello."

She jumped in surprise. "My goodness, you scared me. What on earth are you doing in here?"

"Frau Thiel locked me in. Because of Grandpa."

"I see."

"She didn't want me to go to Barnstorfer Wald with him."

"Well." She carefully arranged the stack of books on the edge of the table. "At this hour, you'd have no business being there either."

She turned toward the door. "This period started a while ago now. You should get to class."

I grabbed my bag, and we left the room. I heard voices in the hallway. Someone said my name.

"Crap," I whispered. "They're gonna kill me. Grandpa made fun of Frau Karlow!"

The voices approached. I tried to run back into the classroom and behind the curtain.

"No, wait." Frau Kröger grabbed my arm and thought for a minute. "Come with me, and keep your mouth shut!"

We went into a small storage room at the end of the hall. She handed me a stack of books. On top was *How the Steel Was Tempered*.

"What am I supposed to do with these?" The books

smelled old. They were very heavy, and I almost lost my balance.

"Don't make such a scene," Frau Kröger grumbled. "You're an athlete, aren't you?"

She took a few books too.

Walking down the big staircase, Principal Schneider, Frau Thiel, and Party Secretary Karlow came toward us. I moved the stack in front of my face so all they could see was the ugly front cover of *How the Steel Was Tempered*.

"There you are," hissed Party Secretary Karlow. Her brown hair was pulled back in a tight braid. Not a single hair could escape. Her skin was irritated from her constant rage and studded with tiny red pustules.

"Mm-hmm," Principal Schneider grunted.

"You're coming with us this instant," Frau Thiel exclaimed.

"Hey there, Klaus. Kind of a bad time." Frau Kröger simply kept walking. "I need Hanna to carry these books for me. They're really quite heavy." She groaned a bit excessively. I followed her. Party Secretary Karlow obviously wasn't on board.

"Your books can't wait?" she asked acerbically.

Frau Kröger didn't look at her. "Afraid not. What with all the classes I'm subbing for. First semester report cards for three classes. That's no small undertaking."

"We need to have a word with Hanna Klein."

Frau Kröger turned to Principal Schneider. "Does it have to happen this very minute, Klaus?"

Principal Schneider's head wobbled uncertainly. We'd already taken another step. The three behind us didn't move.

Principal Schneider couldn't keep up with his club foot.

We put the books in the cabinet in the language arts classroom.

"I'll have to carry all of these back down again later."

"That was awesome!" I sat at a desk. "I think Karlow has evil eyes. So cold and blank."

Frau Kröger rummaged around in the cabinet.

I flipped through *How the Steel Was Tempered*.

Frau Kröger emerged from the cabinet. She looked disheveled. "That's required reading next year."

"The stuff we have to read in school is always so boring. The only book I really liked was *Owlet Hollow*."

A red slip of paper marked a page in the book. I opened to it. A paragraph had been circled. I read it out loud.

"'Man's dearest possession is life, and it is given to him to live but once. He must live so as to feel no torturing regrets for years without purpose, never know the burning shame of a mean and petty past; so live that, dying, he can say: all my life, all my strength were given to the finest cause in all the world—the fight for the Liberation of Mankind.'"

I leaned back.

Frau Kröger gave me a tired smile and took the book. Then she placed a different one on the table for me. "Read this. Another Russian."

Out in the hallway, Party Secretary Karlow was screaming at someone. Frau Kröger winced and straightened her dress. "We'd better wait before we go back out." She sat down beside me at the desk.

We both looked at the chalkboard, where the brown coal mining sites in the GDR were listed in spidery handwriting. Next to it, someone had drawn the Border of Peace between East Germany and Poland formed by the Oder and Neisse Rivers.

In front of me on the table was *Crime and Punishment*, by Fyodor Mikhailovich Dostoevsky.

"Is it any good?"

Frau Kröger folded her arms the way we learned in first grade. Her wedding band glinted in the sunlight coming into the room. She nodded.

"What's it about?"

"Morality. Right and wrong. And about humanity."

"For the whole thing?"

She nodded.

"Sounds really boring."

Things were getting louder outside the room.

Frau Kröger got up, scurried to the door, and carefully opened it.

"Be careful Karlow doesn't see you," I whispered. "Otherwise we're next!"

Frau Kröger ducked and peered through the crack. I slinked up from behind and looked over her shoulder. At the end of the hallway, Party Secretary Karlow had cornered a tenth-grade boy, who fiddled with his Adidas sneakers indifferently as she told him off.

"Great attitude, wonderful. That's all our country needs, FDJ members like you!"

Without warning, Party Secretary Karlow looked in our direction. Frau Kröger snapped her head back, straight into my nose. It immediately started to bleed.

"What next?" she groused, slamming the door shut. She went to the sink and soaked a washcloth in cold water. Then she pushed me onto a chair, held the washcloth against the back of my neck, and pressed a white cloth handkerchief with a green border to my nose.

"Great day," she said.

"How is that my fault?" I mumbled into the cloth. Cold was spreading from my neck through my skull and into my forehead.

"Your grandpa should steer clear of school. You see what happens when he doesn't."

The door opened. Party Secretary Karlow stared at us, her gaze as if she'd spent the last thousand years encased in ice.

Frau Kröger stiffened. It was slight, but I noticed.

"What are you doing?"

By now, the handkerchief was soaked in blood.

"First aid, isn't it obvious?"

Fresh blood shot out of my nose and onto my top.

"Damn it!" Frau Kröger leaned over me. "Do you have a fresh handkerchief, by chance? Mine is completely ruined."

Party Secretary Karlow didn't budge. She was no help at all. I pawed through my schoolbag for my math notebook and pulled out a sheet of blotting paper. I ripped it in half, balled up the strips, and stuffed them in either nostril.

"Good idea," Frau Kröger praised me, patting my shoulder. "Even if it does look ridiculous."

"This will have repercussions!" Party Secretary Karlow slammed the door shut.

The repercussions came the very next day, just as Herr Parek was walking us through the theory of evolution, scribbling all over the board.

"This stuff is way over my head," Saxony Jensie murmured beside me. "*Homo erectus, Homo neanderthalensis, Homo sapiens.*"

Andreas turned around with a dopey grin. "And *homosexual!*"

Saxony Jensie hit him in the back with his ruler. "Have you guys heard this one? How come people in the GDR can't be descended from apes?"

"No idea."

"It's obvious! You ever seen an ape that could survive that long without bananas?"

The PA system began to crackle. Principal Schneider's voice shot into the room: "One, two, one, two!"

Herr Parek stopped scribbling and looked up in confusion. "What is it this time?"

"The voice of God," Andreas said.

The class laughed.

"One, two. Hanna Klein to the principal's office. Immediately."

Herr Parek gestured toward the door with his piece of chalk. "Off you go."

Andreas raised his hand. "May I go to the bathroom, Herr Parek?"

"No, you may not."

"But it's an emergency!"

"Not now."

"But he has to go!" Saxony Jensie crowed. "Do you want him to pee his pants or something?"

"Quiet, damn it. Only Hanna leaves the room. Otherwise I'll be the only one left standing here, and we all know it."

He turned back to the board and added some more fur to *Australopithecus*.

I stepped into the empty hallway. Principal Schneider, Party Secretary Karlow, and Frau Thiel were already waiting in the office. Frau Thiel wore a yellow dress with a hideous floral pattern.

"Ah, yes," Principal Schneider said. "Hanna Klein. We would like to speak with you regarding your grandfather. What is your stance on his behavior?"

Everyone stared at me. I looked at the stunted potted plant on the windowsill. No one ever watered it.

"Take a stance," Party Secretary Karlow spit. "That means now!"

I recalled the opening of Jack London's *The Sea-Wolf*, which I did whenever I wanted to distract myself.

"We're waiting, *Jugendfreundin* Klein!" Principal Schneider limped around the room. His club foot thudded heavily on the linoleum.

Party Secretary Karlow came up closer. "I would hope you are aware that our state only grants its most capable students the opportunity to take the *Abitur*." She circled me. "Do you consider yourself among these capable students?"

I pictured Wolf Larsen and imagined what he might do in my place.

"Do you believe you deserve to receive higher education at the expense of our socialist state?"

He probably would have beaten them all to death. Or squished a raw potato with his bare hands.

"Say something," Frau Thiel hissed.

Party Secretary Karlow seized me by my upper arms. "Do you consider yourself suitable for university matriculation while your own grandfather disparages the educational measures of the state?" She shook me. "Answer me!"

As long as she was ragging on Grandpa, it was best not to say anything. There was nothing Frau Karlow could do to him now since he was already retired.

Principal Schneider signaled her to calm down. She sat down petulantly behind his desk and picked up a pen, as if she wanted to take notes.

"Would you open your mouth already?" Frau Thiel shrieked from the corner.

Everything was so easy all of a sudden. I lifted my gaze, looked out the window at the blue sky, then closed my eyes.

"'I scarcely know where to begin, though I sometimes facetiously place the cause of it all to Charley Furuseth's credit. He kept a summer cottage in Mill Valley, under the shadow of Mount Tamalpais, and never occupied it except when he loafed through the winter months and read Nietzsche and Schopenhauer to rest his brain.'"

The room was silent.

"'When summer came on, he elected to sweat out a hot and dusty existence in the city and to toil incessantly. Had it not been my custom to run up to see him every Saturday afternoon and to stop over till Monday morning, this particular January Monday morning would not have found me afloat on San Francisco Bay.'"

"What's all this?"

I opened my eyes. Principal Schneider looked at Frau Thiel, who shrugged. Party Secretary Karlow clenched her jaw as she stared at the silver ballpoint pen in her hand.

I saw Dad lying before me, smiling blissfully, because he loved *The Sea-Wolf*.

"'Not but that I was afloat in a safe craft, for the *Martinez* was a new ferry-steamer, making her fourth or fifth trip on the run between Sausalito and San Francisco. The danger lay in the heavy fog which blanketed the bay, and of which, as a landsman, I had little apprehension.'"

Party Secretary Karlow got up and walked out the door. Frau Thiel didn't move.

Principal Schneider folded his arms and stepped over to the window. "What is this, the Volkstheater?" he murmured. He turned slightly toward me but didn't look at me. "You are dismissed. Meeting adjourned."

I tore the door open in relief and ran into the hallway. I almost crashed into Frau Kröger.

"Whoa there, careful!" She held on to my arm and eyed me. "Everything all right? Party Secretary Karlow just mowed me down too. Are you the reason she's so angry?"

Frau Thiel strode into the hallway. "You should be very, very ashamed of yourself! There will be consequences! You should be ashamed of yourself! Shame on you!"

She gasped for air as she headed down the stairs.

"How peculiar," Frau Kröger said quietly as she watched her leave.

"What?"

"It's just, if someone asked me to name a student who came into regular conflict with authority, you wouldn't spring to mind."

I puffed out my cheeks.

"Was it bad?"

"No, I used Jack London to get me out of the situation."

She raised her right eyebrow. "Seriously?"

I nodded. "Turns out literature really is good for something!"

She frowned at me. "Of course it is. That's what I spend every class talking about!"

We walked together down the hall.

"It's because of Grandpa Franz. They've got it out for me now, since he acted so stupid."

Frau Kröger remained silent. Then we heard the familiar voice. "Aha! There you are!"

"Ugh, not again," I sighed. "I've just about had it with her."

"Don't treat this too lightly, Hanna," Frau Kröger warned me quietly.

Party Secretary Karlow marched toward us.

"What a delightful performance! Maybe you should become an actress."

She gave me a surly look, then turned to Frau Kröger. "What do you think, Frau Kröger? You're her language arts teacher. Hanna Klein is just made for the stage, wouldn't you say?"

"Could be."

"Maybe we should rethink that biology major," Karlow said. "Could be it's a mistake. Maybe the *Abitur* is too."

"There's still some time before all that," Frau Kröger countered.

Karlow scrutinized her. "Time? Do you mean to suggest that Hanna Klein should take her time in fixing her attitude?"

"Of course not," Frau Kröger murmured. No one spoke for a few seconds. I didn't know where to look. The sight of Frau Karlow made me nauseous.

"Well then . . ." Frau Kröger took me by the arm and pulled me down the hall.

"I have math now, with Frau Bauermeister. That's in the other direction," I whispered.

"Hush," Frau Kröger hissed. "You need to get out of here first."

I was way late to class, of course.

The classroom was silent. Everyone was writing in their notebooks. Frau Bauermeister pointed at the board. "Rewrite the term using the second binomial formula!"

I opened my notebook.

"I'm completely lost," Saxony Jensie said beside me.

I quickly helped him with the problem. When Frau Bauermeister asked who knew the answer, he raised his hand and strutted up to the board with his notebook.

After Saxony Jensie got his A for the day and sat back down, Andreas turned around. "So? How was it?"

"Not too bad. Frau Kröger protected me from Karlow."

"Really?" Saxony Jensie yelped. "Wow! She's pretty great. She doesn't just repeat everything they say at assemblies or on the news. I've noticed that before."

"Quiet!"

"Wanna know what my neighbor Frau Kresse told me?" Saxony Jensie winked conspiratorially. "Frau Kröger's fiancé was in prison because he was bumping heads with the state. They kicked him out of the GDR. Then they told Frau Kröger to renounce him."

"And?" Andreas and I asked at the same time.

"And what?"

"Moving on now to the third binomial formula . . ."

"Did she?"

"Did she what?"

". . . once Andreas, Jens, and Hanna finish their conversation, which I'm sure is very important!"

"Renounce him, dude, come on!"

Saxony Jensie looked up in alarm. "No idea! My neighbor didn't know either."

"I bet she did," Andreas hissed. "They'd never let her be a teacher otherwise."

"That's so sad," I said.

Saxony Jensie shook his head. "At least her fiancé is over there now and can go to Kurfürstendamm. I bet he couldn't care less that she married someone else."

~~

On the platform, by the fountain
stands a man, scooping
the water with two hands.
And those waiting see the
uniform and the boots
caked in dust; there on the tracks
are railroad cars
with cannon. They see:

He goes thirsty
for them,
his boots are

> *caked in dust*
> *for them—*
> *and he approaches the cannon now*
> *for them.*

Stupid poem by Berger, it's got no rhythm.

It's the last one I've got.

Doesn't rhyme. Can't swim to it at all.

"The Drinker." Can't remember who wrote it. Definitely not Goethe. I memorized it at the Baltic Sea Stadium, during breaks between foot races at the children's *Spartakiad*.

Spartakiad champions today, Olympic champions tomorrow.

That was printed on the banner waving over our heads. Illogical. Not every *Spartakiad* champion can become an Olympic champion. It's not even mathematically possible.

That was the day my coach, Manfred Sandhagen, told me I'd been eliminated and wouldn't be attending the sports academy. Wasn't fast enough and showed no potential for improvement.

The Olympics were off the table for me. I sat under that stupid banner and cried my eyes out. I would have loved to try for the team, but there was no chance now. Wouldn't be representing my socialist fatherland in athletic competition, like it said in my aptitude results. It was all over.

The one good thing about that day was Marita Koch. She opened the games and talked to us. Everyone knew her, considering she was the GDR's most famous athlete, and she wasn't even stuck up.

I stood off to the side because I felt like a loser. Didn't want to tell her I hadn't made the cut. She probably would have bolstered me up, but I was too embarrassed.

Around that time, I started practicing with the duck group. That's what the competitive swimmers called it. So embarrassing. The girls from my former training squad gave me pitying looks in the showers, then grabbed their towels and went to their regular spot in the stands. I walked over to the duck group, which gathered a little farther off. My new coach was Ulrich. He introduced me to the others. We did several timed 400-meter swims. Ulrich ran down the side of the pool with his stopwatch, screaming. I didn't see what the point was. Our times were no longer important. We'd never be better than the others.

Things really went downhill for Andreas that year. He couldn't keep it together, started playing hooky and picking fights with dudes he didn't even know. Saxony Jensie and I kept telling him to be careful, but he wouldn't listen. In late September, he disappeared for days and stopped coming to school. Saxony Jensie and I looked for him everywhere—the ramparts, Barnstorfer Wald, even in Warnemünde. At some point, he showed up at my front door, completely filthy, and asked me to walk him home. He was scared of his father, who beat him constantly, even under normal circumstances. After something like this, there'd be no stopping him. We walked to Augusten Strasse with our heads bowed. He quietly told me that, after a fight with his dad, he had grabbed his sleeping bag and taken the train to Stralsund. From there he'd caught the ferry to Hiddensee and roamed around the island for a few days. He'd slept in an old shed at night and used his allowance to buy rolls, processed cheese spread, and soda.

In the stairwell, I asked Andreas why he had run away. He looked at the floor and started to tremble. He shook his head, but all he said was that someday he'd be eighteen, and then he could finally move out.

At that point neither of us knew it would actually happen at age sixteen.

Andreas wasn't at school the next day. I brought over his homework after class. It was the worst I'd ever seen him. His left eye was swollen shut, his upper lip split. He was wearing a long synthetic sweater, so I couldn't see his arms.

The school year continued as badly for him as it had started. He constantly ran away from home and skipped school. Saxony Jensie and I quit searching for him because it wasn't like we ever found him. He would just hop a train to wherever—Wismar, Neubrandenburg, Grevesmühlen. He got tons of demerits and an official reprimand. That winter he broke into the kiosk at the public rose garden and stole cigarettes and liquor to sell to older students to cover the cost of his train tickets. That was the last straw.

Agents from Youth Welfare Services came to school and picked Andreas up, right in the middle of civics class. He had to hand over his ID in front of everyone, then leave the room with the agents. We all ran to the window, even though Frau Grahl yelled at us to stay in our seats. Andreas crossed the schoolyard with his head bowed, a man holding him by the forearm. He got into a yellow Moskvitch, and they drove him off.

Frau Grahl said that Andreas was going to a reformatory, where he would be trained to become a better citizen. No one was listening. He would come back with a greater sense of the collective spirit, she continued, and refrain from such reprehensible acts. Furthermore, the enemy of the state had clearly had a negative influence on Andreas. Saxony Jensie started fidgeting in his seat—I thought it was totally unfair of her to say that too. His father was to blame, not the enemy of the state. I pinched Saxony Jensie's arm so he'd keep his mouth shut. Things were bad enough as it was.

That afternoon Andreas's mother called me. No one had told her Andreas had been picked up. She interrogated me, crying the whole time. At the end, she asked what was going to happen to him. I didn't know.

She asked how this could have happened, as if it were my fault.

I had no clue either.

"He has repeatedly played truant, and for this reason, he has earned himself an official reprimand!" Frau Thiel stood before us with her finger raised. Andreas stared down at his desk. "This is very, very bad!"

Saxony Jensie leaned forward and prodded him with his ruler. "Dude, don't worry about it."

Andreas sat there, hunched over, and shrugged his shoulders. You could see he was scared.

"His grades have suffered considerably since last year! He is not a good example for the class, quite the opposite."

"He's the best in phys ed," Saxony Jensie shouted. Several of our classmates murmured in agreement.

"That may be, but athletic performance is not the sole deciding factor."

Saxony Jensie whacked the desk with his ruler. "Yes, it is!" Then he whispered, "I hate that fat witch! She looks like an old sack of potatoes."

"No whispering! His best friends clearly don't have a positive influence on him either. Hanna!" She lumbered toward me, wheezing. "Just two years ago, Andreas was as good a student as you. How do you explain that decline in performance?"

I was in no mood to answer.

Frau Thiel waited for a moment, then shook her head and returned to the board.

Her brown velvet dress was all stretched out.

"I'm very disappointed in you, Hanna."

It wasn't clear to me what I had done wrong, but it was better just to keep quiet.

Saxony Jensie raised his hand, brash as ever.

"Yes, Jens?"

"Why don't you ask his dad? I'm sure he can explain it!"

"Excuse me?"

Andreas turned around to Saxony Jensie. He was furious. "Shut up!"

Saxony Jensie was very upset. "Why not ask his dear father, seeing as it's his fault Andreas sometimes acts up."

Andreas gaped at him. He couldn't stop him from talking.

Frau Thiel crossed her arms. "Do you intend to bad-mouth Herr Kuschwitz here, in front of everybody?"

Saxony Jensie clasped his ruler stubbornly. "I'm not bad-mouthing him. He is bad."

In a flash Andreas lunged and smacked him. Saxony Jensie screamed.

I held Andreas's arm back to stop him. We both slid out of our chairs, onto the linoleum.

"Out, all three of you!" Frau Thiel boomed. "Take your things and go. I don't want to catch sight of you again today. There will be consequences, I assure you!"

We stuffed our books into our schoolbags and passed by Frau Thiel. She looked about ready to thrash us.

Saxony Jensie slammed the door behind us. "There will be consequences, there will be consequences," he mimicked Frau Thiel.

Andreas had calmed back down, and he left Saxony Jensie alone.

We stood stupidly in the middle of the hall. It was really quiet. Everyone was in class.

"We'd better go someplace else before Schneider hobbles by," Saxony Jensie said.

We left the building and crossed the schoolyard to the gym. We sat down on the steps. Saxony Jensie kicked around his brown gym bag like a soccer ball, and Andreas pelted little rocks against the mountain of coal heaped by the furnace room. The pile sat there and never got any smaller. They heated the whole school with it.

Finally, the bell rang for recess. We had PE next. We trudged to the smelly locker rooms and changed. Our classmates were starting to warm up to us again.

In the gym, we all lined up before Frau Kröger. A few girls sat on the benches to the side. They weren't participating because they had their period.

"You look thrilled as ever, class," Frau Kröger shouted and clapped her hands. "I'm happy to boost your enthusiasm." She called on Sabine. "What did I promise last class?"

"No idea."

"Exactly! Timed two-hundred-meter dashes!"

Everyone groaned.

"You each have two tries to earn a good grade for the day!"

Saxony Jensie puffed out his cheeks. "Ugh, I don't want to!"

"I'd've been shocked otherwise, Jens Blum!" She clapped again. "Let's go! Everyone outside!"

We filed into the schoolyard and lined up by the flag poles. It was cold and windy.

"Let's go, let's go," Saxony Jensie mimicked angrily.

Andreas whistled through his teeth and pointed at Frau Kröger. "Nice tracksuit she's got there!"

"Dude, that's from the West," Saxony Jensie whispered. "The three stripes mean it's real. At a socialist school, too."

"Jens Blum, Andreas Kuschwitz, Frank Kötter. You're up first. Then we'll have a girls' group. Once round the school; that's about two hundred meters."

"It's way too cold to run," Saxony Jensie said. "And has anyone ever actually measured it? 'Cause I'd say it's at least two hundred twenty meters."

He always found something to complain about. Frau Kröger ignored him, pulled up the zipper on her navy-blue tracksuit, and put the silver whistle in her mouth. Saxony Jensie, Andreas, and Frank went to the starting line.

The whistle blew. Andreas shoved Saxony Jensie to the side and scrambled to the front. All three disappeared behind the school.

We watched the other side of the building. Andreas shot around the corner first.

"28.42!"

Then Saxony Jensie came into view. He wasn't paying attention and ran straight into a flag pole. He hobbled up to us, griping.

Frau Kröger shook her head. "45.13. Not exactly a stellar performance."

He clutched his head. His red hair was a mess. "I can't help that it's an obstacle course!"

"You've been at this school long enough to know that the flag pole is there. That'll be a C for today." She wrote something in her grade book.

Saxony Jensie burst into tears. "Not fair!"

I ran against Karin Meier and Susanne Buhrmeister and was fastest.

"31.21," Frau Kröger called out.

Karin and Susanne were dorky and held hands as they strolled over the finish line together. Neither wanted to be the loser.

Frau Kröger shook her head irritably. "48.90. Marita Koch would not be impressed."

"Yeah, but she didn't run smack into a flag pole either," Saxony Jensie yelled, rubbing his head.

Everyone laughed, including Frau Kröger, but Andreas was looking past me in horror.

I turned around. Herr Kuschwitz was crossing the schoolyard. Andreas's father.

Andreas turned white and looked at the pavement. His father didn't even glance at him but walked straight into the building.

"What the heck's he doing here?" Saxony Jensie asked.

"Who cares?" Andreas replied. "Not me."

Frau Kröger's whistle chirped. "We're going to run the

same race again, to give Jens here an opportunity to avoid the flag poles. Let's go, let's go!"

She blew the whistle, and Saxony Jensie took off like a madman. This time, he didn't even round the corner. We waited for several minutes.

Frau Kröger sighed. "What obstacles could there possibly be behind the school?"

"The coal pile," Andreas grumbled.

"I'll go look for him," I volunteered, and ran off.

Saxony Jensie stood by the back entrance and waved. "Come quick!"

I sprang up the steps to join him. "Now we'll both get a C in gym! What is going on?"

"Kuschwitz is meeting with the principal. We're going up there, and maybe we can figure out what that asshole is doing here!"

We ran up the two flights of stairs, tiptoed to the door, and listened for a while. Luckily, the hallway was still deserted.

We kinda just stood there. Nothing happened.

"Andreas's dad is creepy. That's what I imagine people from the Stasi are like," Saxony Jensie whispered.

"They were at our house a few days ago," I whispered in return.

He reeled. "What? Why?"

"'Cause of Grandpa. He always rants against the state when he goes grocery shopping. Someone snitched on him."

"And what'd they do?"

"Nothing. They just talked to Frau Lewandowski, our neighbor. She told the Stasi that Grandpa sometimes belches in the stairwell, and that he's really clumsy and always trips over her laundry bag."

Saxony Jensie giggled. "I'm sure they really cared about all that."

"Frau Lewandowski told me later that she eavesdropped on what the other neighbors said. The only one at home was Frau Block, though, who's practically deaf, and she screamed at the top of her lungs that, unfortunately, she couldn't understand what the nice gentlemen were saying but that she would like to invite them in for a glass of egg liqueur. Then they left."

Saxony Jensie held a hand to his belly, he was laughing so hard. "Great neighbors!"

Suddenly we heard voices approaching inside the door. We quickly hid behind the big potted palm. The handle was pushed down.

Andreas's father came out of the office but turned back again on the threshold to face Principal Schneider, who stood behind him. "I'm sure it's the best solution for everyone. Things can't go on this way with him."

Then he closed the door, passed by us, and took the stairs down.

Saxony Jensie elbowed me behind the palm plant. "What was that supposed to mean?"

"Whatever it was, it can't be good."

Andreas's father's solid, decisive steps echoed through the school. He was now one floor below.

"What an asshole," Saxony Jensie hissed. "I hate him. He's arrogant and mean." We slipped out from behind the palm. "How could anyone be so horrible they'd criticize their own son to the school principal?" Without warning, he lost it. "You stupid asshole!" he screamed down the hall.

The footsteps slowed.

"Crap," I said.

Saxony Jensie kept yelling. "That's right, I mean you, you asshole!"

Andreas's father froze.

The sound carried better than Saxony Jensie had expected. He looked at me fearfully.

I shook him. "Have you lost your mind?"

We could hear the footsteps again. They were louder and approaching fast.

"Shit, he's coming!"

We ran down the hall toward the classrooms.

"I'm sorry," Saxony Jensie panted. "Where are we running?"

We couldn't go into any of the rooms because class was in session.

"Up to the attic!"

We used to have shop class there, but it was usually empty. We sprinted to the top floor. I took the stairs two at a time and pushed down the handle on the wooden door. Thankfully, it wasn't locked.

A class had just been there. It still smelled of burnt plastic and adhesive.

We closed the door behind us. I watched the stairs and hallway through a crack in the wood.

I couldn't see much.

Steps echoed through the schoolhouse. Then I saw Andreas's father. He stopped by the stairs to the attic.

Saxony Jensie leaned into me. "I'm going to pee my pants," he whimpered. "Do you see anything? What's he doing?"

"Looking up."

"Crap!"

"How could you be so stupid?" I whispered.

"At least he didn't see us! What's he doing?"

"He's waiting."

Saxony Jensie groaned softly. "What do we do if he comes up?"

"We hide."

Saxony Jensie's gym clothes smelled like feet. I could barely stand it.

Then a sharp voice shattered the silence. "Get out here, Saxon!"

Saxony Jensie stared at me, wide eyed. We didn't dare breathe.

"Come on, Saxon! Or do you want me to come get you?"

Saxony Jensie pinched my arm in fear. "Ow!" I hissed and pulled away.

At that moment the bell rang for recess. Doors opened and students flooded the hallway, roaring and laughing loudly.

"I'll get you, mark my words," Andreas's dad yelled up the stairs. Then he disappeared. We exhaled and leaned our backs against the door.

"That was close," I said, relieved.

Saxony Jensie banged the back of his head against the wood frantically. "How did he know it was me?"

"How do you think? You should be able to answer that stupid question yourself."

"My grandma says that I talk like one of you fish-heads now and don't even sound like a Saxon anymore."

"As if. Once a Saxon, always a Saxon."

"And now we've got stupid FDJ prep. I really don't want to go. I wish we could go to the ramparts instead."

We opened the door to our hideout and went down the stairs. We expected to find Andreas's father around every corner, so we had to sneak through the building, which made us late to the special class, called Under the Blue Banner after the color of the FDJ flag. Our civics teacher, Frau Grahl, led the sessions, which meant they were always boring in the extreme.

Because we were late, we immediately got red entries in our homework planners. What's more, we were still wearing our gym clothes, which Frau Grahl didn't appreciate in the least.

"Your clothing is highly inappropriate," she said.

"We didn't have time to change," Saxony Jensie retorted. "We had to do ten four-hundred-meter dashes in PE today. That takes longer than a regular school period."

The class giggled.

Frau Grahl knit her brow, as though doing the math, then shook her head in defeat.

Andreas was already there and clearly in a bad mood. "Your bags are still in the gym," he said sullenly.

We took our seats.

"Man, something stinks," Frank said, glaring at Saxony Jensie.

Frau Grahl opened a window. "Punctuality is the very least one must demonstrate to be accepted to the FDJ," she said.

"Yeah, yeah," Saxony Jensie muttered. "We get it."

Andreas raised his hand.

"Yes, Andreas."

"What happens if you don't even want to be accepted?"

"Dude," Saxony Jensie whispered and looked around anxiously, as if disaster were about to strike.

Frau Grahl blanched. "I don't believe my ears."

"Hypothetically speaking," Andreas said. "Let's say I'm asking for a friend."

"In that case the question is irrelevant."

"Why?"

"You'll have to tell me who this is in reference to, if you want an answer." Frau Grahl turned to the board and picked up a piece of chalk.

"Donald Duck," Ronny murmured. "He doesn't want to join the FDJ."

Saxony Jensie chuckled.

Frau Grahl's hand trembled as she started writing.

Andreas read along loudly. "Principle of democratic centralism."

"Just one more mean question, and she'll start bawling, like always," Saxony Jensie whispered.

Frau Grahl turned around and looked at us. "What's all this whispering?"

Andreas sat up straight. "Jens Blum has an important question."

"That's right," Saxony Jensie said. "The other day in geography, we were learning about Africa. Then we started wondering if the FDJ exists in Burkina Faso too. Can you tell us?"

Frau Grahl turned beet red and narrowed her eyes.

"Or is that also considered irrelevant?" Andreas asked.

Frau Grahl dropped the chalk and stormed out of the room.

"Told you," Saxony Jensie sneered. "Total crybaby."

Water flows around me, holds me up.

Waves come and go, the steady movement moves through me, and I flow with the water, at its mercy. My hands plunge in, and I hear the flippers splash. Beneath me are the depths, dark and scary.

Breathe. In and out, in and out. Again and again, endlessly.

I'm not moving forward. The waves toss me back, and I swim against resistance, not budging from the spot.

Everything is different than at practice. Nothing but cold, waves, and wind for hours on end. My coordination is off. At times, I can't control my fingers, allowing water to flow through and rendering the arm stroke utterly useless. I have to hold my fingers together better or I'll waste too much energy.

"We're almost there!" Andreas yells.

I look up. There's nothing in sight.

"Why do you say that?" I ask.

"Just 'cause."

His mouth twitches, which might be his attempt at a smile.

He's in a good mood, unlike me.

"Know what I'm gonna do first thing when we get to the West?"

I don't feel like thinking, and I don't feel like talking. I'm cold.

"Eat a bockwurst! If they have them there."

Great, now I'm nauseous too. I can't think of food right now, least of all bockwurst. I hate that kind of sausage.

"With lots of mustard."

"Stop it."

"Why, what's up?"

"I feel sick."

"Come on, don't be that way." He touches my arm, and I pull it away. "What's up with you? We're almost there."

"Leave me alone and let me swim. I don't feel like chatting."

I do a long arm stroke to get away from him. I tug at the string. Andreas isn't swimming. I stop and stare at him, super annoyed.

"Lie on your back and take a break," he says, like a pro.

Maybe he's right. Maybe I do need a break. But then I'll fall asleep. It won't work.

I shake my head. "I want to swim."

He nods and swims on with me.

I need to focus on technique and find my pace again.

Lift your arms out of the water, plunge them back in, parallel to the shoulder and in front of the head, then pull strongly. Regular kick, careful that the amplitude isn't too large; otherwise you'll start spinning. The body can't be allowed to roll; it's bad for your positioning in the water.

One stroke after another, then we'll reach our goal.

Slight pain in my right knee. How are you supposed to concentrate when you're in pain?

One, two, one, two. Salt burns the corners of my mouth.

One, two. Counting is all I can do. The poems have all slipped away.

The string holds me back again. I'm furious.

Andreas looks cheerful for no reason. "We've got the current at our backs," he shouts.

I look at the water and try to find a reference point,

which doesn't exist out here. But Andreas is right—we're being pushed north. I can feel it too.

"Some good news for a change," Andreas yells. "Denmark, here we come! See ya later, GDR!"

In the train to Bad Kleinen, Saxony Jensie kept playing and rewinding the cassette in his Stern tape player. We must have listened to "Take On Me," by a-ha at least ten times. The batteries eventually ran out from all the back and forth, and the song began to lag.

That immediately sent Saxony Jensie into a funk. "The batteries lasted longer on our field trip to Bad Doberan last spring, when we visited that memorial to victims of fascism."

Andreas had still been in our class at that point, before they sent him to the reformatory. The train ride there was so much fun. Thomas had brought along his tape player and was showing it off since he was the only one so far who'd gotten one. Everyone else had to wait till the *Jugendweihe* ceremony. As always, Saxony Jensie made a total fool of himself, because he was obsessed with hearing "You Can Win If You Want," by Modern Talking. He drove everyone crazy, including Frau Grahl. She kept telling us to shut off the Western music and listen to some of "our" songs. But no one wanted to listen to the Puhdys or Stern Meissen, and unfortunately, no one had brought any Karat tapes. Andreas liked them a lot.

Saxony Jensie grinned. "Remember when Frau Grahl and Sabine laid the wreath at the memorial, and Thomas was standing in the back row, playing 'Live Is Life'? Talk about a solemn event."

We transferred to the bus and sat down. We were bored.

"I don't even know what to expect from a reformatory," Saxony Jensie said. "Just the way it sounds." Then he enunciated each syllable. "Re-form-a-tor-y."

We were the only ones who got out at the stop. It was cold and wet outside.

"Pretty bleak," I said.

The bus drove off through deep puddles and splashed water high onto the sidewalk.

"At least we have mountains back home in Dresden," Saxony Jensie sighed, staring at the row houses. "There's really nothing going on here."

We walked along the glistening cobblestones. Windflowers blossomed in a meadow. Saxony Jensie carried the tape player on his shoulder. "Honestly, things are way nicer in the Elbe Sandstone Mountains!"

An old man was approaching.

"Could you please tell us where the reformatory is?"

He pointed. "Past the church, then take a right at the electrical substation onto the tarred road. Have you been misbehaving?"

"No," Saxony Jensie said, like a good boy. "Just visiting!"

After walking for fifteen minutes, we finally reached a heavy wooden gate and peered through the cracks. Behind it was a two-story, red-brick building. Standing around the front courtyard were wheelbarrows piled with more bricks. It smelled like smoldering wood. There was no one in sight.

Saxony Jensie took a deep breath. "So this is where Andreas lives."

I reached for the iron handle.

"Stop!"

We turned around. A man in baggy corduroy pants was headed our way. He had black hair and an enormous hook nose. He didn't look friendly.

"What do you want?"

"We're here to visit Andreas Kuschwitz," I explained.

Saxony Jensie set the tape player on the pavement and prattled off, "Blond curls, about five-five, athletic build."

The Nose stood before us and folded his thick arms. "No one's allowed in without prior registration."

"And where do we register?"

"With one of the organs of Youth Welfare Services."

Saxony Jensie shook his head in confusion. "Huh? What the heck is that? 'Organs of Youth Welfare Services.'"

"Are you family?"

"No, we're his best friends."

"In that case, get the hell out of here. Only family is allowed. Now get out of my sight!"

"But we came all the way from Rostock," I told him.

"Tough!"

We didn't move. The Nose spread his arms threateningly. "You deaf or something?"

"Just a minute, please!" Saxony Jensie bent down. He fumbled awkwardly with the player, then got the tape out and held it up.

"Can we give this to you? I made it specially for Andreas. 'Take On Me,' by a-ha, is on one side, and 'Cheri, Cheri Lady,' by Modern Talking, is on the other! Each song is on there eight times." He boastfully waved the cassette around.

"You recorded Modern Talking eight times for Andreas?" I blurted.

He puffed up with pride. "Yeah!"

"Are you mental? He thinks they suck!"

"But I like them. So when Andreas listens to the tape, it'll remind him of us."

"Brilliant idea." I shoved him.

"Ow," he screamed and hit me in the back with the cassette.

"You'll have to take that back home with you," the Nose said sternly. "He can't listen to that here."

We stopped tussling. "Why not? Isn't there a tape player?"

"No."

Saxony Jensie scratched his head pensively. Then he picked up the Stern tape player and held it out to the Nose. I couldn't believe my eyes.

"You're gonna give away your parents' player?"

"Just lending it." He looked up at me sadly.

The Nose slid back the bolt on the front gate. "Personal music isn't allowed, let alone Western music! You should have known that!"

"That sucks!"

"This isn't an FDGB vacation resort, you know. Now get out!" The Nose opened the gate and went in.

"I can't tape the Puhdys for him," Saxony Jensie whined. "He'd whup me the minute he gets out."

"You could have taped Karat."

"But he already has all their songs on tape!"

The Nose closed the gate without another word. Through the cracks, we saw him approach the building.

"Come on, let's check out the area," I suggested.

Saxony Jensie hoisted the tape player onto his shoulder and trotted behind me. Garbage and debris lay all over the place. The grounds were fenced in. Several windows in the red building were barred.

"Man, it's like a prison."

We reached a broad ditch filled with water and couldn't go any farther. We tried to cross it but sank in the ground and got our feet wet.

"God damn it," Saxony Jensie yelled. "We can't get in!"

"And Andreas can't get out. For half a year."

When we got back to Rostock, Saxony Jensie insisted on treating me to ice cream. I didn't feel like it but gave in and went with him to the Seafoam Café and ordered a pineapple sundae.

Saxony Jensie inhaled his ice cream. "Did you know that's not real pineapple? It's just sugar beets soaked in pineapple juice," he said, like a total smartass. "My dad told me. They sell the actual pineapple for Western currency!"

"I don't believe that. They'd have to sell the juice with it."

"No, you idiot!"

The two blue-haired grandmas sitting at the next table, each eating an enormous sundae, turned around to look at us. He leaned forward and whispered, "Man, that's the whole trick!"

Suddenly he turned bright red.

"What's wrong?"

He turned away and looked out the window. There was a man chasing after his umbrella, which sailed down the street.

"Did you see that?" Saxony Jensie laughed falsely.

He tipped more than a mark. As soon as the waitress left, I laid into him. "Are you mental? Tipping an entire mark! What's gotten into you?"

"Nothing!" He jumped up and furiously pulled on his blue jacket. I followed him outside. He stood by the Brunnen der Lebensfreude and gazed at the bronze figures that made up the fountain. "My favorite is the fat wild boar. Will you go out with me?"

"What?"

He stared at his sneakers. "You know," he murmured.

I was so annoyed. First that stupid trip to the reformatory, now this. "No, I don't know."

"But I want to go out with you," he said defiantly.

"No!"

I took off toward Friedrich Engels Strasse. Saxony Jensie carried the tape player on his shoulder and fortunately kept his mouth shut. On the corner of Paul Strasse, we stopped. He awkwardly turned various knobs on the player.

"The batteries are dead!"

"No duh!" he snapped. "And the store is closed. What a shitty day!" He pouted, staring sadly down at the pavement.

I didn't know what to say, and so I beat around the bush. "Did you do math yet?"

"Of course not," he yelled. "What do you think? When would I have done that?"

"Fine, all right, I get it!"

Saxony Jensie started messing with the tape player again, refusing to look at me.

"Come on, Jensie, what would Andreas think if he came home to you spewing nonsense like that. We're friends. We don't go out with each other."

"Oh, okay." It didn't look like he actually got it.

"Promise you'll be back to normal by tomorrow." I elbowed him in the side.

"Ow," he yelled and stepped back.

"Come on, that wasn't even hard!"

"It really hurt. Shit, man!"

He set the tape player on the ground and rubbed his ribs.

"You really are crazy. I don't have time for this crap." I left him standing there and walked down the street alone.

"And you have no idea what it's like," he hollered at me. "All you ever think about is your stupid swimming and your weird dad."

I didn't react.

"And besides that, Dynamo Dresden just beat Hansa Rostock in their latest soccer match!"

I was greeted by the standard chaos when I got home. Dad lay facing the wall, his hands clutching the edge of the blanket. Grandpa was trying to pull it away from him.

"Mr. Activist will never meet his quota if he lazes about in bed all day!"

I shoved him aside. "Leave him alone!"

"Frau Meier was pounding on the wall like crazy earlier." Grandpa opened his flask and took a swig.

"It's no wonder, the way you get Dad all worked up."

I searched for the right book on the shelf and sat down on the bed. "*White Fang*?"

Dad turned over and smiled happily at me.

By the next morning, Saxony Jensie had fortunately pulled himself together and was acting normal again.

He whispered in my ear, "We have to talk to Frau Thiel. There's no way she knows that Andreas was sent to an actual prison."

Herr Kowalski opened the class roster. "Last class, we discussed electrical resistance." His finger wandered down the list. "Jens Blum."

He stiffened. "What's going on?"

"Performance assessment!"

"Oh no," he groaned.

As Saxony Jensie shuffled to the front of the room, Herr Kowalski erased the board. He sighed because his back was hurting again. "A company is developing an immersion heater with an electrical resistance of sixty ohms. How strong is the current?"

Saxony Jensie gaped at him in confusion.

"Which formula would you use?"

He looked at me helplessly. I pointed at Ronny, Enno, and Inge, which only confused him more. As usual, he was completely clueless.

"We covered this extensively last class! Resistance is the ratio of voltage to current."

Saxony Jensie glanced at the piece of chalk in his hand.

"What is the symbol for resistance?"

"Well, R."

"Then write that down. Along with the symbols for voltage and current."

R and E and I were now on the board.

"Oh!" Saxony Jensie pointed at Ronny, Enno, and Inge in turn. Now they looked confused.

"And now the formula!"

Saxony Jensie had no idea what came next.

"It's like pulling teeth with you! I just said it. Resistance is the ratio of voltage to current."

He nodded broodingly, finally wrote the formula on the board, then waited for further instructions.

"Now, which variable are we solving for?"

"Well, for the current. I."

"And which variables have been given?"

"Resistance. R. Sixty ohms."

"And?"

Saxony Jensie shrugged.

"Immersion heater! Household!"

Since he didn't react, Herr Kowalski flew off the handle. "Is it really that difficult? It's clear that yet again, you haven't studied!" Saxony Jensie cowered before him. "Would you just think, for once? What voltage do we use in everyday life, that is, on the rare occasions that we're not hanging around a substation or dangling from an overhead power line?"

Saxony Jensie teared up. "Two hundred twenty volts." He sniffed.

"Thank you!" Herr Kowalski pointed at the formula. "You are finally equipped to solve this highly complex problem! All you have to do now is rearrange the formula. Let's see if you get it on your first try."

Of course he didn't.

It took Saxony Jensie ages for that too.

"Three point seven joules," he finally whispered.

"Amps, for God's sake! That's a C for today! Sit down!"

When the bell rang for recess, we hunted for Frau Thiel. Saxony Jensie was in a terrible mood because of his C in physics.

"What a load of crap," he vented. "I'm already on thin ice. There's no way I'll manage an A-minus now."

We found her downstairs, where it reeked of chlorine, as always.

"Andreas is in jail," Saxony Jensie shouted down the hallway.

She stared at us. "I beg your pardon?"

"We were there."

We stopped in front of her.

Frau Thiel set down her leather doctor bag and glared at us. She was in no mood to talk.

Saxony Jensie hopped back and forth. "They have bars on the windows and aren't allowed to listen to music!"

Frau Thiel grabbed his arm. "Would you stand still! What on earth were you two thinking?"

"He didn't do anything to deserve this."

She looked at me in disbelief. "I beg your pardon?"

"He doesn't deserve this."

Her blond perm quivered. "Of all people, I would expect you to understand, Hanna!"

"Go there and see for yourself."

"I'll do nothing of the sort! It's out of my hands, and Andreas has only himself to blame!"

"But it's like prison there!"

She snorted and reached for her bag but missed the

straps and almost lost her balance. Now she was really pissed off. "I'm certainly not discussing this with you!"

Frau Thiel left us standing there. We watched her billowing bright-green skirt as she walked away.

"'Of all people, I would expect you to understand, Hanna!'" I mimicked her.

"Fat old cow," Saxony Jensie said.

We heard noises coming from the little storage closet at the end of the hallway. We went to the door and peered in. Frau Kröger was arranging a stack of books on the shelf and jumped when she noticed us.

"My goodness, must you sneak up on a person like that?"

Light came in through the tiny window under the ceiling. She straightened her pale-blue sweater.

"You wash with Perwoll detergent, huh?" Saxony Jensie grinned like a dope.

"Insolent as ever, eh, Jens? What do you two want?"

"Um," I began, and Saxony Jensie traced a crack in the linoleum with his shoe.

"Come in and close the door."

It was a tight squeeze for three people in there.

"Like the elevator in the Stasi building!" Saxony Jensie chortled.

"So," Frau Kröger said, clearly a bit annoyed.

I pulled myself together. "Well, we went to visit Andreas. At the reformatory."

Saxony Jensie launched into the story. "But not inside. They wouldn't let us in. This guy with a huge nose blocked us. We walked around a little. There are bars on the windows. And Andreas isn't allowed to listen to music either. Or have visitors."

Frau Kröger crossed her arms and looked at him thoughtfully.

"We're worried about him," I said.

"I can see why."

"What can we do about it?"

She shook her head in resignation.

"But you're a teacher. Can't you get him out of there?"

She laughed out loud. Then her voice hardened. "No. Do you honestly think that?"

We stood there awkwardly. She suddenly looked very tired. "Please leave now."

We didn't move. We just looked at her. She angrily pushed past us and opened the door. Before we knew it, we were back out in the hall.

"I don't get it," I said. "What's up with her? She usually isn't like that."

Saxony Jensie bent over and tied his shoe. "I would have expected more from her. I can't believe this. Who else can we ask?"

"I dunno."

There were two boys in the hallway, trying to help each other tie their blue neckerchiefs.

"Well, would you look at the Young Pioneers!" Saxony Jensie scoffed and strutted toward them. "You look like real morons, you know that? Need a little help?"

They turned away. Saxony Jensie grabbed one boy's neckerchief, while I untied the other kid's messy knot.

"This looks downright counterrevolutionary."

The little blondie gazed up in horror.

"Around like this, and like this, and like this. It's easy!" I smoothed down his white Pioneer dress shirt. "Your mom might want to wash this sometime soon. Your collar is all greasy."

"Thank you," he quavered.

"Don't mention it," Saxony Jensie said. "You'll have plenty of opportunity to practice tying your neckerchiefs! On May first, October seventh, December thirteenth, March first, and so on."

"January twelfth! Be prepared!" I exclaimed.

The little kids flung up their arms. "Always prepared!"

I burst out laughing.

"What happened January twelfth?" Saxony Jensie asked, bewildered.

"Jack London was born. 1876."

"Ohh! In that case, we can celebrate May seventeenth too. My dad always drinks a bottle of schnapps that day."

"What for?"

"World Maritime Day."

"World Maritime Day," one of the Young Pioneers repeated, giggling.

Suddenly Saxony Jensie burst out, "Run along now and collect the recyclables!" He waved his arms and shooed the Pioneers down the hall.

At that moment Frau Kröger came out of the storage closet and watched him in bewilderment. She didn't look at me as she passed.

⌒⌒

There's an intense stabbing in my thigh. It takes my breath away, and I stop swimming. I lie on my back, grab my knee, and hug it tight to my belly and hold my breath. The tiniest movement worsens the tearing pain in my leg.

Without meaning to, I turn onto my side in the choppy water and have to reposition. Waves splash against my head. Water, everywhere I look is water. I can't stand the sight of it anymore.

Andreas is quiet beside me, doesn't say a thing. He can tell what I'm doing. Back on land, I showed him the movements to relieve cramping.

My lips are raw and burning; my whole mouth hurts. My gums are torn to shreds from the snorkel, and it hurts like hell whenever salt water gets in my mouth.

I stretch out my leg, then hug my knee back, till the pain gradually subsides. Because of my gums, I'm not using the snorkel anymore but breathing normally on my right side. That makes my neck hurt because the repeated movement is too one sided.

I can't breathe on the left, though it would really come in handy right now, especially since the water on the left is calmer than on the right.

I keep swallowing water on each breath.

I stretch out my neck and try to relax for a second.

Andreas takes off his goggles. "I just peed. It wasn't that bad. Actually kind of enjoyable. Nice and warm."

I couldn't hold it anymore either and went a little while ago. Strange feeling, to pee your pants, as if you were a baby. The urine was like hot water on my cold body.

"I hope we won't fall asleep now, like your grandpa said."

I shake my head. "We'll keep each other awake. With the string."

Andreas studies the string on his left wrist skeptically.

"Come on, let's go," I say. "We'll cool down if we stop moving."

"I cooled down a long time ago," Andreas says quietly.

So did I, but it's no use. We have to keep going—keep our muscles warm.

I start heading straight, but then Andreas shouts, "Do you see that light?"

I scan the waves. "Where?"

"Over there!"

He's right. There's a light to the north, blinking rhythmically.

"What is that?"

It can't possibly be a searchlight. We're way too far out for that.

"Maybe a lighthouse?"

He must be mistaken. There can't be land yet; it's too soon. And if there is, then it isn't the country we want.

"A boat. It must be a boat."

Yes, there's the bow! It's getting bigger, coming toward us. I stop swimming, watch it approach, wait for the engine noise, one second, two seconds. Nothing happens.

I prize the goggles off my face. The sharp breeze hurts my eyes, and they tear up. The boat isn't moving, but it keeps blinking.

"Dude!" Andreas hits my shoulder. "It's a buoy!"

He's right.

Andreas yanks on the string. "We gotta get over there!"

And we start paddling. The closer we get, the more distinct the buoy becomes against the gray of the Baltic. It's red and probably ten meters tall.

A navigational buoy.

We're in the middle of a shipping route.

I imagine touching the buoy long before we reach it.

We swim toward it with purpose and fighting a current that pushes us in a different direction. Finally, I touch the cold metal and search for something to hold on to.

The buoy is enormous, its underside rusted, the red paint chipped. It rides the waves and sloshes up and down in the water. A chain underneath leads to the bottom of the sea. When I was small, I would dive and try to follow buoy chains all the way down. Not a chance I'll do that now.

Andreas reaches for a metal handle and pulls himself up, but he slips, falls back in the water, and drags me with him.

The string doesn't exactly help right now, but I can't untie it. My fingers are far too numb.

"Stupid," Andreas shouts, coughing.

He tries again, builds up momentum with his flippers, and laboriously pulls himself up. The buoy has a ledge, and Andreas takes a seat and holds out his hand to me.

I grab it but also clutch the handle, which is cold and slippery. Andreas pulls me up. The buoy moves, and I start sliding off. My knees slam into something hard. I just barely manage to hold on. I finally make it up and crouch beside Andreas on the tiny platform. He rubs his ear to get the water out.

Unreal, how amazing it feels to have something solid beneath me.

I touch the metal all over. The buoy pitches in the waves, but otherwise the water can't do anything to it. The buoy withstands it, there in the middle of the Baltic. I look up. There's a spotlight above us, with a ladder leading up to it. I grab one of the rungs so I don't slip off when the buoy occasionally rocks more violently.

"Swimming doesn't agree with us," Andreas yells. "We're seeing ghosts. Boats and lighthouses. A simple buoy—it cracks me up." He stretches out his legs and groans loudly. "God, that hurts." He leans forward and fumbles around his heels.

"Whatever you do, don't take off your flippers. You'll never get them back on."

He sits up and looks at me. "Really? Why not?"

"Same thing happened to me after hours of training. There's a lot going on inside those flippers, all the skin rubbed off and stuff. It isn't pretty."

He frowns at his flippers and appears to hesitate.

"Concentrate on something else, and leave them on. It isn't worth it."

Eventually, he nods and leans back against the buoy. "Man, it hurts so much. I never would've thought."

"How could you? You're not a pro swimmer."

"Don't your feet hurt?"

"Of course they do, but I don't think about it. There's nothing I can do to change it."

He exhales loudly. "As if it were that easy, not to think about something that hurts."

The sun breaks through the clouds and shines down on us. Andreas turns his face toward the light. "Man, that's nice. It really warms you up."

I stretch out my body. I want the sun to warm as much of it as possible.

It feels so good not to have to move anymore.

I feel my wet suit gradually warm up. We dry off in the wind, which has a slight chill. If it weren't for the sun, things wouldn't be quite so pleasant on this buoy.

Heat is just so important. I feel it work its way through my body and quiet my shivering.

I close my eyes, and everything inside me starts to move, as though I were still swimming. The buoy beneath us also sways in the waves.

Up and down, up and down. I feel queasy.

"I hope we luck out and someone comes by," I say quietly. "I hardly dare to dream it."

"I'm sure they will," Andreas says beside me. "The buoy marks a shipping route, and it'll be easier to see us here than in the open water. We can attract more attention."

"By doing what, jumping and waving as if it were May Day?"

He chuckles quietly. "For example. Too bad we can't build a fire like Robinson Crusoe."

We sit in silence for a while.

I hear Andreas sigh in relief. "No more swimming, thank God. We'll just stay here, in the warm sun. I couldn't swim another stroke if I tried. Everything hurts."

I so hope that he's right but don't dare to believe it. That a ship will pass and the captain will see us, that a boat will lower and scoop us up and take us to Lübeck—or even Gedser, for all I care. And that from there, we'll set out for Hamburg, for Saxony Jensie.

"If we're done swimming, then I can take off my flippers," Andreas says, breaking the silence.

No, we can't get ahead of ourselves. I would love to give Andreas a boost, but the flippers can't come off yet.

"Wait'll we're on the ship. Just in case."

Andreas shakes his head. "Fine. I do what you tell me. You're the pro, after all."

I don't feel that way anymore. My body hurts, and everything is so different out here, not at all familiar. I miss the pool, the smell of chlorine and the sounds under-water, the coaches yelling and the impact of my feet against the side of the pool on the flip turn.

I open the canteen, take a big gulp, and pass it to Andreas. I can tell that he wants to drink more too, but he checks himself. We have to ration the water carefully. He gives me a piece of chocolate, which I suck on slowly and allow to melt in my mouth. The sugar feels good.

We sit and rest on the buoy for a while. I feel Andreas twitch beside me and fall asleep. His head drops onto my shoulder.

I nod off too. The waves slap against the buoy, and sometimes I hear gurgling. I pull my swim cap on tight so the wind can't get at my ears. I scan the water from time to time. If a ship does come by, we don't want to be asleep.

If only Saxony Jensie could see us now.

He wouldn't believe it, could never in his life imagine doing something this wild. When he and I went to the beach in Warnemünde, all he did was bum around on his towel and read *Mosaik*. He rarely ventured into the water because he was scared. He refused to put his head under and never made it very far when he did swim. He said he didn't want to mess up his hair because the chicks suppos-edly loved his amazing 'do. In reality, he was just scared of the cold water.

Luckily for him, Saxony Jensie got to leave the country the normal way, by train.

I stretch out my legs and massage my thighs. The muscles are rock hard and feel cold. They've never experienced torture like this before. They have to warm up; otherwise they won't work right. Andreas lifts his head. My movements probably woke him.

"Are there albatrosses out here?"

I look at him incredulously. "What?"

"Albatrosses. Do they have them out here?"

I shake my head. "What?"

"Do you have water in your ears?"

"No, but why are you asking?"

"Just 'cause."

He leans back, and I look at him in confusion.

"I sing to myself while I swim, for distraction."

I didn't know that.

"I know more than a hundred songs."

"Whoa, when did you learn them all?"

He exhales. "Over time. While I was at the reformatory, it helped me to think of a few songs and sing them to myself. No one knew—it was my own little world. 'The mind is free,' and all that, you know. I learned a bunch more later on. Wanted to expand the repertoire just to be safe, in case I had to go back."

I gaze past him at the waves. I'm kind of astounded that evidently we both have our own way of dealing with the situation.

Andreas has his songs. I have my poems.

I've never told him that either.

"I use Goethe or Schiller to distract myself, or some-times Rilke."

"Oh God!" Andreas sits up straight, like he used to in school, when the teacher called on him. "Are you for real? I got my fill of that in language arts class! 'Erlkönig' and 'The Sorcerer's Apprentice' and stuff like that?"

I nod.

"Nope," he says flatly. "I would straight-up drown. Karat and 'Albatross' are way better."

"'Albatross' is a great song."

Andreas nods, then quietly starts singing.

"There is a bird
that sailors have crowned their king of the sky.
He circles the world,
from South Pole to North Pole;
there's nothing too far.
The albatross knows no borders."

He smiles happily and leans back against the buoy. I never knew he had such a good voice.

"Majestically he sails,
he wanders the breeze as if he were a god.
He follows their ships
o'er high seas and past cliffs,
the thrill of the flight.
He finds them their way
o'er the sea."

He falls silent, and his eyes smile as he gazes at the horizon. "It's like everything is easier when you're singing."

He quietly keeps humming the song. The melody drifts over the waves, matches their rhythm, and is stuck in my head now too. I close my eyes and imagine I am an albatross flying over the Baltic Sea, unburdened and free.

"I'm so glad we did this," Andreas eventually says. "We took matters into our own hands and didn't wait around for things to get better by themselves."

"Which they never would have. Things are just going to keep getting worse. They would have put obstacles in our way our entire lives."

"Luckily that's all over now," Andreas says. He sounds relieved.

I can't talk that way—this isn't over yet. I want to be happy, but I can't. I'm scared. While we may be out of the water while sitting on this buoy, we're not yet out of danger.

Andreas hides his fear well. He's had to do that a lot in life.

I wonder what Mom's doing this exact moment.

I'm suddenly very sad. I feel bad for her because she's probably really worried right now. She's known since last night that something's wrong because she would have gotten the note. I've always come home before.

Presumably, she will still call the factory today, but all they can tell her is that I'm not there. Andreas isn't either.

She'll call his parents, who won't know where he is, because he's been out of their house for a long time.

Mom will drive the Trabbi to his apartment on Patriotischer Weg. No one will be home.

Then she'll go to the Neptune Pool to see if I'm at practice.

She'll ask Ulrich about me.

And he'll realize what happened.

And Mom will definitely sense that he knows something.

Will he talk to her? Will he tell her?

What will she do then? Will she run to the police and insist they search the Baltic and bring us back? Or will she just hope that we make it and not say a thing?

I'm sick to my stomach. I have to call her as soon as we get there.

"Picture all the things we can do now. Hitchhike to Paris or Rome, go see the Colosseum." Andreas looks at me. "Where would you wanna go?"

"I dunno." I can't make any plans.

"You've got to have at least one place in mind."

"Maybe Greece," I say so he'll leave me alone.

Other than Saxony Jensie, we won't know anyone over there. At least we'll have each other. Not that that helps much now.

We'll never eat rotisserie chicken in Warnemünde again. And what about Grandpa? And Dad? When will I see Mom again? My stomach tightens.

"We can major in whatever we want now. Biology and computer science. We'll just have to make up the *Abi*, but we can handle that, no problem."

I anxiously knead my muscles, which are still hard and cold. I don't want Andreas to sense how I'm feeling.

"We can stay at Saxony Jensie's place, at least to start. His parents are really nice. They'll help us."

They'll be surprised to see us, that's for sure. They're hardly expecting us to show up on their doorstep.

Saxony Jensie will freak. I'm sure he'll immediately start showing off all his new stuff, his clothes, new records, and the Western chocolate he can eat whenever he wants. There will probably be Nutella for breakfast.

Has he made any friends yet over there? It can't be easy, as a Saxon. Do they even understand his dialect?

He's probably got a BMW already. But his hair will look as stupid as ever.

Andreas glances at me again. "You're not saying much."

"Let's hope he's fixed his hair by now."

Andreas laughs. "I doubt it. When someone suffers poor taste, not even the West can help."

I gaze out across the waves. I'm not sure Saxony Jensie will appreciate it if we start ragging on him as soon as we arrive. We'd better break the habit—he's got the home-field advantage now.

I unzip my wet suit and pull out the bundle containing the copy of *Mosaik*.

"The Black Felucca."

Luckily, the plastic wrap didn't spring any leaks and let in water.

"Looks good. It'll get to Saxony Jensie in one piece," Andreas says.

I feel his elbow in my side. "Remember his pants at the *Jugendweihe* ceremony?"

"Oh God, let's hope he's not roaming the streets of Hamburg in those things. They'll send him straight back to the GDR!"

"You look like you have massive paws!"

Saxony Jensie's powder-blue suit was way too big for him. His relatives in Hanover had sent it to him because they had no use for it. He looked down at his pants, which gathered and bulged out over his shoes.

"The tailor shop was already closed when the package finally arrived last night. And get this—the Stasi stole the Nutella out of the box again. Those stupid jerks!"

I had to wear a red skirt and a white silk blouse. I felt like such a tool. But all of the kids gathered at the Volkstheater that day looked ridiculous. All colorful and overly festive, like for Carnival.

"We will now practice getting on and off the stage," Frau Thiel wheezed.

We walked into the auditorium and past the seats, which were still empty.

"Honecker oughta practice that too," Saxony Jensie whispered.

"Huh?"

"Getting on stage and stepping back down." He turned around as he walked and winked at me with a grin. "Especially the stepping down part!"

I accidentally stepped on his pant leg, and he almost fell. There was a loud ripping sound.

"Shit, man, no freaking way!" He turned around frantically and looked at his butt. "The ass is torn!"

Enrico and Mandy plowed into us from behind and burst into laughter when they saw the mishap.

"Why don't you guys watch where you're going?" Saxony Jensie barked at them.

Frau Thiel scowled at us. "What is it this time, Jens Blum?"

"I have to go home and change my pants!"

"We don't have time for that. You should have picked out your favorite pants beforehand."

"That's not why. These ripped!" Frau Thiel didn't care.

"That fat lavender witch doesn't get it," I whispered. "You can even see your tighty-whities."

"Crap," he murmured anxiously. "What'll Frau Kröger think if she sees me like this? This is so embarrassing. You have to walk really close behind me!"

He'd recently developed a crush on Frau Kröger.

"The lineup is different today, though," I said. "You're standing on the side because you're the shortest."

He blushed. "First of all, that's not true. Heiko is shorter. But either way, you have to help. Everyone will laugh at me!"

We were on stage by that point, and Frau Thiel was tugging around at us. "Let's get one thing perfectly clear: you will all need to straighten your clothes later and stand at attention, like at assemblies!"

She reached us. "Rather a large suit, isn't it, Jens? Nice to see you in a skirt for once, Hanna. You won't be standing on the left edge, remember. You know the lineup. That's Jens's spot."

"No, it's Heiko Kruse's!"

"He's standing on the right edge because he's an inch taller."

"Nuh-uh!" Saxony Jensie insisted.

I poked him in the side, because I felt like he had bigger issues to deal with.

Frau Thiel hurried off the stage and waved exaggeratedly. Her arm flab jiggled from side to side. "Everyone now sit down in the fourth row, in the correct order you'll stand on stage later!"

I took a seat between Sabine and Ronny. In his suit he looked like J. R. from *Dallas*.

"Where's your cowboy hat?" I asked him.

"Ha ha," he muttered irritably.

Sabine was dressed in white, like it was her wedding. Saxony Jensie hunched over beside her and gave me a hand signal.

I looked around. Herr Parek and Frau Kröger were sitting behind us, whispering to each other. Saxony Jensie gazed up at the ceiling when Frau Kröger glanced at him.

The auditorium was filling.

Someone kept turning the music up and down. The recording alternated between "Tell Me Where You Stand," by Oktoberklub, and the first movement of Beethoven's *Eroica* Symphony.

I stood up and looked around. Mom and Grandpa sat five rows behind us. Grandpa lifted his cane and waved it above his head.

"One, two, one, two, three," someone said into the mic.

Saxony Jensie practically lay down on top of Sabine because he had a joke to tell me. "Have you heard this one? A stutterer applies to be a radio deejay in Berlin. When he comes back from his interview at the Berliner Rundfunk station, his friend asks, 'So, did they hire you?' 'N-n-n-no,' the stutterer says, "c-c-cause I'm n-n-n-not in-in-in th-the p-p-party!'"

We both snickered. Sabine shook her head.

Our class was up first.

The *Eroica* started, and we all stood. There was a bit of a tussle as we neared the stage because I had to cut in front of Sabine in order to be right behind Saxony Jensie. Sabine obviously didn't get it, and Saxony Jensie got so mad, he tried to trip her. She almost stumbled down the stairs and was so embarrassed that she stopped caring about what order we were in.

"You have to stay right by me," Saxony Jensie ordered. He held a hand over his butt as we climbed the steps. It looked like he had pooped his pants.

We lined up beside one another. Frau Thiel glared at Saxony Jensie and me. She was furious because we had messed up the formation. I was taller than both Saxony Jensie and Sabine, yet now stood between them. That was not allowed.

Frau Thiel stiffly approached the podium. The *Eroica* quieted, then blared suddenly from the loudspeakers. People sitting in the front rows plugged their ears. There was a repeated clicking, till finally it went silent. I heard Grandpa cough.

"The young citizens of the German Democratic Republic standing before us today feel fortunate to play an active role in shaping this era, over the course of which all peoples, under the leadership of their revolutionary parties, shall consummate the transition from capitalism to socialism."

Saxony Jensie fidgeted next to me, tugging at his pants.

"Our young friends know that as the custodians of tomorrow, there are certain tasks that history has set before them, tasks for which they will require both extensive general knowledge and solid specialist training. The youth of the German Democratic Republic is an ever-learning youth."

Saxony Jensie whimpered softly and tried to give his parents a sign. They didn't understand and shot him dirty looks, because he was making such a fuss during the speech. Mom, who was sitting with them, smiled at me. She was happy about the skirt too. Grandpa hoisted his cane in the air.

Frau Thiel went on for ages and raised her index finger at the end. It was now time for the pledge.

"Dear young friends! Are you prepared as young citizens of this, our German Democratic Republic, to join together with us and, honoring the constitution, do you vow to work and fight for the mighty, noble cause of socialism and to cherish the revolutionary legacy of the people? Affirm with 'This we vow!'"

She read a whole bunch of idiotic sentences like that. After each one, we had to yell, "This we vow!"

The boys intentionally made their voices sound deeper to impress the little Pioneers standing along the walls of the auditorium.

After the final "This we vow," Frau Thiel turned to us. In a tone of voice that sounded like we had all just gotten married to one another, she said, "We have heard your vows. You have set yourselves a lofty, noble goal. We solemnly accept you into the great collective of working people, who—under the leadership of the working class and its revolutionary party, united in will and action alike—constitute the advanced socialist society of the German Democratic Republic. We confer a tremendous amount of responsibility on you. We are ever prepared to assist in word and deed as you productively shape our socialist future."

Then she left the podium, and the Pioneers joined us on stage. The music was turned back up.

Tell me where you stand, tell me where you stand, tell me where you stand and what direction you have planned . . .

"What a joke. All this just for a tape player!" Saxony Jensie whispered in my ear.

Backward or fore, you must make up your mind! We are carrying time onward piece by piece . . .

"I'm buying one too," I responded quietly.

Frau Thiel was pissed off, you could tell, but Saxony Jensie just kept babbling away. "I have a hundred fifty marks saved, and I'm getting a thousand marks from all my relatives. That's enough for the player."

Whenever you speak, it is fully apparent you've given no thought to the route you take . . .

The Pioneers presented us with flowers and copies of *The Meaning of Our Life*. A little blond girl shook my hand and smiled.

"And my uncle Arno in Dresden is sending me twenty marks to get a cassette."

We have a right to know who you are, we have no use for your nodding masks . . .

"Off the stage!" Frau Thiel shrieked.

"I can finally tape the hit parade on NDR 2 and don't need to worry about accidentally taping over my dad's ABBA cassette."

I wish to use your real name when I call, so now it's time you showed your true face . . .

"Off the stage!" Frau Thiel screamed again.

"Column right, march!" Saxony Jensie cried out boisterously. Several people in the front row laughed. Frau Thiel stormed past us and off the stage.

"Man, do I feel grown-up now," I said when we finally got back to our seats and the music turned off.

"Frau Thiel needs to use the formal *you* with us now," Saxony Jensie exclaimed. "Isn't that funny?"

"No way, our homeroom teacher doesn't need to do that. It only applies to the others."

"Nuh-uh! If I say so, she has to use the formal *you* with me!"

It was 8b's turn on stage. They were all dressed as stupidly as we were and dragged themselves up the steps. Left and right, they tripped one another in time to Beethoven's *Eroica*.

"I don't actually need to be embarrassed." Saxony Jensie pointed at Heiko Kruse. "He looks even worse than me."

It was true. I had never seen a boy in a purple velvet suit before. He looked sad, and I felt bad for him.

"Must be his relatives in the West wanted to unload that hideous thing too," I whispered.

They started playing "Tell Me Where You Stand" again. Saxony Jensie leaned in so I could hear him above the god-awful racket.

"They'll probably never tell their family how stupid Heiko looked, 'cause they're scared they'd never get another package."

Heiko Kruse stared at us.

"Quiet," Frau Kröger said behind us.

Saxony Jensie gave her a pained smile and simply kept talking. "We take whatever they give us," he whispered. "The GDR gobbles it all up. We're like the pet pig of the West."

I exploded with laughter.

"Would you be quiet!" Frau Kröger and Herr Parek hissed at the same time.

Outside, Grandpa clapped Saxony Jensie on the shoulder. "Ha ha ha, the pet pig of the West! Good one! I'm going to remember that! I should have thought of it myself! I'll put it on a poster for May Day."

"You have fun with that!" Mom adjusted my mussed blouse and smiled. "Very pretty, sweetheart!"

"Shaped like a pig, colored pink. Red lettering: 'The East is West Germany's Pet Pig.'"

"I wouldn't do that if I were you, Herr Klein," Saxony Jensie's dad droned. "I'm afraid you might be asking for trouble."

"Besides, no one will understand what it means," Saxony Jensie's mother added.

"That doesn't matter, Frau Blum," Grandpa snapped. "I don't understand any of the posters either. Like, 'To Learn from the Soviet Union Means Learning How to Win.'"

"What's so confusing about that?" Saxony Jensie's father grumbled. "They beat us."

"*Freed* us," Saxony Jensie corrected him freshly. "From fascism under Hitler."

Mom clapped her hands. "Enough of that! Let's get something nice to eat now."

"Off to the Sun Hotel," Grandpa announced. "Chop-chop. I don't want to run into that fat wench!"

Every table in the hotel restaurant was taken by families who had just attended the *Jugendweihe*. Grandpa ordered a glass of schnapps and leafed through the book I'd been given, *The Meaning of Our Lives*.

He laughed bitterly. "Oh, children, you still have so much to learn. I'm glad I get to enjoy my socialist retirement." He downed two shots of schnapps, one after the other. "Stop me if you've heard this one. At a local assembly, a little old lady asks the chairman, 'Excuse me, comrade, but was it humans or scientists who invented socialism?' The chairman is dumbstruck. 'Excuse me?' he says. 'I don't understand your question.'"

"Eight orders of Kaliningrad meatballs!" the waitress hollered from across the room at a large table. Grandpa waved her over enthusiastically. She had enormous breasts.

"'Well, was it regular people who invented socialism, or was it scientists?'"

Saxony Jensie stared slack-jawed into the waitress's cleavage and spilled his Club Cola. Grandpa stabbed a meatball and shoved it into his mouth. You could barely understand him now. "'Well, generally speaking, it was regular people, of course!'"

"Generally speaking?" Saxony Jensie's father looked up from his plate.

"'That's what I thought,' the little old lady responds. 'Because scientists would have tested it on their rats first!'"

"Wow," Saxony Jensie howled, clutching his belly. "That's a good one! I'm going to remember that!"

"Do not tell that one at school," his mother warned him, placing a hand on his arm.

"I could go for a schnapps now, myself!" Saxony Jensie's father flagged down the waiter. His Saxon accent was even worse than Saxony Jensie's. "I've got one too. Reagan, Gorbachev, and Honecker ask the good Lord what the world will look like in the year 2000. The good Lord tells Reagan, 'In the year 2000, the US will be communist.'"

"A likely story," Saxony Jensie's mother grumbled as she mashed a potato.

"At that, Reagan turns away and bursts into tears. 'What about the Soviet Union?' Gorbachev asks. The good Lord responds, 'The Soviet Union will no longer exist. It will have been absorbed into the Greater Chinese Empire.' At that, Gorbachev turns away and bursts into tears."

"Those Chinese!" Grandpa picked the capers out of his gravy.

"'What about the GDR in the year 2000?' Honecker asks." We stopped chewing and stared at Herr Blum. "At that, the good Lord turns away and bursts into tears."

Mom slammed her silverware on her plate and pressed her napkin against her mouth.

"Hard to believe our *Jugendweihe* was only three years ago," I comment into the cool breeze, which still blows steadily across the Baltic. It only warms up when the sun comes out. "And now here we are, sitting on this buoy, even though we swore we would productively shape our socialist future."

"But that's what we're doing!" Andreas makes a fist. "We're getting the hell out. That's highly productive."

He's still acting cocky, looks very pleased with himself.

We rock back and forth on the buoy.

Where's he getting his optimism from? We haven't achieved a damn thing. We're stuck here, waiting.

"We wouldn't have been much help anyway," he says. "Well, maybe you, but certainly not me."

"I wasn't much better than you. I was disciplined with a transfer too, you know!"

"But they never targeted you, like they did me. Remember that thing we did with the recycling? That was my idea. You never would've done something like that on your own."

That's true. Working in that horrible factory, we came up with some pretty dumb ideas. Andreas suggested that we earn a little extra cash on the side with recycling. I thought he meant like back when we were cheery little Pioneers, going door-to-door with a cart. But that wasn't the plan. Instead, he scaled the wall outside the SERO recycling drop-off center on Friedrich Engels Strasse in the middle of the night and stole recyclables. I had to stand guard. It was silent and spooky. I still remember that the streetlight was broken and flickered the entire time I waited there in the dark. Andreas tossed bundles of paper recycling over the wall, which I stacked on the other side. Then he passed me coal sacks filled with glass jars and bottles. I was so scared, I almost wet myself, while he was totally clinical about the whole thing.

We hauled the stuff into our basements, being super careful no one saw us. We would have been busted on the spot. No normal person runs around with old bottles in the middle of the night.

The next day, we just acted normal as we brought everything back to the SERO. The dude working there was wasted. He counted the jars and bottles, weighed the bundles, scribbled something on his smeared piece of paper, and handed over cash. He didn't register that this had all passed through his hands before.

The next night, we re-stole it and dropped it off again. This went on for some time.

The whole thing was pretty risky. After all, we could have been caught red-handed and sent to jail for stealing public property. Andreas didn't seem to care in the least. It wasn't till we decided to flee that we stopped stealing.

I can't keep my eyes open, I'm so tired. Andreas never would have learned to conform. I may have, but who knows. No point in thinking about it now. I wouldn't have acted up all the time, though, like Andreas, that's for sure. I'd be way too scared. Maybe I would've become like Dad at some point, distant and not quite right in the head. Sitting on this buoy is preferable to that any day.

If only a ship would pass by.

I want to get out of here, dry off and warm up. We can't sit on the buoy forever. It'll get dark at some point; that will be awful. I can't do a whole night on this thing.

Better than another night in the water, though.

The pitching makes me nauseous. I open my eyes and search for a fixed point. Two tankers on the horizon, way too far away.

But what's that thing closer to us? I sit up straight.

Something white, looks like a sail.

Am I crazy?

I blink several times, but the sail doesn't disappear.

I grab Andreas's arm. "Over there!" He twitches but doesn't move. It's like he's turned to stone.

"It's real," I insist. "It's not a mirage!"

Andreas pulls himself up by one of the metal rungs. He groans because something hurts, then starts to wave. Hesitantly at first, then with increasing vigor.

The sail approaches us. It's a sizable yacht, and it glows brightly in the sunshine. Suddenly something changes about the Baltic—it no longer appears as threatening or infinite as before. Blue water beyond a white sail. It's like in a movie. It's like vacation!

"He saw us!" Andreas keeps waving, and I pull myself up too and watch the yacht. My flippers bang against the metal buoy.

There's someone standing at the wheel.

"A vacationer," Andreas bellows. "We did it!"

It's a man in a light-blue shirt.

The yacht cruises by with full sails, not slowing down at all. The man doesn't move, doesn't wave back, just stares at us from behind his sunglasses. He can't be more than fifty meters off.

"Hey," Andreas roars, continuing to wave. "Come pick us up!"

The man still doesn't move.

We turn our heads and watch the yacht retreat.

Huge waves slam into the buoy.

"What's wrong with him? Is he messing with us?"

The yacht doesn't turn back.

"What an idiot! That was our chance," Andreas screams.

I sink back onto the platform and stretch my aching legs. I can't believe it. We watch the yacht for a long time, till it disappears among the waves.

I've got a hollow feeling in my stomach.

"I don't believe it. What an asshole!" Andreas continues to rant. "Why didn't he stop?"

I don't know what to say.

"Just floats by, as if there were nothing strange about two people on a buoy in the middle of the Baltic. We were obviously waving, weren't we?"

I nod, lost in thought.

"Maybe he was scared we would rob him, since we look so shady, all dressed in black, like pirates. But doesn't he have to pick us up because we're stranded?"

"Yeah, you're right," I say. "His flag was red and white. Did you see that too?"

"No clue, but there was definitely some red."

Crap. I knew it. "He was from Poland."

"Oh!" Andreas sits back down on the platform. "In that case, whatever. We don't wanna go there anyway. Too bad. We'll just have to wait for the next boat to come by."

It's not that simple. Not anymore. I gaze out across the waves.

How to explain it to him? I can hardly believe it myself.

We're no longer safe on our buoy.

"I just don't understand it. Is he allowed to pass by us without doing anything? I thought there was some sort of treaty about helping people in trouble at sea." Andreas looks at me reproachfully, as if it were my fault.

"He's also doing his duty if he tells someone."

"Oh, well that's fine too! Then someone'll come back for us soon."

I take a deep breath and muster all my courage. "Which is why we need to leave the buoy."

Andreas stiffens. "What?"

I search for words.

"Why?" he shouts.

"A Pole," I say. "Who do you think he'll inform?"

His questioning expression tells me it hasn't hit him— not yet.

"It certainly won't be Denmark or Sweden," I say resignedly.

Andreas looks at the horizon. His eyes darken as he finally understands.

"We can't just wait here till they come."

He stares down at the waves and starts to tremble. "I can't."

I don't respond. I can't speak anymore.

Andreas shakes his head. "I can't get back in there."

Neither of us says anything while the water below crashes into the buoy, over and over. A constant, endless rhythm, as though we aren't even here. I feel the cold metal against my hands. I would much rather stay here too. "Then we'll just sit and wait for them."

Andreas crumples beside me and shakes his head. "I can't believe this is happening."

Me neither.

We have to keep going, but I don't have the strength to convince him of that. He doesn't want to get back in the water. And there's no way I'm swimming alone.

We're going to jail. Andreas said he'd never survive that. I know I wouldn't.

What should I do? I have a lump in my throat and wish I could just cry.

One thing's for sure. If we stay on the buoy, we'll end up in jail. If we keep swimming, we still stand a chance.

Need to stick it out till the right boat comes along. How long will that take? How much time is left?

I stare into the gray water. It's our only option.

We have to get back into the cold. Into the uncertainty.

"Fuck this shit!" Andreas curses next to me and jumps up. "We're in international waters! If they come, we'll just refuse to leave the buoy! What'll they do then?"

I've regained my composure, and I answer him calmly. "They'll hold a gun to our heads and force us onto their boat."

"That isn't fair, though," Andreas screams. "They can't do that."

He moves so violently that the buoy tips to the side, and I have to hang on with both hands to keep from slipping off. Andreas abruptly doubles over and vomits into the water. Poor guy. On top of everything else.

I look up at the sky. What were we thinking? Seemed like a good idea when we were warm and dry. But now? Pretty shitty.

Andreas sinks beside me on the platform and doesn't say a word. He's very pale.

I wish we were back in Rostock, in his apartment. We could be sitting there now, drinking hot tea and talking. But instead, we're here. And we have our reasons for that.

"Do you remember what you said last winter, when the Stasi tried to bribe you?"

They had offered to let him return to school if he agreed to work for them.

He nodded. "The one thing we can do is leave."

The wind has grown stronger, and the Baltic is choppier. A gray mass that stretches out before us and seems to engulf everything. A mass we can't escape.

"I don't want to get back in the water either," I say softly. "But we have no choice. If they catch us here, we're going to prison. For years."

"Maybe the Polish guy won't do anything," Andreas murmurs.

"Maybe," I respond quietly. I can't encourage this kind of thinking because I don't believe it's true. I hope it is, but we can't count on it.

We have to leave the safety of the buoy if we want any of this to have been worth it. There's no backtracking now. It's far too late for that.

We gaze at the horizon in silence, sit quietly for a long time, thinking, weighing the situation. Each of us processing it for ourselves.

After a while Andreas turns to look at me. His eyes are clear. He smiles sadly.

Then he grabs the canteen and takes a big swig. I do too, then attach it to my belt.

"Think about tomorrow," I say. "And Saxony Jensie."

Andreas doesn't react. He pushes himself up to the edge of the platform, till his legs dangle over. His white hand clasps a metal rod on the buoy.

He slowly lets go of the rod. I drop into the water at the same time as him so the string doesn't rip my hand off.

Hitting the cold water is pure hell. I don't want to be here.

I move my legs and start to swim.

Everything hurts.

There's no way. I can't move another inch! I can't swim, have to go back to the buoy.

But then they'll get us.

Keep going. Swim.

I don't want to; it's so cold.

But I have to; otherwise it's all over. Years in prison. No one to help, nothing.

My whole family will be punished for what I've done. They might even lock up Grandpa because he rants against the state whenever he goes grocery shopping. Mom will be booted from the *Kombinat*, and Dad will be moved to Gehlsdorf forever. They'll have it in for Ulrich too because he didn't inform on me.

I have to keep going, but I turn around one last time and glare at the buoy.

Why is it even there?

I wish it would disappear. I don't want to think about it. I hate it!

Things would be easier if it weren't even there.

I follow Andreas, who's doggedly swimming straight ahead. My arm movements are halting, and I can't find my pace.

Andreas turns around and looks first at the buoy, then at me. I ignore him.

The waves crash into my right side, and it's hard to breathe. I stop doing the crawl and swim the breaststroke instead. It doesn't actually help me see any better. The swell has intensified.

Wave crest, wave trough. Andreas's arm sometimes appears in my line of vision—it shoots into the air, bends, and plunges back into the water.

I feel bad. Guilty.

We should have stayed. He won't make it.

Swim, just swim. The buoy is in the past.

The ships on the horizon are our goal.

The string between us barely tightens. We swim steadily beside each other, as if we were born doing this. Just go, keep going, keep straight ahead.

A burning sensation shoots through my body, which is cold as ice.

We don't speak. There's nothing to say, and besides, it's a waste of energy.

I've lost all sense of time. The sun is high in the sky, probably late morning.

Wave crest, wave trough, wave crest, wave trough.

The water is murky, the Baltic Sea a desert, barren and bleak. No life anymore, not even jellyfish.

I see ships on the horizon, but they don't come any closer.

"Good of you to come shopping with me, kid. I can't carry that much anymore."

Grandpa needed food. He didn't even have bockwurst or pound cake in the pantry.

"Have you heard this one?" Grandpa asked as we passed by the empty shelves in the grocery store. "Sigmund Jähn has been appointed the new director of the GDR's largest shopping center. As a cosmonaut, he knows a thing or two about empty spaces! Ha ha!"

We stopped in the produce section. All they had was lettuce.

"They don't usually have lettuce," Grandpa said in bewilderment. "At least, I've never seen so many heads in one pile before." He shuddered. "I don't want to eat that."

"I'm not allowed to," I replied. "Mom says so."

"For once, she's right about something," Grandpa muttered.

A man in a blue work smock shoved past us, pulling a cart. "Do you mind?"

He grabbed one head of lettuce after another and pitched them into the cart.

"What are you, mothballing all this contaminated stuff? No one wants it, huh?" The man looked at Grandpa in amazement. He lifted his cane threateningly. "And why might that be?"

I tugged at his sleeve.

"Just send it back to Siberia. The atomic disaster is their fault, after all."

The man kept tossing about heads of lettuce. "Ukraine," he mumbled.

"Same difference," Grandpa yelled. "I was there, you know!"

I pulled on his sleeve again.

The man shook his head in resignation. "As if I didn't have enough to do."

"I want to know, young man. This instant! Where is this poisonous stuff going?"

The man held a head of lettuce with both hands and responded in a strange tone, "Why, to an assortment of institutional kitchens, sir."

Grandpa was so shocked, he forgot to pound his cane on the tile floor. He launched straight into full-blown screaming. "Institutional kitchens?"

Several people turned around. Two women collided with their shopping baskets and started telling each other off. Another head of lettuce soared into the cart.

"You mean to say that this poison will end up in hospitals, schools, and kindergartens?"

The next head of lettuce flew through the air, then another, then two at once. The cart was finally full, and the man pushed past us. "For instance."

"For instance?"

Grandpa stormed after him, brandishing his cane. A woman yanked her pudgy kid out of the way, and the man shoved the cart into the storeroom.

"Employees only!"

He slammed the door shut. Grandpa jiggled the handle, but it wouldn't open.

"Think about it. Hospitals. Old folks' homes! Good idea, comrades, great. No need to worry about socialist pensions if they all croak! Fantastic! We're governed by idiots!"

Everyone in the store was staring at us now. I brought Grandpa outside, while he kept ranting. We hadn't bought a single thing.

"Why don't they hawk the lettuce to the West? Sell it for foreign currency? They could make a killing and kill the enemy of the state at the same time."

"The West has its own contaminated lettuce. It rained there too."

"I'll tell you something, kid. The Russians let that nuclear plant explode on purpose, to shift the balance of power in Central Europe."

He hobbled beside me.

"Shift it where?"

"All the way to the Atlantic. They want to incorporate Germany into the Russian Empire. I bet you anything this is just part of their bigger plan! There's only one thing that would help: bombing Russia. Like Ronald Reagan wanted."

"What do you mean?"

"Kid, didn't you hear about this? Ronald Reagan was delivering a radio address to the American people. He was practicing on the microphone beforehand and didn't know he was already on-air. But he was. He said he was launching an attack on Russia in five minutes. It was just a joke, but folks got pretty upset."

"Well, it isn't funny."

Grandpa dragged his cane across the cobbles. He was completely drained. He waved me off at his front door. "I'm going to watch *Medicine to Music* for my exercises and hit the hay."

At lunch in the cafeteria the next day, there was more salad than they'd ever served before.

"The man with the cart was actually right," I said when I saw the other students' plates.

Saxony Jensie gave me a funny look. "What man? What cart?"

"At the store yesterday. Because of Chernobyl. Oh crap, the red goat is here too!"

Party Secretary Karlow stood by the serving counter, checking plates and taking notes.

"Have you heard this one?" Saxony Jensie asked. "So, Brezhnev is standing at the Pearly Gates, and he goes, 'Hey, Saint Peter, I'd really love if you sent me to Eastern heaven.' 'No problem,' says Saint Peter. 'But you'll have to come back for meals. I'm not cooking for one over there.'"

Ronny and Ulrike laughed loudly behind us.

"Everything looks exactly the same outdoors as always," Frau Karlow screamed at one tenth-grade boy. "There's no reason to turn down this beautiful lettuce."

"Doesn't the red goat know that you can't see

175

radioactivity?" Saxony Jensie asked me belligerently. "She seems to think it's like in Bitterfeld, where laundry turns black on the clothesline from all the pollution."

I reached the front of the line.

"Do you want salad?" the lunch lady asked me.

"No."

"Oh really," Party Secretary Karlow howled. "And why is that, Hanna Klein?"

"I never eat salad. I don't like it." I thought of my mother and her rule. No lettuce, no fruit.

She looked daggers at me. "You are clearly being influenced by enemy media."

I reached for a plate of potatoes and hard-boiled eggs in mustard sauce.

"Salad?" the lunch lady asked Saxony Jensie, who had hidden behind me.

"No, no," he crowed loudly. "I have diarrhea, and when you have diarrhea and eat fresh lettuce, things can get really—"

"That's enough, Jens Blum," Karlow spit.

Then she turned to the lunch lady. "Don't even bother asking if they want salad. Just put it on their plates, Fräulein Schmitt."

The lunch lady rolled her eyes as soon as Karlow turned back to the others in line.

"I, for one, would like a double helping of salad!" The lunch lady heaped lettuce onto a plate. Karlow took it and gave her a nod. "It's nothing but propaganda!"

"Yeah, yeah," the lunch lady replied wearily.

As Karlow walked past Herr Münchmeyer, he looked shocked by all the greens peeking over the edge of her plate.

"'You're clearly being influenced by enemy media,'" I mimicked her when we sat down.

"Karlow's gonna grow five ears now!" Saxony Jensie stuffed a mustardy egg in his mouth. "My dad says I'm not allowed to eat any lettuce. If I do, I can't watch *Dynasty*. I'm not idiotic enough to risk that!"

Everything is gray. Inhale, right arm, exhale, left arm, inhale, right arm. My hands are soft, bloated from the salt water.

The Baltic isn't blue, like the postcards would have you believe. It's gray nothingness, an infinite rushing that surrounds me, permeates me. I hear it constantly. Sometimes I kick off and float through the grayness, as if I were dreaming.

There's nothing to keep me awake. Nothing happening.

But I've found my pace and the pain has subsided.

I'm warmer too. Exhausted but not completely wrecked. Can't actually tell how I'm doing.

A sudden jerk on my wrist.

A loud cry.

I stop and look up.

"There!"

Andreas bobs up in the water, waving.

I pull off my goggles.

A ferry, just a few hundred meters off.

"The flag!" Andreas bellows.

Black.

Red.

Gold.

Without the garland of corn.

"Hello!" Andreas waves, screams. "Hello!"

I do the same. "Hello!"

The ferry is headed our way.

"They saw us!" Andreas shouts.

We yell and wave and yell. I kick my flippers like crazy to rise as far out of the water as possible. I inhale water and start coughing. Andreas chokes on water too and clutches my shoulder because he's seized by a cramp. He almost pulls me under. I shake him off and kick up again, continuing to wave at the ferry.

It's close now. I can see the people onboard.

"Hello! Look down!"

I suddenly realize how loud the engine is. I hadn't noticed it before, I was so excited.

Yelling is pointless.

But Andreas doesn't stop—he churns up water, screams, and thrashes his arms against the waves. The ferry is level with us. We're looking at its broadside.

This mighty ship, right there.

It could easily run us over.

They have to see us.

Portholes, funnels, the bridge.

The waves carry us up and down.

We're two specks in the sea. Unless someone happens to look in our direction, they'll never see us.

Andreas screams, increasingly desperate. I join him in solidarity.

But our screams are drowned out by the engine noise.

There has to be someone standing at the railing, looking out over the water.

There! A child, blond hair, probably a boy. He's holding the railing with both hands, looking straight at us through the rails.

He sees us!

Standing beside him is an adult, maybe his father. He's smoking and looking in the other direction.

"Tell someone!" Andreas roars at the boy.

But he doesn't move, doesn't signal his father, just stares at us, frozen. I wave and wave and suddenly, the boy lifts his arm and waves back.

"No, kid, don't wave. Go get someone!" Andreas shrieks, his nerves shot.

The boy doesn't understand what's happening, doesn't realize we're in danger. He's still too young. He turns his head slowly with the movement of the ship so he can keep his eye on us as the ferry passes.

I wave at him, and he waves back again.

"Idiot! Shit! He fucking saw us," Andreas yells and pounds the water with his hand. "Why the hell didn't he do anything?"

"He's just a kid. He doesn't get it."

"Neither do I." Andreas is beside himself. "We're going to die out here! First the stupid Pole, now this kid. As if there were nothing unusual about two people paddling through the Baltic in wet suits and goggles." He starts coughing, inhaled water. "God damn it! We should have stayed on the buoy! Great fucking idea to keep swimming!"

"We'd be on our way back to the GDR this very minute if we had," I scream back. I don't want to think about the buoy anymore. It's in the past.

"And how the hell do you know that?" Andreas won't let it go. "What if that ferry passes the buoy? It would have seen us! You're not the pro you think you are. Practicing in the pool hardly makes you an expert on the high seas!"

That's not fair. "I never claimed to be an expert. You were the one who wanted to run!"

"So did you! I—"

At that moment, water slaps him in the face, silencing him. I curl up and try to ride the wave, but this one is nothing like the smaller wake created by the patrol boats.

The sea begins to seethe.

Water crashes down on us. Andreas spins around, as if he were caught in a whirlpool. The powerful pull on the string hurts my wrist.

I can't see.

"We have to stay together," I roar.

A powerful undertow from the ferry. My snorkel is full of water; there's no air, and I cough. The engine noise is unbearable. The ferry's propellers are so loud.

Waves tear me up and down.

I'm underwater. I hold my breath.

Suddenly Andreas is beside me, and his elbow collides with my ribs as he fights the waves, which then sweep him away again. He pulls the string with him.

Which way is up?

I finally surface. I cough and spit out water.

The waves have calmed somewhat.

Burning salt water runs down the back of my throat. I gag. I turn away from Andreas and puke in the water.

Disgusting. My entire mouth is on fire. I vomit several times till my stomach is empty. I close my eyes, and lights dance across my lids.

Everything is spinning. I feel so sick.

"You okay?" Andreas asks after a few seconds.

I shake my head. My heart races. I'm shivering and sweating at the same time. My body is going crazy.

"It's better to get it out," Andreas says, trying to help.

Unfortunately, he's wrong. That might be true when you're drunk, but not here. I've lost a lot of energy and warmth. And fluids.

Something's different. I touch my stomach. The canteen! I feel for it all over my body.

It's gone. I lost it. I don't see anything on the surface of the water, and besides, it wouldn't float; it's too heavy. It must have come loose in the waves, and I didn't notice.

We don't have anything to drink. My heart races faster.

It's my fault we're swimming and not on the buoy, and now I went and lost our drinking water.

How could this happen?

I don't dare tell Andreas.

He's on his back, floating. I copy him and look at the sky. I don't want to move. Finally, there's some peace and quiet. I can hear my heart pounding. I don't know what to do; I wish I could dissolve and disappear into the sea.

I need to calm down.

Andreas is eating chocolate and offers me a piece, but I can't eat.

Water seeps into my ears, and sounds become muffled, then clear again. There's nothing to hear now but the water lapping and gurgling. We're going to float off course.

Fat white clouds above, and the sun burns my face. Somewhere out there is the beach. Somewhere out there, kids are playing, splashing in the warm water, chasing beach balls, hopping through the surf.

With solid ground underfoot.

And here we are, in the middle of the sea.

Our strength gone.

Our water gone.

I'm not shivering from the cold.

It's because I'm scared.

182

I feel like I'm going to cry. The lump in my throat grows, making it hard to breathe.

What have we done?

We'll never make it.

Why didn't we just stay put?

It was warm and dry there, not horribly cold like here.

I want to go home and crawl into bed. Want to read to Dad. Mom will make hot chocolate.

I'm sobbing and can barely breathe.

I want this to be over.

Andreas grabs my shoulder. "We have to keep going."

I look at him. His face is ashen, his pupils dilated.

"I can't."

Does he really think there's any point in trying?

"Don't give me that bullshit. If I still have energy, there's no way you don't."

Andreas keeps nudging me, won't leave me alone.

I apathetically roll onto my front; nothing to see but water.

No more gazing at the sky—that was comforting.

I want to roll onto my back again, look at the sky, close my eyes, sleep.

"Let's go," Andreas barks. "You have to fight like a soldier! Think of your grandpa! Or Major General Karton. Imagine if he could see us now! There's gotta be something that stupid military defense training was good for."

My muscles are hard and cramped as I swim against the cold.

"Major General Karton is unfortunately sick today. Drills will be held in the schoolyard."

Frau Thiel opened the schoolhouse door. We followed her outside.

"I thought you weren't allowed to get sick while defending the fatherland," I whispered.

Saxony Jensie grinned. "It's all a cover. He fled to the West! Too bad he's out today; I would have liked to watch that lame movie again."

Almost every class, Major General Karton played the same video about the armed forces. The quality was so bad that you could hardly tell what was going on. Tanks were dropped out of airplanes with parachutes. Sometimes the ancient film would tear and he had to fix it with tape. We were supposed to be learning to defend our fatherland, but something always got in the way. The major general, wearing his uniform covered in medals, would give commands from where he stood at the board. We had to stand up when we spoke in that class.

Frau Thiel put her hands on her hips. She was out of breath. "Well, don't just stand there. Start drilling."

Everyone looked around at one another. No one really knew what to do.

"It's always four per row, marching in step. I'm sure Major General Karton has shown you how it's done."

We lined up in the schoolyard but took our sweet time

doing it. Andreas stood behind me, Saxony Jensie to my side.

"I'm gonna step on Sabine's heels and get her good," he whispered in my ear.

"And straighten out your clothing. This is unacceptable!"

Everyone tugged around on their garments.

"Where's Frank?" Frau Thiel asked.

He grudgingly raised his hand.

"You're the agitator. Deliver the commands."

"Oh no," he groaned.

"Don't talk back!"

Frau Thiel stepped aside and clapped rhythmically. "Go! Sing 'Freiheit'! One, two, one, two ..."

"Attention! Forward ... march!"

Off we went.

"The Spanish sky unfurls its countless stars ..."

"Right!"

"High above our trenches at night ..."

"Forward!"

"When the morning dawns from afar ..."

"Mark time!"

"We are prepared to meet the new fight ..."

"Column right ... march!"

Saxony Jensie stepped on Sabine's heel. She turned around. "Ow! That hurt!"

She then stumbled onto Patricia's heels, and Patricia crashed forward. The formation became hopelessly jumbled.

"Though far from home, we won't leave you alone ..."

"Ouch!"

"Forward!"

"We fight and win in your name . . ."

Andreas jostled me from behind and almost died laughing.

"Free . . . dom!"

"These damn pants," Saxony Jensie cursed. They were sliding down again, and he had to hold them up by the waistband.

"This is a disgrace," Frau Thiel screamed across the yard. "Thankfully, Major General Karton isn't here to see this. It would make him even sicker!"

We stopped singing and stumbled across the yard. Frank murmured commands that no one followed. Frau Thiel ran past our platoon, waving her flabby arms.

"Sing a marching song! The rhythm will set the pace for you. 'The Internationale'! Do you need everything spelled out?" She began sweating heavily. "This is painful to watch!"

She didn't take her eyes off us as she waddled back to the building.

"Oh man," Andreas groaned irritably behind me.

"We could sing the 'Ode to Joy,'" I suggested.

We were studying Beethoven's Ninth in music, so everyone knew the lyrics.

"Yeah, let's do that," Saxony Jensie exclaimed. "Something new for a change! Something nonpolitical!"

We got into formation and started marching.

"Joy, beautiful spark divine, daughter of Elysium, drunk upon the flames we find your sacred realm, O heav'nly one!"

"Forward!"

"Thy magic powers bring together that which custom else divides. All of humankind are brothers where thy gentle wing abides."

"Right!"

"You've got to be kidding me," Frau Thiel brayed. She spun around and stormed back toward us.

At that moment Frau Kröger came out of the building. She watched our troop in amazement.

"He who knows life's greatest treasure, that of being friend to friends, he who's won a lady's pleasure, join us in our merriment!"

"Column left ... march!"

Frau Thiel tried to catch her breath and looked at Frau Kröger for help. "This isn't a marching song!"

Frau Thiel couldn't reach us as quickly as she wanted. Frank intentionally gave commands that led the troop away from her.

"He with but a single friend in all the world from sea to sea! While who yet remains alone shall weep and leave our company!"

"Mark time!"

Frau Kröger rushed across the schoolyard. Saxony Jensie poked me in the side.

"She was laughing. I saw it myself! She was laughing her head off!"

187

Frau Thiel crashed into the middle of our group. "Mark time!"

Saxony Jensie kept singing. *"Ev'ry living thing doth sup on joy, the yield of Nature's breast. Creatures good and those corrupt follow her rose-strewn trail with zest."*

"Quiet, Jens Blum!" Frau Thiel screeched. "If this is what the party's reserve guard looks like, well, that's just great! Beethoven! I don't believe it!"

"Why? It's just something new for once. Something nonpo—"

I elbowed him sharply.

"'Something new for once?' I don't believe it!"

"Forward . . . march!" Frank bellowed.

We trotted off, with Frau Thiel caught in the middle. She stumbled and caught herself on Susanne, who shrieked.

"Frank, quiet! Drill complete!"

Frau Thiel grabbed the students standing closest. "Back into the building, everyone! In silence!"

But we hummed away.

"Silence! Do you hear me!"

Frank the agitator grumbled, *"Gladly, as His suns do hurry . . ."*

Frau Thiel's head whipped around. "Who was that?"

"O'er the heavens' mighty swath . . ."

She spun around again.

"Everyone gets a C in civics! You should be very, very ashamed!"

Since we had all gotten Cs for the day, we burst back into song in the hallway. *"Joyfully, as heroes t'ward victory, as heroes t'ward victory!"*

Frau Thiel obviously told Major General Karton everything once he was back. In our next military defense class, he stood at the board and spoke sharply to us. His name really fit. He was fat but somehow angular at the same time.

After he ordered us never to mock military achievements by selecting inappropriate musical material again, he called every last student to the front of the room and worked us over. First we had to recite military ranks. Sergeant, navy warrant officer, colonel, army general, fleet admiral. Then we had to answer a bunch of stupid questions, like which countries belonged to the Warsaw Pact, which ones were in NATO, and which nations in Africa were socialist. We had to point to the countries on the world map as we answered.

Andreas pretended he couldn't find Cuba, even though he was the best in geography in our class. He was trying to annoy the major general and hovered over South America with the pointer, tracing the Andes till he landed in Patagonia.

Several classmates snickered.

"That's the Strait of Magellan. Can you be serious?"

Andreas feigned surprise. "Oh really?"

"You don't know where our brethren socialist state of Cuba is located?" the major general thundered.

"I'm not sure."

"Cuba is located on the very doorstep of the enemy of the state!"

Andreas didn't move.

"Point out the United States of America!"

Andreas drew back his arm and whacked the tip of the pointer into the Mid-Atlantic Ridge. The entire class stared at the spot—there was nothing but water there on the map. And an enormous mountain range below sea level, which we had learned about in geography.

The major general's bald spot turned bright red. He dashed out of the room and returned with Frau Thiel.

She theatrically opened her fat, pale arms. "I should have known you just had to step out of line again, Andreas Kuschwitz."

The major general stiffened like a board and screamed across the room, "*Jugendfreund* Kuschwitz, since there are no grades in this class, you will receive a C in civics for your pathetic and dishonorable performance."

Andreas shrugged and sat back down.

Saxony Jensie leaned forward and whispered, "I've got a great joke for the major. A guy comes home and finds a military tank in the living room and yells: 'Wow, look! My friends have come to visit!'"

I feel better now. Had a breakdown back there, wanted to quit.

It's happened to me before, at practice. Things can get weird when you're exhausted.

It's usually right before the end—it's easy to flag at that point, no big deal. When you know you're about to reach the end of the pool and that soon you'll be grabbing the lane divider. Then loosening your knotted muscles under a hot shower.

I don't know how much longer this will last, how many meters lie ahead now. What we're doing now is insanity; you can't practice for that beforehand.

But at least I pulled it together. It's a good thing Andreas was there for me and didn't allow me to let myself go.

My calf hurts—there's a cramp coming on, and soon. When it does, I'll have to lie on my back and remain calm. It'll help to imagine I'm in the pool, the side of it within reach. Just don't be scared—things are hard enough as it is. Recite a poem in your head, ease the cramp, flex your muscles, relax, don't think about what's underneath you. Nothing.

My mouth is full of the revolting taste of salt. And these stupid goggles don't keep out the water; my eyes burn. I can hardly see.

If only the boy had said something to his dad.

If only the dad had glanced at his son and noticed him waving.

Then we'd be safe on the ferry now.

And not out here on the open water.

The water is getting colder. Feels like less than sixty degrees.

There's a sound underwater, somewhere in the distance, a tremendous rumbling. A ship's propeller. It's quiet above water when I take a breath, but the rumbling returns when I go back under. Over and over and over.

There's a lot happening in the Baltic, but the ships aren't coming any closer.

Fucking flippers. The sides cut into my feet. The nylons are shot, so now it's straight skin. In salt water. Just don't think about it.

Andreas curses. He's very close and sometimes whacks his arm into my side. His movements are uncoordinated. He's slowing down, and the slower he swims, the more he swears. He should save his energy and focus on swimming, but I don't have the strength to stop and tell him that.

"Why am I doing this shit?" he rages.

The string tightens for a second, then slackens again.

Fortunately, he keeps swimming, doesn't stop.

What would I do if he suddenly couldn't swim anymore?

He knows all too well why he's doing this shit. He doesn't want to go back to prison. The reformatory was more than enough of that. He was so thin when he got out, with his hair short, curls chopped off. He barely spoke while he took the train with us to Warnemünde. Saxony Jensie told all the latest jokes, but Andreas couldn't laugh at them. Me neither; it just didn't feel right anymore.

To celebrate his return, we were going to Hotel Neptun for rotisserie chicken.

Andreas wolfed down his half chicken, followed by his fries and then the salad. One after the other, at reformatory speed. We watched him in shock, almost forgetting our own chickens. They only got five minutes for lunch, he explained when he sensed us watching.

Later, we walked past the seagull statue and Tower 3 down to the beach.

Andreas gazed out over the waves and quietly described a day in prison, as he called it. Wake up, morning exercise, wash up, make bed, breakfast, march to the steelworks, march back, dinner, dorm cleanup, lights out.

"You have to fly under the radar, like a spy," Saxony Jensie blurted. We laughed. Of course he'd go and say something like that on a stormy day when his hair looked even more ridiculous than usual.

Flying under the radar didn't exactly work.

It was 'cause of Grandpa. It was basically his fault, though it wasn't on purpose. He didn't even realize what he had set into motion.

And that was it. From that point on, all we knew was the factory. From six in the morning till four in the afternoon. Can openers every single day. Assemble the pieces, tighten the screws, package them up.

No more *Abitur*, no more biology major. Every single day that old perv would grab my ass. Uwe told him to stop, but it didn't help.

Andreas was stationed at the drill press, wearing blue work coveralls and shapeless plastic safety glasses. Every single day, he manufactured the exact same piece for ship propellers.

Who knows, maybe even for the one I keep hearing.

The underwater droning continues.

Something grabs my arm. It's Andreas's hand. I stop swimming and lift my head. My neck hurts. Several ships on the horizon, headed for West Germany. Probably tankers. Way too far away.

I shake my head. It's pointless to wave or yell; they'd never notice.

"I feel sick," I say. "I might puke."

Andreas is also very pale. He's shaking.

There's a stabbing pain in my calf, the wet suit is chafing my wrists, all my muscles hurt and refuse to move.

I have a pounding headache. "Give me the canister."

Andreas lies on his back and opens the bag attached to his weight belt. The canister of painkillers. He fumbles with the top and shakes a pill into his hand, then puts it in my mouth.

I force it down with a little seawater. Andreas watches me and seems confused.

I have to tell him now, however hard it is and however guilty I feel. "I lost the canteen. Back there in the waves."

He stares blankly.

"I'm so sorry."

"Shit." That's all he says.

I'm not hungry or thirsty. I'm just in pain.

The pill isn't working.

"I can't stop shaking," Andreas says.

His body is fighting the cold, sending the muscles into spasms to produce heat.

We start moving again. Neither of us can crawl anymore, so we're both swimming the breaststroke. I can't get my arms out of the water. It's like swimming in slow motion.

Ulrich would lose his shit if I swam this slow at practice.

I can barely concentrate anymore.

Suddenly the compass needle shoots toward the east.

A powerful current. Andreas doesn't notice, and I reach for his arm.

"We're drifting east. We have to swim faster!"

I kick my legs harder and pull the string to help Andreas along and get us back on course. It's almost impossible. The current keeps pushing us back. The compass needle also jumps around and won't settle.

My pace is thrown off completely. I can't coordinate my movements. My body doesn't know what it's doing. Commands from my brain get lost somewhere along the way to the muscles.

Andreas is struggling to keep up with me. He can barely do it.

I want to scream at him, even though it's not his fault.

We battle the current for an eternity, giving it everything we've got, till everything hurts.

No fixed point, no way to determine our position.

The compass eventually calms down. We don't know how far off course we've gone.

"Which way is north?" Andreas asks.

I look at the compass and point.

"Let's swim straight west," he says. "We're out far enough. No way we'll land in the GDR at this point."

We don't actually have a clue where we are. But I don't argue. The endlessness of the Baltic is killing me.

The thought of swimming west gives me hope.

No one was in the mood for the May Day demonstration. The only good part about it was that we didn't have school.

I picked up Saxony Jensie and Andreas at home, and together we walked to Kröpeliner Tor, where our class was meeting to get into formation. Andreas wasn't wearing his FDJ shirt and immediately caught heat from Frau Thiel about it.

"Andreas, where's your shirt?"

"Dirty. We didn't have any detergent left."

"Let's make one thing clear—you will be in the very last row today!"

Who should round the corner then but Party Secretary Karlow, who could immediately tell something was off. She had a nose for that, like a dog.

"Kuschwitz, why am I not surprised? Here without your shirt. What do you have to say for yourself?"

"What I have to say is that I'm also capable of representing the socialist worldview without a special shirt."

Her face went white. "That's of no value here. Get out. You're not participating in the demonstration with an attitude like that. This country doesn't need people like you."

"Great, I'm going for ice cream."

Andreas gave her a thumbs-up and vanished into the ramparts.

"You're a disgrace!" Frau Karlow screamed at him.

"Lucky," Saxony Jensie sighed. "I want ice cream too."

Instead, he had to carry the red flag down Lange Strasse and yell, "Long live Soviet friendship!"

"But you know what?" he yelled in my ear. "Things aren't looking so good for our friendship with the Soviet Union. Ever since perestroika and glasmost, suddenly Honecker doesn't want to copy everything they do anymore. Says my dad."

"It's called glasnost."

"What?"

"Glasnost, not 'glasmost,' like it was the most glassy thing. That doesn't make any sense!"

But Saxony Jensie didn't care and overzealously waved his flag around. The demonstration was thankfully done by noon, and we could take off. Andreas was waiting for us at the Steintor city gate because our plan was to go to Warnemünde.

Saxony Jensie and I ran home quick to change because we obviously didn't want to wear our FDJ shirts to the beach. That would have been way too embarrassing.

There were lots of people selling stuff on the pier in Warnemünde. One guy had set up a bunch of Christmas pyramids, even though it was early May.

Andreas and I quickly scrambled up to the wall from the rocks.

"Great spot!" Saxony Jensie yelled, and took a running start but didn't make it. Andreas and I grabbed him by the waistband and hoisted him up onto the walkway.

That's where we spread out our posters. And whatever else we could sell—articles about bands, stickers, ads.

"Now, let's see how much money we can make off this *Bravo*," Andreas said to Saxony Jensie.

His grandma had been in the West and brought him the latest issue of the magazine. Of course, she thought he'd be keeping it for himself and not selling it on the black market.

We were immediately swarmed by people. Two girls who looked almost identical, from their blond hair to their pink T-shirts, stood before us, whispering.

"What'll it be?" Saxony Jensie opened his arms out over our treasures.

They both pointed at the big Depeche Mode poster.

"Twenty marks exactly!"

They looked stunned and dug in their pockets. Each held out a ten-mark bill.

"What, you gonna cut it down the middle?"

They stared at us.

"Or take turns every week?"

They put their heads together, whispering again, then took the poster. They ran off.

"Who the hell cares what they do with it? Don't scare off our customers with your stupid questions," Andreas snarled at Saxony Jensie.

I looked around the pier. If the People's Police came, we'd have to split.

A boy with lots of zits bought the George Michael poster for fifteen marks. Madonna and Prince went quick too. Andreas shelled out twenty-five for Sting, because Jennifer Rush was on the other side. A woman Mom's age bought a picture of Don Johnson's knee from the celebrity puzzle in *Bravo* magazine.

"You hangin' Don Johnson's knee on your wall, er what?" She nodded politely and placed seven marks on the ground. Then she left, looking in every direction as she went.

Andreas punched Saxony Jensie in the side. "Shut your freaking trap, man!"

"But how stupid is that, hanging someone's knee on your wall?"

"Maybe she already has the thigh," Andreas said.

"Ooh, I know!" Saxony Jensie squealed. "Let's take pictures of my knee and say it's Bruce Springsteen's. We could make tons of money that way."

"That would never work," I said. "Your knees are way too scrawny. And too dirty."

"So? I bet Bruce Springsteen sometimes gets dirty knees from rocking out on stage."

Andreas paged through *Bravo*. "Whoa," he said suddenly.

Saxony Jensie's red shock of hair spun around. "Huh? What?"

"Whoa," Andreas repeated and disappeared behind the magazine.

Saxony Jensie slid over to him and looked over his shoulder. His bushy eyebrows shot straight up. "Whoa is right!"

"What is it?" I asked.

"Concert for Berlin," Saxony Jensie read in English. "Next weekend! David Bowie, Genesis, and the Eurythmics!"

"Whoa!"

"They're playing right outside the Reichstag. That means we'll be able to hear them over here in the East too," Saxony Jensie screamed in my ear, as if I were deaf.

"Let's not sell this article for the time being," Andreas decided.

Pretty much all we had left now was ads. A man gave us five marks for the lot, then began asking questions.

"Where do you live?"

"Rostock," Andreas answered.

"Address?"

Andreas gave him Sabine's address, the teacher's pet in our class who lived in the Stasi building.

"And you?" The man stared in my face.

"Seven nine eight Allee der Bauschaffenden. In Dierkow."

"Five Braunkohlenweg, in Riesa," Saxony Jensie brayed in the most hideous Saxon accent.

The man took a few notes and moved on to the next group.

In the train later, we reread the article about the concert. Saxony Jensie crossed his arms and griped, "Why is everything always better in the West? Can anyone explain? And why don't the Eurythmics ever come play for us?"

"Why would they?" Andreas asked, angrily staring out the window. "Don't hold your breath."

To cheer us up, we counted our money. We had earned 261 marks and 30 pfennigs. That meant 87 marks and 10 pfennigs each.

Saxony Jensie was astounded. "What should we do with it?"

"Buy Western chocolate at the *Delikat*," I suggested.

"That's stupid."

At the Marienehe stop, a mother got in with her crying kid. She sat down diagonally across from us.

"We could go to Berlin!" Andreas slapped Saxony Jensie's leg. "Dude, what do you say?"

"Ow! What'll we do there?"

"Go to the concert, man! Obviously!"

"Are we even allowed to?"

Andreas leaned forward and whispered, "We'll just take the train Saturday after school. We'll get there in time for David Bowie."

"I don't have money for the ticket," Saxony Jensie tried to talk himself out of it.

"Don't bullshit us, you wuss. You have eighty-seven marks and ten pfennigs!"

I laughed. "What a dumb excuse!"

He got all offended and stuck out his tongue at me. "We won't even see anything. The Wall is right there!"

The woman with the kid kept giving us weird looks. It was getting dark out.

"But we'll hear them," I countered. "If you want to see them, just watch TV."

"I would come along if I could see them!"

"Whatever, you're just scared. Wimp." Andreas turned to me, ignoring Saxony Jensie. "And on Sunday, we'll go see the Eurythmics."

"Yeah!"

Saxony Jensie slid his butt around in his seat. "So where'll we sleep?"

"In a park or something. It's not cold at night anymore. We could take our sleeping bags!"

"I don't think that's allowed. We'd probably be arrested. Or robbed. Like on that recent episode of *The Prosecutor Has the Floor*."

"I know someone in Berlin, where we could stay."

They both looked at me in surprise. "Really?"

"My Aunt Elke and Uncle Jürgen. It's just been a while since I saw them."

"When was that?"

"At my Uncle Wolfgang's funeral. Nineteen eighty-two or so."

Saxony Jensie's mouth twisted. "Do you think they remember you?"

"Of course. We're related."

When I got home, I opened the desk drawer where Mom kept her little notebook of addresses. Uncle Jürgen was in there too. Sixteen Dimitroff Strasse, Prenzlauer Berg, Berlin. City of Peace and Friendship Among Nations.

When I told Mom how much money we made on the pier, she said she was going to quit her job at the fish *Kombinat* and start selling junk on the black market of Warnemünde.

"Fuck!"

Andreas feels around his neck and down the front of his wet suit. "Fuck this shit! I can't believe it!"

"What's wrong?"

"There's water coming in at the top, and it's fucking freezing."

I swim over to him, take off my goggles, and check it out. I can't believe it either. His suit is busted, with a huge tear down from his neck to his chest.

"When did this happen?"

"Just now. God damn it, how could this happen? What do I do now?"

"Do you have the tape?"

Andreas nods, turns onto his back, swings the bag around to his stomach, and opens it. He hands me the adhesive tape and dive knife. "It's waterproof."

We have to make this work.

I peel off a strip of tape and try cutting it with the knife. I balance in the water, kicking my legs to keep me steady and the tape dry. But what's the point—the suit and the spot we have to tape are wet as it is.

"More. You'll need more for it. Shit, this sucks. Water gets in every move I make." Andreas is breathing rapidly. "This would be easier on the buoy," he murmurs.

I tear off a strip, even though I don't think it will work.

"The cold is running from my stomach to my legs, God damn it. I didn't realize before how well insulated the wet suit was."

"Come a little closer," I say. Andreas paddles toward me.

I press the strip of tape over the tear as well as I can and hold it down for a while. It sticks in some spots, but not in others. I add another layer to those loose spots.

The repair doesn't inspire confidence. A few movements, and the tape will peel.

Andreas's face has an odd sheen to it. "Well? Did it work?"

I nod mutely. What do I say?

He won't last another hour like this.

What do I do? We can't return to the buoy. We'd never find it.

I look around, as though help might come from somewhere.

There's nothing out here. No one.

Everything inside me constricts.

Just keep encouraging him. That's the least you can do. Act like you believe it yourself.

But I can barely speak. "The water in your suit has to warm up again," I stutter.

Andreas nods. "Thermodynamics. We had that in physics." He circles his arms in the water and looks at the horizon. "Never really got it in school. Out here, I do."

I have water in my left ear, and my neck aches.

"I'm so cold," Andreas says quietly.

I can't look him in the eyes. What the hell do I do? I can't warm him up. I can't do anything.

Andreas closes his eyes, leans back slightly in the water, and feels around his stomach. Then he opens his eyes again and appears relieved.

"What're you doing?"

"Just ditched my weight belt. It pulls me down too much. I don't care about body position anymore. I need better lift." He inhales deeply, lies on his back, and floats.

But we need to keep going.

How could his stupid wet suit just rip like that? It's from the West. Without insulation, Andreas won't last much longer. Heat loss occurs much more rapidly in water than in the air, and you have to convert a lot of energy in order to keep warm. He can't even move fast enough for that. If only I hadn't paid such close attention in physics. I'd rather I didn't know all this stuff.

He has to hang on somehow.

Has to distract himself with his songs or memories.

Has to think of the good times and our new life in the West.

And I have to talk to him as we swim, keep encouraging him. I can't forget to do that, even if I barely have any strength left myself.

I squeeze his arm. "We have to swim now."

He nods and looks me in the eye. "Promise me we'll make it."

I swallow and blink quickly. I'm sure he can tell I'm lying. "I promise."

He rolls onto his stomach, looks out across the sea, and shakes his head, as though none of this made any sense to him.

The present has nothing to give—only the future can strengthen him.

I gently touch his shoulder. "Think of Hamburg and Saxony Jensie. Think of our trip to Berlin. We want to go back there together some day!"

He chews his lips, which have gone blue, and nods silently.

We need a miracle.

We need a boat.

The train departed at 1:28 p.m. Saxony Jensie and Andreas were waiting for me outside the Intershop. Saxony Jensie had an NVA canteen and binoculars around his neck.

"On the lookout for enemies of the state?" I said in greeting.

"You never know!" he responded.

We walked down the long hallway to the platform. The train was pretty full, but we managed to find three empty seats.

"Think they're all going to Berlin?"

"Duh, they're all going to Berlin, you stupid Saxon. That's where the train goes."

Andreas messed around with the Walkman he had gotten for Christmas.

"Dude, I mean to the concert."

"No clue."

Saxony Jensie paged through the new issue of his *Mosaik* comic, this one called "The Golden Pillar."

I had brought along *The Adventures of Werner Holt*, which we had to read for school. I had expected it to be way worse, but it turned out to be about war and friendship, which was finally something more concrete.

Lots of people boarded the train in Neustrelitz. A guy in a parka with long black hair adjusted the dial on his portable radio.

"RIAS doesn't come in here yet."

Saxony Jensie stared at the guy, who pulled out two bottles of beer from his bag and handed one to his buddy. I hid my embarrassing schoolbook.

He looked over at us. "What's up, Olsen Gang? Where you headed?"

"To see David Bowie!" Saxony Jensie hooted.

The guy laughed and turned to his friend, who looked just like him. "Imagine that, the Olsen Gang wants to see the Wall! Careful you don't accidentally hop over, you hear?"

Saxony Jensie hid behind his comic book again.

"It's probably a better idea to stick with the nice tales of Califax, Abrax, and . . ." He turned to his buddy again. "What's the third one called?"

"Brabax!"

"That's right, Brabax. Maybe you should focus on them instead. Berlin is too big and dangerous for Young Pioneers."

"We're in the FDJ," Saxony Jensie boasted.

"Wow, did you hear that? They're in the FDJ!" the guy said to his friend. They both laughed.

Andreas tapped his temple at Saxony Jensie. "Quit embarrassing us!" he hissed.

All that came out of the radio was static. The parka

208

dude turned the dial some more and found Berliner Rundfunk.

"Turn that off. I'd rather listen to the static of the free world."

His friend belched.

We got out at the Lichtenberg stop and simply followed the guys on the city train to Marx-Engels Square. It was my first time in Berlin. It reeked of exhaust fumes. Everything was so big—the buildings, the streets. When we crossed the Spree River, we passed by a monumental structure.

Saxony Jensie stopped, right in this old man's way. "Whoa, what's that?"

"Berlin Cathedral, you hick!"

Saxony Jensie pulled out his compass.

We laughed our heads off. "Are you mental? Who wanders around Berlin with a compass?"

"Well, in case we get lost, we can check our cardinal direction."

"You don't need cardinal directions in Berlin! Everything's east."

"Have you heard this one yet?" Saxony Jensie asked. "The Berlin Wall needs to be replastered. Seventeen million and three people volunteer. Three for the inner side, seventeen million for the exterior."

"Look!" Andreas exclaimed. Right there was the Palace of the Republic. Andreas wrinkled his nose. "Yeah, I had a feeling. It really is ugly!"

Saxony Jensie turned a full circle, looking through his binoculars. "There's the Brandenburg Gate," he screamed, pointing west.

At this point, we were part of a crowd walking in the same direction up the street. By the time we reached Humboldt University, there was no more moving on.

"Shit," a man in front of us cursed. "It's cordoned off up there."

Andreas jumped up. "Vopos!"

"Shouldn't we get out of here, then?" Saxony Jensie paled at the mention of Volkspolizei, the People's Police.

"Why? We're not doing anything," Andreas said.

Suddenly the parka dude from the train appeared beside us.

"What's up, Olsen Gang. Having a nice trip? Not only can we not see David Bowie, now they won't even let us hear him."

His buddy was furious. "Turn on your radio, at least."

Then we could faintly hear music coming from the Brandenburg Gate. I couldn't tell what it was.

"He's playing 'Let's Dance'!" Saxony Jensie roared.

"No, that's 'Absolute Beginners'!"

"'Heroes'!"

Someone behind us screamed, "This is some real socialist bullshit here!"

Saxony Jensie yanked on my arm. "We gotta get out of here. I'm gonna lose my dad's sleeping bag in this crowd!"

People were yelling up front.

The parka dude cranked the volume on his radio and hoisted it over his head.

"You're listening to RIAS Berlin, a free voice in the free world."

"Whoa." Andreas gazed into the sky, as if the announcer were sitting right there.

"I wanna go!" Saxony Jensie screamed.

Andreas climbed onto Saxony Jensie's back. He almost collapsed.

"They're fighting up there! With batons!"

Saxony Jensie squirmed, and Andreas fell. "What the hell is wrong with you?"

"I want to leave!"

"Wuss!"

"I don't want to brawl with the People's Police either," I said.

The parka dude was right in front of me, moving strangely to the music on the radio. I nudged him. "How do we get to Dimitroff Strasse from here?"

"Had your fill of socialist realism, huh?"

"That's right!" his buddy yelled in my ear, then danced around me.

"We want to go home. My uncle's waiting."

"Hang on a sec." He stared at the radio. "David Bowie's saying something." Then he burst out, "David Bowie just said hello to his friends on the other side!"

Everyone clapped and cheered.

Saxony Jensie stared at him with his mouth open, then

looked toward the Brandenburg Gate. "Whoa, and that's live!"

Andreas scrambled onto Saxony Jensie's back again, to get a better view.

The parka dude turned to me. "Walk to Alexanderplatz, which is back there." He pointed at the street the Palace of the Republic was on.

"Just keep heading for the glittery drumstick!" his buddy hollered. "Then take the subway to the Dimitroff Strasse stop."

"Maybe we'll see you again tomorrow," Andreas yelled.

"You know it! In the name of peace and socialism!"

We shoved our way through the crowd and set out for the television tower.

A friendly lady explained which way to go through the subway station. Saxony Jensie got in the wrong train and would have ridden off alone toward Otto Grotewohl Strasse had Andreas not yanked him out right before the doors closed.

We rode underground first, then the train climbed into the light and continued above ground. We got out at the Dimitroff Strasse stop and took the stairs down to street level. We crossed an enormous intersection.

We found number sixteen and took the stairs all the way to the top floor. We couldn't find Uncle Jürgen's name anywhere. We went back down.

"Guys, look. One street number applies to three buildings!" Andreas pointed at a big metal panel in the entryway. Front building, rear building, side wing. All of the tenants' names were listed there, some in old-fashioned script. Kowalski, Ebert, Schrader, Nuske.

Finally, we found Köppke. Rear building, fourth floor.

I told them to wait one floor down. I didn't want to give Uncle Jürgen a heart attack.

"Doesn't your uncle know we're sleeping over?"

"No, he doesn't have a phone."

"Oh my gosh," Saxony Jensie cried in panic. "What if he's not home?"

I rang the bell. No one opened the door. We sat on the stairs.

"Hopefully he's not on vacation, or something." Saxony Jensie pulled out his canteen. "It's a good thing I brought this!" He took a big swig and passed us the water. We waited for two hours till Uncle Jürgen finally came up the stairs. He had long black hair and wore faded jeans and a red-and-white plaid shirt. He looked like a rock star.

"Hanna?" he asked in surprise.

"Hey, Uncle Jürgen."

"What are you doing here?"

"I wanted to come visit you."

He looked at Andreas and Saxony Jensie, who jumped up and wiped the dirt from the seats of their pants.

"Hello," they both said at once.

Uncle Jürgen looked at me again and scratched his three-day stubble. "Well, why don't you all come in first."

213

We sat in the small kitchen. Uncle Jürgen opened the fridge and pulled out a bottle of Berliner Pils. "You thirsty?"

We nodded. He opened a cupboard.

"You'll have to split a warm bottle of Vita Cola." He placed three glasses on the table. Saxony Jensie poured the drinks while Andreas watched to make sure he split it evenly.

Uncle Jürgen raised his bottle. "Cheers!"

"We're hungry too," Saxony Jensie said meekly.

Uncle Jürgen set his beer on the kitchen table. "Then I'll fry up some potatoes. It's what I would have made today anyway."

"Hurray!" Saxony Jensie cheered.

The walls were all wood paneled.

"Did you make that?" Saxony Jensie pointed at a painting of a church.

Uncle Jürgen nodded. "That's the church up on Stargarder Strasse."

He tossed potatoes into the pan and chopped bacon. Saxony Jensie got up from the table to watch.

"Where's Aunt Elke?" I asked.

He added eggs to the mix. It smelled so good.

"Visiting her mother in Thuringia."

As he cooked, we told him why we were in Berlin. Uncle Jürgen shook the pan, which Saxony Jensie's eyes followed attentively.

"And the Eurythmics are playing tomorrow?"

"Yeah. So awesome."

Uncle Jürgen split the food between four plates and set them on the table. We ate hungrily.

"And you want to go?" Uncle Jürgen asked with his mouth full.

"Duh," Saxony Jensie said.

"Duh," Andreas mimicked him. "You would say that, wouldn't you? And who's the one pissing his pants out there, he's so scared?"

"That's not even true!" Saxony Jensie pointed at Andreas. "He's in love with Annie Lennox."

"Keep your mouth shut," Andreas growled.

Uncle Jürgen stood up. "Dessert?"

He pulled two packages of Leckermäulchen yogurt cups from the fridge.

"No way, you have Leckermäulchen!" Saxony Jensie exclaimed. "You can't find those in Rostock!"

"Capital city supplies," Uncle Jürgen said.

"What does that mean, 'capital city supplies'?"

"It means that the capital of the GDR has to look good in the eyes of the world, while the rest of the country's going down the toilet," Andreas murmured. We all looked at him in surprise.

"Well, yeah. That pretty much sums it up," Uncle Jürgen said, still taken aback. He turned to me. "Hey. So, Elisabeth does know you're here, right?"

"Yeah, 'course."

Saxony Jensie looked at me, perplexed. "Who's Elisabeth?"

215

"My mother."

"Well, let's make one thing clear here: You're not going to the Wall tomorrow. Way too dangerous."

"But that's why we came to Berlin!" Saxony Jensie whined in outrage.

"Tough luck. You've got no business down there."

We looked glumly at our dessert cups. "But the Eurythmics are playing," Andreas said in a small voice.

"Tough!"

Saxony Jensie and Andreas slept on the old couch in the living room, and I was on an air mattress. Saxony Jensie told a long story about the Abrafaxes before we fell asleep, while Andreas snored softly.

Saxony Jensie completely flipped out the next morning when Uncle Jürgen set a jar of Nudossi spread on the table.

"So awesome!" he yelled and slathered a thick layer on his crisp bread.

"You can never get enough, can you?" Andreas snapped.

After breakfast Uncle Jürgen went to church for Pentecost services, which seemed weird to us.

"Doesn't he know that religion is the opium of the people?" Saxony Jensie asked as we sat watching *Tom and Jerry* on TV. Tom was being sawed in half after Jerry had outsmarted him yet again.

"Why don't we just split?" Saxony Jensie suddenly asked.

"We can't—it's rude," I said.

"But he won't let us go to the Eurythmics show; he said so himself!" Saxony Jensie ran into the hallway and pulled on his sneakers. "I want to see them!"

"But you won't see them."

Andreas got up too. "For once, the Saxon's right. I'm going too. I can watch *Tom and Jerry* at home."

I had no choice but to follow. I left a note for Uncle Jürgen, telling him not to worry. Unter den Linden, leading to the Brandenburg Gate, was blocked off again. There were way more people than the day before. We couldn't hear any music. We weren't even standing near a radio.

"Well, so much for that," Andreas sighed.

We waited an eternity for something to happen. We were starting to get bored when suddenly Uncle Jürgen popped up beside us. He had somehow managed to find us in the crowd.

"Caught ya!"

He was only kind of mad and even smiled a little when he saw Saxony Jensie with his canteen and compass.

"All right, pals, we'd better turn back."

Andreas glared at him furiously. "No!" Then he disappeared into the crush.

"What's with him?" Uncle Jürgen craned his neck and tried to see where he'd gone.

"He's got a mind of his own. I'll go get him."

Uncle Jürgen called something out to me, but I couldn't hear him anymore.

I found Andreas just a few rows farther on, and together we fought our way to the front. We were surrounded by people a lot bigger than us pounding their feet on the pavement. We heard a loud scream in front of us. Andreas jumped onto my back. "They're fighting!" He slid down and pulled me forward.

"I don't want to go up there!"

There were only a few people now between us and the Vopos. They were attacking the crowd. There was blood. Many people were being hauled off and arrested.

"Shit!" Andreas was finally scared too.

Someone behind us started chanting, "The Wall's got to go!" Another voice joined in. "The Wall's got to go! The Wall's got to go!" Then: "Gorbi, Gorbi . . ."

"Why are they saying 'Gorbi'?" Andreas screamed into my ear.

"I don't know!" I yelled back. "I want to go!"

The batons were getting closer. The Vopos stomped on people. A delivery truck pulled up just a few meters away. Even more policemen, this time with German shepherds, leaped down the ramp and onto the street. The dogs dragged screaming people out of the crowd by their feet.

"I want to get out of here! Now!"

I grabbed Andreas's arm. He followed me. For once, even he had had enough. We ducked down and squeezed past people's legs. It was really hard because the crowd was packed and churning. A knee slammed into my ear, and another caught Andreas in the nose. It started to bleed.

We managed to reach the side. Everywhere we looked, police were loading people into trucks. We sprinted past Humboldt University and down the street. Other people were running that way too, so we had police on our heels the entire time. At one street corner, Andreas pulled me between two parked Trabbis. We hunkered down and waited. I was completely out of breath. Police darted past and didn't see us.

He punched my shoulder. "Ha! Now we finally know what the point was in winning the *Spartakiad*."

I had a side stitch. We stayed crouched there for what felt like forever; police officers kept charging past.

"I can't get caught, or they'll send me back to the reformatory," Andreas whispered as the city train rattled overhead. That was all we needed.

It was starting to get dark.

"Marx-Engels Square isn't far," Andreas said. We ran to the entrance and up the stairs. The train platform was teeming with policemen. Two immediately accosted us.

"They can't do anything to us," Andreas whispered.

"What are you two doing here?"

"Spring break," I blurted.

"Let's see some identification!"

We pulled our IDs from our pants pockets. They studied them for a long time.

"What are you doing out so late?"

"We've been trying to get back to my uncle's house, but we got lost. We're from Rostock."

The policeman looked at me sternly.

"Where does your uncle live?"

"Dimitroff Strasse."

"Number?"

"Sixteen."

"And your uncle lets you roam the streets of Berlin alone at this hour, even though you don't know your way around?"

Andreas helped me out. "We spent the entire day together, ate rotisserie chicken and fried potatoes and stuff. Then Hanna and I went to the milk bar, which took a little longer than expected. We don't have stuff like that in Rostock because the capital city supply doesn't reach that far!"

The policeman stared at him.

"We lost sight of him at Alexanderplatz because there were so many people."

"Which milk bar?"

Andreas kept a straight face. "You know, the one by Alexanderplatz. I don't know how to describe it. I'm not from here."

The policeman turned to his partner, who was checking a young couple's papers.

"Hey, Krusche, do you know of any milk bar by Alexanderplatz?"

"Nah," he muttered absently.

"It just opened, right next door to the bookstore," I said to distract him. My dad had told me about that bookstore, where years ago he had bought lots of Jack London.

"When are you going back to Rostock?"

The officer finally gave us back our IDs.

"Tomorrow," we said at the same time and shoved the IDs into our pockets.

"Well, then, send my best to the fish-heads!"

Twenty minutes later, we rang Uncle Jürgen's doorbell. He didn't open the door, though—it was Aunt Elke. She was wearing a loose yellow dress and looked furious. She had short brown hair.

"Aha!" She stepped back.

Saxony Jensie sat in the kitchen, sobbing into an enormous checkered handkerchief.

"Where's Uncle Jürgen?"

"Good question. Where do you think?" Elke put her hands on her hips. "Go ahead, young man, tell them!"

"Arrested," Saxony Jensie wailed.

"Shit!" Andreas and I said at the same time.

"You can say that again!" Aunt Elke dropped into a chair.

Sniffling, Saxony Jensie told us what had happened. "Your uncle Jürgen was worried because you guys didn't come back. So he went after you. All I saw then was three men dragging him away."

Andreas and I just stood there awkwardly.

Elke gave me a punishing look. "Jürgen never would have gone to the Wall, especially not when it was obvious there would be trouble. What's gotten into you, Hanna?"

221

"We just wanted to hear David Bowie and the Eurythmics."

She opened her arms. "Ever consider playing a record?"

"The Amiga label doesn't represent them," Andreas said. "And besides, they were actually here. That's better than listening to a record."

"Exactly!" Saxony Jensie waved the handkerchief. "It's, like, totally live!"

"'It's, like, totally live!'" Elke mimicked him. "Do you want to know something? This isn't 'totally live,' it's totally terrible."

Saxony Jensie stopped waving and looked sorrowfully at the blue waxed tablecloth.

"And for what? To stand around, just waiting for music to spill over the Wall? That's demeaning."

Andreas talked back. "No way. There's nothing demeaning about hearing David Bowie."

"Still better than hearing *and* seeing the Puhdys." Saxony Jensie sniffed.

Elke didn't laugh.

"And now look. Jürgen's in jail, God damn it!" She stood up. "But what's the point of telling you three. You've no idea what this means."

She went to the sink and started washing dishes. She was so mad she broke one, which made her even angrier, and she threw the sponge at us.

On the couch later, Saxony Jensie whined about how hungry he was.

"Shut up, Saxon," Andreas kept repeating, till he finally did.

In all the turmoil, none of us had eaten. No one dared to ask Aunt Elke for a couple sandwiches. She had gone to her bedroom and was listening to Chopin.

"Nothing to eat, but plenty of damn tinkling," Andreas grumbled as we fell asleep.

The next morning Aunt Elke woke us at seven. "All right, boys and girls, field trip's over! Time to go home!"

She drove us to Lichtenberg in their Trabbi and waited till we had boarded the train to Rostock. No one spoke on the ride back. I felt guilty about Uncle Jürgen. We all bought flowers for our parents at Rostock Central Station. Mom yelled at me for over an hour. She wouldn't let me watch TV or go to the Reifer. I read aloud some of *Burning Daylight* to Dad. He hadn't even noticed I was gone.

The next day in civics, with her index finger raised, Frau Grahl condemned the events in Berlin.

"Counterrevolutionaries attempted to denigrate our country at a rock concert held directly on the border to the GDR. The West provoked the situation by pointing the speakers directly toward the East."

Saxony Jensie and I stared at our desk and didn't let on to anything. Andreas raised his hand. I poked him in the back with my pencil. I wanted him to keep quiet.

"Yes, Andreas, you have something you'd like to add."

"What does a counterrevolutionary look like anyway?"

"What a stupid question!" Frau Grahl looked around helplessly.

Saxony Jensie's arm shot into the air.

"Yes, Jens."

"There's no such thing as a stupid question, only stupid answers."

She was immediately shaken. "Why yes, of course. Thank you. Who here knows the answer to Andreas's question?"

Sabine raised her hand. "A counterrevolutionary is not identified by his or her appearance but by his or her actions."

"Very well put. Thank you, Sabine!"

Andreas stretched.

I leaned forward and whispered, "Keep your mouth shut, man!"

"What are you whispering about, Hanna? Is there something you'd like to add to this discussion?"

I looked out the window and didn't respond.

"I'm very surprised at your behavior," Frau Grahl peeped.

Saxony Jensie raised his hand yet again and laid his Saxon accent on thick. "When I was little, a man on the train in Dresden said that counterrevolutionaries all have black beards. Is that true?"

Everyone laughed.

224

Frau Grahl flushed. She turned to the board, and her hand shook as she wrote the words *productive forces* and *means of production*.

⌇

I lie motionless on my back.

The clammy cold sinks deeper into my body.

I don't care if we float off course. I can't do this anymore.

Water slaps against my ears, which are covered by the swim cap. Still, I feel the impact, hear the sound. It hurts.

Just the cold and the water, that's all there is. It pours down me, surrounds me, burns my lips and throat. I am so nauseous.

I blink up at the thick cloud cover, and my eyes hurt. Want to close them again immediately. Several clouds are very dark. That means bad weather is on the way.

Andreas floats next to me. He can't swim anymore either. He's dozing.

Something else is up there in the sky.

Something black.

It emerges from the clouds. Maybe there's something on my lenses. A fly. That's impossible, not in the middle of the Baltic. I take off my goggles and suddenly hear a droning sound, distant but distinct.

I look at the sky again and force myself to focus on the spot. There it is, that black thing. It's getting bigger, approaching us. What is it?

225

Directly above whatever it is, the air shimmers, caused by a rapid spinning motion. No, it can't be.

I don't believe it.

Andreas grabs my arm. He's not dozing anymore. He saw it too.

I straighten up and stare incredulously at it.

A helicopter.

The engine noise grows.

"Russian attack helicopter!" Andreas roars.

The Pole.

He reported us.

We're in international waters, and they want to take us back in their helicopter.

But can they even see us out in the middle of the Baltic? We're supposed to be needles in a haystack. Maybe it's just coincidence they're flying in our direction.

But why? Maybe it's an exercise. They wouldn't fly all this way just for us.

We have to dive. Now.

I look at Andreas, and he looks at me. He doesn't move. Only then do I realize I didn't actually say anything, only thought it, mistaking thoughts for reality. The lines are all blurred out here.

"We have to dive!"

I put my goggles back on and stuff the snorkel into my mouth so hastily that it tears up my gums again. I take a deep breath, and some water gets in, burning my throat. I cough and dive under.

Have to swim deep enough to make sure my flippers don't upset the water at the surface.

Andreas is close; there's just a quick tug on my wrist, then the string goes slack. We both dive in the same direction, swim several meters into the inky depths, and stay there as long as we can.

I watch bubbles float to the surface, our breathing air.

Up till now the only danger had been below. Now it's above us too.

In the air.

A helicopter.

They're pulling out all the stops to get us.

This is insane. As if we were someone important.

The drone of the helicopter penetrates the water and seems to be all around, as though the helicopter itself were descending upon us.

Andreas pulls the string. He wants to surface.

I blow out air, swim upward, break through the surface, breathe frantically.

From the back now, I can see the little rotor on the tailpiece spinning vertically.

"It passed by overhead," Andreas calls.

It doesn't seem to have seen us.

The sound gets quieter, although it's still deafening.

Andreas takes off his goggles. He's deathly pale, and he shakes his head. "Wild."

"Where could it be headed?" I murmur in disbelief.

It has started to rain.

"They didn't see us, did they?" Andreas looks at me fearfully.

"I don't think so," I say for both our sakes. "Maybe there's someone else out here they're looking for, in a boat or something."

Andreas appears skeptical. It seems unlikely to me too.

I look at the helicopter and suddenly see it from the side, then from the front.

"The God damn thing turned around," Andreas yells. "They're coming back!"

I see two big eyes under the rotor blades. Probably jets.

"You gotta be kidding me!"

The eyes approach, along with the rattle and roar.

Andreas grasps my arm and looks around frantically, as though he wants to hide somewhere. Like we used to at the playground. Ready or not, here I come!

I'm paralyzed. We have to do something.

"Let's go! Dive!"

Panic in his eyes. He's still clutching me.

I shake him off and dive, dragging on the string. My wrist hurts. He's not following. I swim back up and yank on the string as hard as I possibly can.

Finally, he gets it. The resistance lets up, and Andreas follows me into the depths.

I don't get far, though. I don't have enough air.

What is the point of all this? There isn't one, not anymore. I'm done.

The West can't be that great. What a stupid idea.

What's up, what's down.

It's time we quit. It's no use. Jail time beats dying. We have to surrender now.

I'll tell him as soon as we surface.

Andreas pulls the string. The roaring in my ears intensifies as we swim upward.

The noise at the surface is unbelievable. It's so loud, pure madness.

This is what Hell must be like.

I can't breathe, and my heart is racing. I feel my pulse in my neck; I cover my ears, wish I could close my eyes so I didn't have to see anymore, didn't have to be here anymore.

The helicopter is directly above us, its belly a bluish gray, every last rivet visible. A vast expanse of shiny metal.

It lowers even more, like it wants to force us underwater. What the hell?

I hear several things at once—spinning blades, the engine, and, cutting through everything else, a high-pitched whine that drives me insane.

I can't see the sky anymore. The helicopter skids are so close, I could touch them.

I'm paralyzed. My body is failing.

The force of the rotor blades whips up water.

Andreas pulls me down, away from the helicopter hovering above us in the air.

Everything around us crashes and roars, and I can barely get any air.

229

Water shoots straight up, like a wall, climbing toward the helicopter.

I gaze upward. What is happening here?

Suddenly the wall collapses, and all the water crashes down on us.

Waves come from every direction, and we battle the undertow and try to stay at the surface. Andreas kicks me several times—I'm thrashing my legs about too in an effort not to lose control entirely.

Pure thundering chaos, and Andreas is screaming something.

The helicopter turns, and I see a man by the window. He's moving his arm.

What does he want?

I plunge down and come right back up. There's water in my nose. I cough.

Andreas won't stop screaming.

There's a flash across the water, then another.

Are they shooting at us?

Another flash.

Get away from that thing!

I dive down, tugging Andreas behind me.

Giving it all I've got, going as deep as possible.

But I don't have it in me. I can't do it. My lungs hurt, and I have to swim back up.

Back up.

His face is right in front of me. We're at the surface again. Andreas moves his lips.

"Do you hear that?"

What does he mean, the sound of the rotor blades above?

Is the sound even there anymore?

That's when I notice that things have grown quieter. A lot quieter.

All that surrounds us now is the endless splash of waves.

Strange.

"They're gone!" Andreas seizes my shoulder. "The thunderstorm chased them off!"

I look at the horizon. Choppy water ahead, black clouds above. Where's the helicopter?

"That was one of those helicopters that can land on water. It must have been too risky for them in these waves."

Andreas grimaces, probably trying to grin.

There's a rumbling in the distance. The storm is approaching.

Those weren't shots. The helicopter wasn't shooting at us.

It was lightning.

The sky above is dark and threatening.

No one else is around. There are more cracks of thunder, and the waves surge. Out of the frying pan and into the fire.

Is it even possible to swim through a storm? What if we're struck by lightning? The lifeguards at the beach in Warnemünde would be ordering everyone out of the water right now.

"We gotta move," Andreas urges.

Heavy raindrops fall on me, just a few at first, then more and more. Hopefully the storm will pass quickly. Maybe we'll just catch the edge of it.

If only Saxony Jensie knew.

I plunge my arms into the dark water. I don't look at the sky anymore. Just don't think about what's brewing above. *One stroke, then another. Keep going. Don't think.*

All Saxony Jensie had to do was board a train and ride west. Warm and dry. Maybe he even treated himself to a soda in the dining car. What a champ. We were all thoroughly surprised, even Saxony Jensie. His parents had kept it a secret that they wanted to leave the country with him.

"I doubt he's interested in standing around and having a ball shot at his head."

Andreas dribbled around me. The ball soared and bounced off the side of the building, straight into his hands.

"Ha, cool," he praised himself.

We sprinted up the steps.

Andreas rang the doorbell. "Good thing vacation starts soon. Then we can play soccer every day."

"My mom says I should call it quits soon." I leaned against the wall and some plaster immediately crumbled. "Since I'll be seventeen soon."

Andreas grinned. "Oh, that's right. Real girls play with dolls."

There was a shuffling sound behind the door. Saxony Jensie opened up. He looked pale and thinner than usual. He was in a terrible mood.

"What's up, wimp?" Andreas snorted. "Why weren't you at school?"

"Sick."

"Oh, really? Then how come Hanna's grandpa saw you scarfing down ice cream with your parents at the Seafoam Café yesterday?"

Saxony Jensie scowled at me.

"We just wanted to check on you," I said.

Andreas stormed inside and came to an abrupt halt. The place was filled with crates and suitcases. Clothes were scattered between cardboard boxes. Dishes had been stacked on the floor, and there were books lying around.

Andreas milled around the room. "Somehow this doesn't look like packing for vacation in the Elbe Sandstone Mountains."

"My parents aren't here," Saxony Jensie said.

"'My parents aren't here,'" Andreas parroted him. "What the hell's going on? You really are sick, dude."

Saxony Jensie sadly lowered his head. "We're moving soon."

"What?"

He looked at us shyly, out of the corners of his eyes. "Yeah. It sucks."

Andreas lashed out and punched him in the side. "You're moving, and you don't say a word, you just stop coming to school?"

"I have to help pack."

"That's no excuse," Andreas fumed.

"Where are you going?" I asked. "To one of the new housing developments, like Schmarl or Gross Klein?"

"No." Saxony Jensie gulped.

Andreas punched him again. "Or maybe back to Saxon-ville, where you belong? Back to your darling Heike?"

"No."

Saxony Jensie had a huge crush on this girl he'd met in Dresden during our last vacation. He forced us to admire the picture he had of her. She was blond with blue eyes. He wrote her love letters every day in class, then took them to the post office at the train station after school.

"Too bad. So you're off to one of the hot new housing developments by the city harbor, where everyone wants to move," Andreas concluded.

I stepped toward Saxony Jensie. "So, when do you leave?"

"Not yet. This is all just in preparation."

I looked at him in surprise. "Preparation? Your entire apartment is boxed up!"

"'Cause we don't exactly know when it'll happen. That's why everything has to be ready."

Andreas laughed. "What, are the asbestos boards not installed yet or something?"

Saxony Jensie looked at the floor. Something was wrong.

"At least it's happening right at the end of tenth grade. You won't need to get settled at a new school." Andreas inspected the books that had been set aside. "You're not taking *The Seventh Cross*? Or *The Journey to Sundevit*?"

He toppled the stack.

"Dude, watch it," Saxony Jensie chided him.

"What do the stickers on those boxes mean?" I asked.

"Fragile," Saxony Jensie muttered. "Meissner porcelain that my grandma buried in her backyard in 1945. Everything was such a mess back then. The Americans were supposed to come to Saxony, but then it wound up being the Russians. The Yanks got a piece of West Berlin in exchange."

"Sucks for you!" Andreas bounced his soccer ball on the floor and caught it. It echoed in the empty apartment. Saxony Jensie ran to his room with his head hanging.

I looked at Andreas in surprise. "What's his problem?"

The wood creaked under our feet as we followed him. Saxony Jensie was sitting on his bed, bawling.

"Not again," Andreas griped. "You gotta get tested, man. All this crying just isn't normal!"

Andreas went back into the hallway and slammed the ball against the floorboards. "This floor is totally rotted. You should be glad you're getting out. You almost break through in spots."

I sat down next to Saxony Jensie. He blew his nose into his brown-and-white checkered handkerchief. "I don't want to go."

"It's high time you guys got that new apartment!" Andreas knocked on the wall. "Everything's falling apart in here! There's straw poking out of the ceiling! And the electrical wiring! These cables must've been installed before the war. Before the Great War most likely."

Saxony Jensie dug his hands deeper into his pockets and kept sobbing.

I placed a hand on his shoulder. "Come on, Jens, stop crying. Honestly, there are worse things than moving to the city harbor. It isn't even that far."

"He always cries. He doesn't need a reason," Andreas complained out in the hall.

"We'll still go to the movies and the wave pool together," I said, trying to cheer him up.

Andreas dribbled the ball into the room. "And like every other year, we'll still go swimming in the polluted Warnow!"

"Alster." Saxony Jensie sniffed.

Andreas held the ball with both hands. It was suddenly very quiet. Saxony Jensie sat there rigidly and blinked frantically.

"What did you say?"

"Alster, the Alster River," Saxony Jensie screamed. "You deaf or something?"

Andreas looked at him. "You must be crazy."

"We're moving to Hamburg."

The silence was awful. Andreas dropped the ball and sat down next to us on the bed. No one said a word. We all just stared straight ahead, while the ball rolled into the hallway. Then Saxony Jensie pointed at a box in the middle of the room. "That one's mine! My only one! Guess what's inside."

We eyed the box. "That's not hard," Andreas said.

"Guess!"

"Your *Mosaik* comics," I said quietly.

"Exactly. I'm taking them all with me," Saxony Jensie announced defiantly, then started babbling. "Out of all the years, I'm only missing five issues. 'The Secret of the Grotto'—that was the very first issue, from 1976. 'The Black Felucca,' from November 1982. 'The Mistaken Prince,' from September 1978. That's the one where people think Califax is Prince Rudi, and he goes and conquers Vienna. Then there's 'The Bogus Buffoon,' from April 1980, where he has to eat a bunch of dumplings in a contest. And 'Across the Pyrenees,' from December 1980."

"I have 'The Mistaken Prince,'" Andreas said quietly. "And the dumpling one too."

Saxony Jensie rubbed his eyes and looked at his sneakers.

"You can have 'em."

"You're kidding me." I turned to Andreas in surprise. He had never even traded a copy of *Mosaik*, let alone given one away.

237

"For real?" Saxony Jensie exclaimed.

A spring in the mattress was poking me in the butt. "And I have 'Across the Pyrenees.' My grandpa has been hiding a copy of 'The Secret of the Grotto' at the back of his kitchen cupboard because he thinks he'll be able to sell it for foreign currency someday. I'll just steal it from him. He won't even notice."

"Whoa. Then all I'll need is 'The Black Felucca.'" Saxony Jensie sat up straight. He was suddenly in much better spirits.

Andreas jumped up. "Is that all you care about, your stupid *Mosaik* comics? You're leaving for the West, and all you can do is bug us about first editions and shit?"

He hit Saxony Jensie in the head.

Saxony Jensie raised his arms in defense. "How is this my fault? My parents only told me a few days ago!"

Andreas kept hitting. "So? Just stay here! Wuss!"

Saxony Jensie angrily shot his fist into the air. It hit Andreas in the nose, which immediately began to bleed.

"Crap," Andreas said, leaning back.

Saxony Jensie stood up sheepishly and pulled his handkerchief out of his jeans pocket. Andreas held it against his nose.

Then they sat down next to me on the bed again.

"Your parents can't just decide for you like that," Andreas mumbled into the handkerchief.

A bird chirped outside. "So, you really don't know when you're leaving?" I asked.

238

Saxony Jensie slumped. "No. They won't tell us till the day before. I hope it isn't till after our graduation dance. I've been so excited for that."

There were kids playing on the street outside, and we could hear their voices all the way up in the apartment.

"Well, now you can finally drive your stupid BMW up and down stupid Kurfürstendamm, just like you've always dreamed," Andreas grumbled.

The very same day, I took "The Secret of the Grotto" from Grandpa's cupboard and brought Saxony Jensie all four issues of *Mosaik*. Andreas didn't come because he was still too angry and sad that Saxony Jensie would soon be gone.

Within a few days, he was back to normal.

When we went to pick up Saxony Jensie to play soccer two weeks later, he was simply gone, the apartment empty.

The Blums had received official permission to leave at short notice, and Saxony Jensie hadn't had time to say goodbye. The door wasn't locked, so we could walk in and look around. It felt dismal.

There was a note lying on the old floorboards in his room. "I'll send you guys Raider bars and records. Please send me 'The Black Felucca,' then my *Mosaik* collection will be complete."

Andreas crashed around the apartment, freaking out. "This shitdump country! We'll never see him again!"

In the kitchen where several old pots had been left behind, he asked me if I remembered the joke Saxony Jensie had told us.

"What does GDR stand for? God damn remnants."

I couldn't bring myself to laugh.

⌒⌒

Frigid wind sweeps across the water.

The current pulls us back, then pushes us forward. The waves grow, slowly carrying us up and down, the distance between the peaks and valleys increasing.

Heavy clouds in the sky, piled layer upon layer. None are white anymore, all gray and black. They shift threateningly, changing shape.

White wave crests break around us, build anew, then break again.

Wind drones in my ears.

The lifeguards at Tower 3 will definitely have pulled the gale warning ball up. Swimming strictly prohibited.

I can barely see the sky, and I look at the compass, which is also totally pointless since the water keeps turning me around. We'll never stay on course at this rate—we'll be thrown off by kilometers.

We're doing what we can just to stay afloat.

I spiral through the water, hopelessly disoriented. The wind plows waves in one direction, and they erupt where they collide with the oncoming storm surge. White sea foam flies around us, like breakers at the beach.

It's a storm like the one depicted in the *Mosaik* comic stuck inside my wet suit. When the Abrafaxes follow the black felucca onto the high seas, they almost go down with their ship.

The string yanks on my wrist. It's impossible to stick together. The waves drive us apart.

If it weren't for the string, we'd have lost each other a long time ago.

The Abrafaxes were saved when they washed ashore on a pirate island that appeared suddenly in the middle of the sea.

Nothing like that out here.

Andreas bobs inertly in the water—I barely have the strength to swim anymore either. How must he be feeling? His insulation is shot.

If the water were calmer, we could rest on our backs.

I'm so cold. I can barely bend my arms, they're so stiff. My heart is racing, and I'm shivering so badly, I hear my teeth chatter. Cold or fear, I can't tell the difference.

What would Ulrich say right now?

He's standing by the side of the pool, looking down at me, wheeling his arms, egging me on.

Go, go, don't give up. You two can do it!

But we're not in the pool, we're in the middle of the sea. And there's a storm raging!

Ulrich waves off my excuses, refuses to accept failure. He looks at his stopwatch reproachfully.

The pull of the string hurts. I'm sure the skin has broken, that salt water is seeping in. Don't think about it.

I can't swim anymore. I want this all to end.

Peace, quiet. No more fighting.

There's water everywhere. It shoots straight across the surface, robbing your vision like a smoke screen. I can barely breathe, can only see a few inches in front of my face.

I don't want to do this anymore.

How could we be so stupid?

And why did they have to give us such a hard time? We never hurt anyone! And now we're here, sinking, in the middle of the Baltic!

"Bullshit!" I bellow into the storm. "Dumbest idea ever!" Andreas still doesn't move. Can he even hear me?

"It's impossible. There's no way," I scream. "Grandpa's stories were all bullshit!"

No one's ever made it to the West.

Yet here we are, and there's no going back.

The waves close in over us. The sky disappears.

We won't make it.

I'll never see Grandpa again.

Mom.

I can barely breathe, I'm so scared.

I just want to get out of here, doesn't matter where.

This can*not* be happening.

Saxony Jensie. We have to tell him about the helicopter! And I brought along the *Mosaik*, just for him.

My heart races even faster.

I managed to find the *Mosaik* at a used bookstore. It was pure coincidence.

I have to calm down, can't let myself get upset.

Easier said than done.

An old man spread out the comic books before him. There was "The Black Felucca," sandwiched between "The Imposter Archduke," and "The Devil's Playground." Before the seller emerged, I hastily offered the man three marks. He wouldn't have gotten more than twenty pfennigs for it, selling to the bookstore. It was the final issue for Saxony Jensie's collection. I took it and ran home.

I need to make it. Then he'll have every last tale of the Abrafaxes, from 1976 up to today, over 150 comics total.

The pull on the string gets stronger, and I lift my head.

The sea is dark and raging, water everywhere.

Andreas is beside me. He's not swimming, his eyes trained on the water.

His hand moves through the waves, as though trying to grab something.

What's going on?

He's holding the knife, and he pulls it through the water, again and again.

It takes me a minute to register.

I grab his shoulder and shake him.

"Are you insane?" I scream into the gale.

Pale face, blank gaze. He seems distant, far off, opens his mouth, tries to speak.

Fragments of what he's saying reach me through the bluster. ". . . need to swim alone . . . can't anymore . . . you'll make it . . . I won't . . ."

I shake my head.

"... remember the albatross ..."

He's trying to cut the string.

Never.

"Give me the knife!"

He turns away. I move toward him.

"The knife! Right now!"

Andreas's shoulder touches my arm. He scowls at me through the plexiglass. His pupils are extremely dilated.

He unzips the bag, and the knife disappears into it.

"Give me the bag. I'll take it!"

He hands it over.

I tie it to my stomach but can barely tighten the knot. I can't move my fingers.

The current tears at my legs. The compass needle is all over the place.

I go to put the snorkel in my mouth and feel around my neck for the mouthpiece.

It's gone.

Lost in the storm.

I tucked the tube under my goggle strap, but apparently that didn't help.

I look around, look out over the water.

I can't remember if the snorkel was heavy and would sink or if it would float.

I don't see it. If it is floating somewhere on the surface, it'll remain hidden among the waves.

Swimming without a snorkel. Need to be careful not

to swallow any water, need to breathe very carefully, not freak out.

I kick my legs, but the string holds me back. My wrist hurts badly. Andreas has to keep going, though, or he might come up with more crazy ideas.

Cutting the string? So stupid.

How could he even dream of something like that.

Does he think he'd be able to swim faster then?

We have to stick together.

We should consider ourselves lucky to have each other out here in the void.

I grab his upper arm and haul him through the waves so he can tell I'm there. He goes along with it and tries to help, kicks his legs, keeps going.

Good, that's good. We have to keep going.

For a second the roiling cloud cover breaks, and I can see the sun.

I lift my arm out of the water to point at the light. Something tears in my upper arm, the muscles hurt, and I drop it quickly.

But now I know which way is south.

The sun blazes through the gray of the storm clouds like a beacon. It appears someone means well for us after all.

"We have to go west," I yell into the wind whistling over the water and whipping it into the air. Although the storm around us rages on, I have the feeling it's letting up a little.

Andreas is really close beside me.

He smiles, his face masklike. His wide eyes don't see me. It's as if his gaze got caught inside his goggles. Suddenly he doubles over in the water.

"What's wrong?" I cry. "Are you in pain?"

He doesn't respond, floats at the surface, curled in a ball, dips his chin in the water and turns a little, in order to breathe.

"How're you doing?"

"Okay," he says. "A little cold."

"Does anything hurt?"

He shakes his head.

"How about your wet suit?"

"It's staying shut."

Crazy, I never would have thought that.

"Can you swim?"

"Yeah, 'course."

"Then let's go!"

I spur him on, although I have barely any strength left myself.

What was it Ulrich always said? Let yourself fall, glide through the water, don't fight it. It will always win. Respond to it. You won't stand a chance otherwise.

We cannot take on the full force of the water.

"We should dive through the waves," I call out.

"Crazy, we shook the helicopter," Andreas says. He's not listening to me.

"We have to dive whenever a wave comes!"

"Saxony Jensie will love that." He's slurring, as though drunk. "Like James Bond! In the middle of the Baltic! You'll have to tell him."

"Sure! But right now we have to keep going!"

Andreas kicks his legs harder, follows me.

Swim, just swim.

And dive when the waves come.

Steady rhythm, swim, breathe, dive.

Ulrich by the side of the pool.

An iron will is important to have.

The body is quick to signal that it's reached its physical limit, but it's never true, not by a long shot. Any good athlete can tell you that. These signals come and go, with a lot of performance left to give.

You just have to want it.

It's only over when you stop wanting it.

I'm so weak.

But it feels like things will be over soon.

Ulrich shakes his head. Not yet. You'll make it a few more meters. Just keep swimming, like always. You've practiced so much, you're not giving up now.

I can't move anymore.

He flies into a rage, strides alongside the pool as I go. Don't wilt on me, he screams. Keep swimming!

I shouldn't have lied to him. He was always so nice to me. Maybe not during practice, but he had to be a hard-ass there; otherwise we'd never become good athletes.

He recently asked me when it was happening, my last

big swim, straight across the Baltic. Told him it was TBD. I was scared he'd rat on us. Silly of me. He'd never do that.

But better safe.

There's no more tug on my hand, which is good. Andreas is right next to me and has found his pace again.

Now we can continue and finally make it there.

I look up and see his arm lift out of the water.

He's swimming the crawl stroke.

Amazing he pulled himself together so quickly—he was not looking good just now. Pale and hypothermic. We have to get there soon so he can warm up.

I blink. There's his arm again.

You see, Ulrich says, you've just gone several strokes without thinking about the fact that you're swimming. That's how it works. Distract and occupy your mind so you focus less on the body. Otherwise you'll immediately sense pain or weakness again.

He's right. Suddenly there's a yank on my hand, even though Andreas is right there.

Don't think about it, Ulrich says.

The tugging lets up in a second.

I swim and sense that the waves are getting smaller. I no longer need to dive through them all—their resistance is easing.

I can breathe better too. The air is no longer filled with water.

Andreas's arm.

It's gone.

I blink.

Or maybe not? I see it right there.

No, his arm is gone.

It doesn't reappear.

I just imagined that.

Andreas must be next to me. Is he diving?

The string isn't taut.

I wait, but nothing happens. Andreas is nowhere to be seen.

Maybe behind me.

Nope.

I lift my hand, grab the string, pull on it.

It gives easily, as though he were swimming toward me.

A loose end.

What the hell?

I stare at it. Then I stare at the spot in the water I pulled the string from and can't look away. A wave splashes me in the face, and I can't breathe.

What happened?

Where is he?

I gaze at the string. Did it maybe come undone without him noticing?

I tied it to his wrist at the very start.

Did I not do it right, not pull it tight enough?

I kick my flippers to lift out of the water, and I look around, then sink back into the waves.

I kick up again.

There! Something black.

Wave trough, my view blocked. By the next wave crest, the black speck is gone.

Where is Andreas?

I don't see him anywhere.

In front of me, behind me, beside me—nothing.

Just a gray expanse.

And above, the stormy black sky. The sea churns in the rain that falls on my face.

Water, water everywhere. I occasionally spot something between the wave crests and swim toward it, but I can't keep my eye on it, and by the next wave, it vanishes.

Andreas is nowhere to be seen.

I didn't tie the string tight enough.

"Andreas."

It's my fault.

"Andreas."

No response.

"Andreas," I howl over the water.

I kick to lift myself out of the water again and try to scan the waves. I hold on for a second, then fall back.

No strength left.

He's not there.

I have no strength left to search.

This is the end.

He can't just take off like that! He can't leave me alone!

My heart races, and I'm sweating, even though I'm so cold.

I'm scared.

I've never been so scared.

He can't leave me alone. I need him.

A wave slaps me in the face, and I swallow water and start coughing.

He can't just disappear like that, can't just be gone.

I'll never make it without him.

I have to search for him, have to swim in every direction, from a central starting point.

But how am I supposed to establish that point in the middle of the sea?

I can't. I'm the only thing out here. I'm the only point in space, without anything else to serve as reference. I'm floating through chaos.

The waves lift me up and back down, and I spin around and peer across the water, swim a little in one direction, then another.

Is it actually another direction? Or is it the same?

Doesn't matter.

I have to find him, and he has to be here somewhere.

There's nothing left to see, though, but endless gray.

My right quad cramps, and I double over.

Cold water shoots into my throat, streams down my esophagus, and lands in my stomach, which immediately reacts.

I vomit.

Not much comes out.

I can't do this anymore.

I flip onto my back and pull in my leg to ease the

cramp. Once the pain subsides, I extend my arms to the side and float on my back.

I gaze up at the sky.

I see the sun emerge from behind a puffy white cloud. It blinds me.

Water seeps into my ears.

I close my eyes.

This is the end.

Water roars in my ears.

Or is it my blood?

The sound calms me.

I inhale deeply and exhale, in and out.

Float up and down on the waves, up and down.

They're carrying me.

Up and down.

I don't want to be here anymore.

Up and down.

I want to just let myself fall, down into the depths.

Where it's peaceful and quiet.

Where I no longer need to fight.

I hear music.

Where's it coming from?

Loud and clear. It's music.

From a boat maybe?

It's a song by Nena.

It played at our graduation dance.

Lighthouse has disappeared from sight.

I open my eyes.

There's no boat.

Mirage.

Wherever you go, I'll go too.

I hear them.

Even to the ends of the earth.

People laughing.

I close my eyes again.

The music keeps playing.

Sunny beach or ocean blue.

Pretty nice actually.

Saxony Jensie got hammered that night.

I want to be alone with you.

Up and down, up and down.

Saxony Jensie's suit was way too small.

"How come you always look so stupid?" Andreas ribbed him. "Your clothes never fit right!"

We were slurping orange-juice-and-blue-curaçao cocktails.

"We've stopped getting packages, since we'll be over there soon. No point."

Mom sat at a table with Saxony Jensie's parents. She kept looking over and waving. Grandpa was drinking schnapps and kept falling asleep in his chair. Whenever he started to snore, Mom would jab him in the side with her elbow.

"It's a miracle they even let me come to graduation," Saxony Jensie said bitterly.

I sucked on my straw. My head felt funny. "Why wouldn't they? You did manage to pass tenth grade, amazingly enough."

"And I barely ever studied," he said.

"Guys, guess what! My mom gave me a bike for graduating tenth grade. It's a silver Diamant. It's truly awesome."

Grandpa yelled something and looked over at me.

"What'd your grandpa give you?" Andreas asked.

"Ugh, so embarrassing. He gave me the book *Man and Woman, Intimately*."

Saxony Jensie and Andreas both gaped at me and said, "Really?"

Of course they would be into that.

"He and Mom argued about it yesterday, because he just plonked the book on the coffee table and said it was time I start reading up on what it takes to be a socialist woman. Mom was super pissed and took the book. His other gift wasn't much better."

"What was it?"

"Jesus sandals. 'Cause I'm taking the *Abitur*. He said that everyone who takes the *Abi* and goes to university in the GDR wears them and that they're famous for that, even abroad."

"Horseshit," Andreas scoffed. "Not like we'll ever make it abroad anyway."

Saxony Jensie looked at the floor.

"Except for the Saxon here. He'll be there soon. Why not give him your Jesus sandals? He can show them off in the West."

"I don't want 'em," Saxony Jensie murmured.

Frau Kröger suddenly appeared beside us. Andreas stood bolt upright and smoothed down his dark-blue suit.

"Very sharp," she said approvingly.

He stared shyly at the floor and shuffled his feet in place.

Saxony Jensie came to the rescue. "You look amazing too!" Frau Kröger wore a burgundy dress. Her black hair looked fuller than usual and had a bit of a wave. She also smelled of Western perfume. No wonder the boys were freaking.

"Would you all join me for a glass of bubbly?"

"Of course," Saxony Jensie crowed eagerly, and she headed for the bar. She came back a minute later with four brimming glasses and handed each of us one.

"Lots of changes coming for you three." She raised her glass.

"Data processing technician," Andreas grumbled.

"School," I said.

"Hamburg."

"Here's to you," she said quietly.

We clinked glasses.

Suddenly Saxony Jensie sniffled loudly, and Frau Kröger looked at him in surprise. "What's wrong?"

He was about to start crying again. "They don't want me to go. I don't even know if I want to go either."

"Of course you do," Andreas murmured in a deep voice. "Cruising down Kurfürstendamm in your BMW."

"But that street's in Berlin, not in Hamburg," Frau Kröger pointed out.

Saxony Jensie nodded. "Yeah, that's just an example."

"Metaphor," she corrected him.

He stared at Frau Kröger awkwardly. Then he giggled stupidly. "Do you realize you're the best teacher in the world?"

She smiled and looked at him attentively.

"Like all the Homer and *Odyssey* stuff, that was so awesome. I really didn't get it at first, but then it kept getting better. I'm going to buy that book and read it."

I laughed out loud. "Don't kid yourself! There's no way you'd ever buy yourself a book!"

"Yuh-huh. In Hamburg. And then I'll think of Frau Kröger and her great clothes that she always looks so good in."

Frau Kröger took his glass of sparkling wine. "That's enough of that. And do yourself a favor and buy the book in Rostock. It'll be much cheaper here."

Frau Kröger's husband came over. He had a mustache and looked like Magnum.

He pulled her happily to the dance floor, and they danced to "You're My Heart, You're My Soul."

"Excellent!"

256

Andreas smacked him in the head. "Excellent? I have an important piece of advice for you, Saxon. When you get over there, whatever you do, don't tell people your favorite band is Modern Talking. Tell them you're a Russian spy or something so at least they'll take you seriously."

I nodded. "You'd better not tell your GDR jokes anymore either. No one will get them."

Frau Kröger spun on the dance floor and beckoned us over. Her husband hopped around her in white shoes that were clearly from the West.

Saxony Jensie was immediately distracted. "I want to marry her!"

Andreas shook his blond curls. "She's already married, in case you hadn't noticed. Besides, she thinks I'm hotter."

"Nuh-uh!"

"Take a look at yourself. Your suit's way too tight, and you still have zits!"

"So what? Heike says you can't even see them 'cause of my freckles."

"What's happening with her now?" I asked.

"She can come visit me in Hamburg," he said, suddenly aloof. "That is, if she makes it across the border."

"You suck," I yelled. "Does the same apply to us?"

"I was just kidding," he replied feebly.

Andreas punched him in the side. "Besides, we'll see you on TV."

"Really?" Saxony Jensie asked in surprise.

"Yeah, on the news after you wrap your BMW around

a tree on Kurfürstendamm, 'cause you were too stupid to drive it!"

I snorted and sprayed my drink everywhere.

"Albatross," by Karat, was playing. It was Andreas's favorite song. He looked really sad all of a sudden.

Saxony Jensie started babbling. "Well, I'll send you care packages of Mars bars and Nutella. Then you'll go to the post office at the train station, pick them up, and it'll be awesome."

"Great," Andreas grunted.

"Don't bother sending Nutella," I said. "The Stasi will just steal it. Aunt Brigitte always includes it on her lists, but it's never in the box."

Saxony Jensie wasn't listening. He was fixing the swoop of his preppy hairdo, which he had put a lot of time into styling.

"And get a normal haircut before you leave. Yours is seriously embarrassing."

"You guys need to send me something every month too," he said distractedly.

"What do you want? Green cabbage?"

"No!"

"Red cabbage?"

"No!"

Saxony Jensie looked at us dejectedly. "You're just gonna laugh."

"Candy drops, A&O bars, Schlager chocolate bars."

"Stop! No, it's something more meaningful."

"Meaningful? What, the *Manifesto*? Are you mental?"

"Or maybe records?" Andreas guessed. "Puhdys or Berluc? Ute Freudenberg and the Gruppe Elefant?"

"No way!" Saxony Jensie cried out in alarm.

"Stern Meissen!"

"No, no, no! I mean *Mosaik*. I'm sure they don't have it in the West. And I don't want to miss a single issue."

We stared at him.

"And feel free to send along some Block chocolate bars with the *Mosaik*. Only milk chocolate, though. The bittersweet stuff makes me nauseous."

"You gotta be kidding me." The words escaped my mouth.

Andreas was beside himself. "They have *Donald Duck*, *Asterix*, *Superman*, Milka bars, Tic Tacs, Sarotti chocolate, and all this other stuff over there, and you want us to send you Block chocolate and *Mosaik* comics?"

"It's what I'm used to! The other stuff is great too, but it's just not the same."

We looked at the packed dance floor. Ronny was flailing to "It's a Sin," by Pet Shop Boys. He waved his arms around like a fool and grabbed Sabine's butt. She cackled stupidly.

Saxony Jensie suddenly covered his mouth and bolted for the door.

"What a champ," Andreas said.

I eyed the gold hoop earring he'd recently gotten. It made him look like a pirate.

We ambled through the room toward the exit. Saxony Jensie stood right beside the door, staring into the bushes.

"Man, do I feel sick," he groaned and leaned forward.

"We could easily mix up some bottles of OJ and blue curaçao and send you those," Andreas suggested cruelly.

Saxony Jensie raised his hand. "Stop it."

Frau Kröger appeared behind us. "There you are. I wanted to say bye." She studied Saxony Jensie curiously. "That is, to the extent possible."

He was pale and gave her a tortured smile.

"He had at least ten cocktails," Andreas explained.

"Because I'm so nervous," Saxony Jensie managed to say.

"Why is that?"

"Because we're migrating," he groaned.

"Emigrating," Frau Kröger said. "You're leaving this country."

"Whatever," Saxony Jensie muttered and puked into the bush.

I giggled.

"Dude, get excited!" Andreas yelled. "At least you don't have to waste away here, like us!"

Frau Kröger made a threatening hand gesture. Andreas shut up immediately. She was the one teacher he listened to.

Saxony Jensie looked up at her as he wiped his mouth with his checkered handkerchief. "Do you think we'll ever see each other again?"

She smiled sadly. "I don't know, Jens."

When she noticed her husband heading over, she extended her hand to each of us. "Good luck with the *Abitur*, Hanna. I'm sure we'll see each other around Rostock. Us too!"

She winked at Andreas. He smiled happily.

"And I'll send you a postcard from the Reeperbahn in Hamburg!" Saxony Jensie promised. "Have you heard this one? 'Soviet achievements in scientific research will benefit all of mankind,' a Russian guest lecturer at Humboldt University proclaims. 'Our Sputniks were just the beginning. The day will soon come when you can go to Schönefeld Airport in Berlin and buy a ticket to the moon or Venus!' A student raises his hand. 'That's fantastic,' he says. 'Super! Congratulations! But tell me, my good man, can we catch a connecting flight from the moon to Hamburg or Cologne?'"

Frau Kröger's husband had a booming laugh. She squeezed his arm in warning. They took the steps down to the street.

"They'll never let you on the Reeperbahn with that hairdo," Andreas said. "Forget about it!"

"I get it, I get it. The first thing I'll do when I get there is go to the hairdresser's."

"Go in Rostock! It's cheaper!"

Down on the street, Frau Kröger turned around one last time. Saxony Jensie waved, lost his balance, and crashed butt first onto the ground.

We gazed after her for a long time. When she

disappeared from sight, I raised my hand solemnly. "Let's pledge right now to see one another again soon."

"What the hell for?" Andreas asked, taken aback.

I stuck out my hand. "Pioneer's honor!"

Saxony Jensie struggled up from the pavement and furrowed his pimply brow. "How come Pioneer's honor? We're in the FDJ now."

"We're making a promise."

He stared at my hand, scratched his head, and shook on it. "Pioneer's honor!"

We looked at Andreas expectantly. He was totally bewildered. "And how exactly are we going to get there?"

"Pioneer's honor first," Saxony Jensie said. "Then we'll figure out the rest."

"Saxony Jensie will come get us someday in his BMW," I said quietly.

"Yeah!" he shouted. "Black, lowered suspension, hundred seventy horsepower."

Finally, Andreas shook on it. "All right, fine! Pioneer's honor."

Dark blue skies.

Above me, in the depths of the universe, is a star. I don't know which one.

But it's right there; I can see it clearly. There's nothing in the way, not a single wisp of cloud.

There's still that rushing sound, still that music playing.

I float on my back, up and down, up and down.

I look right, and the sun blinds me.

No more rain. The water is calm.

The gale warning ball in Warnemünde has been lowered again; no more swim ban.

The sandy beach is still hard and damp from the storm. Curious kids run around, their feet tracing the patterns the powerful wind has carved in the sand.

I right myself and gaze across the water.

Barely any waves. The storm has passed.

Andreas is nearby—he's got to be swimming around here somewhere.

But I can't see him.

I hold up the end of the string. It looks cut clean through.

The bag's strapped to my stomach. My hands tremble from the cold and exhaustion as I open it. Chocolate, the canister of pills, adhesive tape.

No knife.

He put it back in the bag, though; I saw it myself.

Did I just imagine it?

Maybe it fell out of his hand.

Or maybe not?

He wouldn't have pretended to put the knife back and then taken the string and—no, there's no way.

He would never do that. Not Andreas.

Andreas doesn't give up.

Ever.

But maybe he just couldn't take it anymore?

A punch in the face.

Don't you dare even think that!

My breath is shallow and rapid. My heart races. Amazed it even has the energy to do that. I try to breathe steadily and stay calm. I focus on the horizon.

He's gone.

I open my mouth, but no sound comes out. I punch the water.

I need something to hold on to, need resistance.

But it's nothingness I grab.

There's nothing out here, no people, no boats, no foothold, no nothing, nowhere.

I'm going insane.

I grab my left forearm and claw myself, clenching my fingers as hard as I can.

Crazy.

I can tell it hurts, but I don't let go.

What have I done?

I throw myself onto my back and sob with open eyes, till I don't even have the strength left for that.

After a while, I lift my hand and study the end of the string again. I gaze at it till my eyes tear up and everything goes blurry.

Maybe the string broke.

Yeah.

The string broke.

That's how we lost each other. He didn't cut it. He would never do that.

I knew it.

The string broke.

These things happen. Defective material. Like his wet suit.

So where is he now?

He must be looking for me, must have called out for me, like I did for him.

We couldn't hear each other in the storm. It was all way too loud.

What'll he do now? He must realize that we'll never find each other out here.

So he'll swim west.

He knows which way is west. He can see the sun too and will follow it.

So I have to swim west.

He probably got a bit of a head start, didn't dawdle like me.

He was doing just fine.

I asked, didn't I? I asked if he could still swim. "Yeah, 'course," he said. Then he said we had to tell Saxony Jensie about the helicopter.

"You. You'll have to tell him," he said.

Why not "we'll"?

I must have misheard.

A story that crazy, of course we'll tell it together.

Saxony Jensie will be stunned.

No way his train ride was as exciting as our trip.

I'm so tired.

But I have to follow Andreas. He'll be waiting for me.

I swim one stroke, then another.

Left, right.

I stop again. Can't do it. No strength.

Ulrich crouches by the pool.

Glucose, he says. Glucose helps against weak spells.

The chocolate.

I lie on my back and open the bag.

The last bit of chocolate. I peel the wrapper and bite into it. It doesn't taste like anything.

Then I take a painkiller. Maybe it'll help.

I chew the pill because I won't be able to get it down with seawater.

It's a good thing we swam together for so long. Andreas knows what to watch out for now. His technique has really improved in the many hours since last night; I'm sure he'll go pro one day. This is the longest workout of his life. Mine too.

Grandpa will be amazed. He knows lots of stories, but not this one, not yet.

It'll be hard to believe, ourselves, that we pulled it off.

And now it's time to keep swimming.

I'm not there yet.

Does Grandpa have any idea what he unleashed with that stunt of his? I doubt it.

266

"Strange, isn't it?"

Grandpa cracked his cane against the pavement on Hermann Strasse.

"Hungary, 1956. Berlin, 1953. Prague, 1968. Chernobyl. All that was just fine. But now they do something reasonable for a change, and suddenly, the big brother isn't the little brother's role model anymore."

Andreas and I were eating Block chocolate and didn't respond. The government had banned the Soviet magazine *Sputnik*, and Grandpa was all bent out of shape. Our entire walk had been like this. It was cold out and smelled of snow.

"Haven't our illustrious heads of state ever heard of the T-34?"

"Come on, Grandpa, it's not like the Russians are going to roll up in tanks just because the government banned *Sputnik*. Calm down!"

"Bah!" He thumped his cane again. "Somebody oughta do something. Somebody oughta let the world know about this lunacy."

"The world doesn't care. Besides, everyone already knows how stupid it is."

"Sure, normal citizens maybe, but not the big wigs. I'm going to do something. We're going to my house and drafting a resolution."

"Don't be ridiculous, Grandpa. All that'll do is cause trouble."

"We're not standing idly by this time. Come with me."

He charged ahead. Andreas and I followed reluctantly.

"At least you know he'll have some pound cake for us," I said encouragingly.

But the cake tasted really old. We sat on the sofa and chewed mechanically. The place was littered with torn newspapers. And the final issues of *Sputnik*. It was unbearably hot in the apartment. Grandpa was burning through all of his coal because he was convinced the GDR wouldn't last much longer anyway.

"Here, for instance!" Grandpa held up a copy of *Neue Deutschland*. "Honecker granted the Order of Karl Marx to that palace-building crook. Marx would turn over in his grave, if he knew!"

We stared at the photo of Nicolae Ceaușescu.

"All right, different topic. Let's take a look at the official statement regarding *Sputnik*."

He dug through his newspapers. There were cake crumbs stuck to some. Grandpa lit up a Juwel. "Do you two know why the October issue wasn't delivered? It simply never arrived, even though people had paid for it. And why didn't it come? Well?"

We shrugged.

"Because they published a piece about the Hitler-Stalin pact. As if it were a state secret no one knew about. But they can't pull the wool over my eyes! I was there!"

"Grandpa, you weren't there when Hitler and Stalin made the neutrality pact."

"No, I imagine I was busy invading Poland at that moment."

Andreas looked at him in astonishment.

"I always hate buying this thing, but what're you going to do. I need it to uncover their lies."

Grandpa rustled the pages of the detested newspaper.

"So, here it is, in the November 21, 1988, issue of *Neue Deutschland*. 'Statement from the Ministry of Postal Services and Telecommunications. Berlin (ADN). The press office at the Ministry of Postal Services and Telecommunications has announced that the periodical publication *Sputnik* has been removed from circulation. It fails to deliver reporting in the service of strengthening German-Soviet friendship, instead publishing distorted historical accounts.'" He leaned back. "They're honestly pulling the German-Soviet friendship card on us!"

He picked up a pen. "Statement from a student at Ernst Thälmann Extended Secondary School and a data technician in training."

"Grandpa, are you nuts? We're not making any statement."

"Yes, we are. Let me think."

He opened his bottle of schnapps. Andreas leaned back and furrowed his brow. His acne had cleared and been replaced by a little stubble, which groomed meticulously.

"In uncertain times, we must not turn a blind eye to our Soviet comrades in arms reassessing their revolutionary history. To learn from the Soviet Union means learning how to win. Those who believe *Sputnik* should remain available to citizens of the GDR, please sign here."

"I gotta get to swim practice." I jumped up from the couch.

Andreas got up with me. "And I have to study."

"Learning for life, are we?" Grandpa took a swig of schnapps.

"Nah, binary code."

We hightailed it out of there.

The next day, Principal Kaselow called for me over the PA system. I had no idea what for.

"Hanna Klein! Upstairs! Now!"

I stood and looked at the board, bewildered. Our history teacher, Frau Steinbeck, had been lecturing about proletarian internationalism. She gazed at me over the tops of her white-rimmed glasses. "I'm sure there's a reason! Get up there."

I knocked on Principal Kaselow's office door and went in. Party Secretary Peters and my homeroom teacher, Herr Kruse, were there too.

They didn't keep me waiting. "Explain yourself!"

Frau Peters held up a piece of paper. I recognized Grandpa's handwriting. This couldn't be happening.

"When did you hang this thing up?"

"I didn't."

"At the very least, stand by your subversive agitation! It says your name right there. Who else could it have been?"

They'll lock him up and throw away the key if they find out, I thought, and studied the linoleum.

"Let's try this again. How long has this thing been on the wall?"

"Not long."

"Be more specific."

"A few minutes."

"When did you hang it up?"

"Before history."

"There will be serious consequences for this. You're lucky we noticed it in time. No one signed it yet. Otherwise you'd be facing immediate expulsion."

I didn't say anything. There was nothing to say.

"For the time being, you are barred from school premises. You will be informed of our decision following deliberation."

I went back to class and shoved my books into my bag. Frau Steinbeck didn't ask any questions as I left the room.

I ran up Friedrich Engels Strasse and turned onto Paul Strasse. Grandpa finally came to the door after the third knock. His hair stuck out in different directions, and there were cake crumbs in the corners of his mouth.

"What the hell is wrong with you? How could you do that?"

"What?"

"That damn resolution! I thought it was a joke!"

He lowered into his chair with a groan. "Did a lot of people sign? Did it give the party secretary a good scare?"

He looked at me expectantly. He truly didn't get it.

271

I sat down on the couch and put my hands in my lap. "They're probably going to kick me out of school."

Grandpa lit up a Juwel and tossed the match into the ash bucket by the stove. "That's ridiculous. Your grades are too good. I'm not so sure about that Andreas, though. He doesn't seem quite as bright. There's a chance he'll get in some trouble."

I gaped at him. Grandpa exhaled smoke. "I'm sure some workers will sign, though, which will give him a leg up at work."

"Tell me you're joking!"

Grandpa dragged on his cigarette and looked through me. He was completely out of it. I leaped up and ran out of the apartment. I sprinted as fast as I could toward the train station.

When I got to the tunnel, I saw Andreas approaching. Even at a distance, I could tell it was too late.

"Stay the hell away from me," he screamed.

I hung back a few meters as I ran after him.

"Get lost!"

His voice reverberated loudly in the tunnel. A few shipyard workers turned around.

"It isn't my fault. He hung the resolution up at school too. I've been suspended!"

"Suspended must be nice!" Andreas stopped and glared at me. "They kicked me straight to the curb. No more apprenticeship now, no more computer science major later. That's it."

He sprinted up the stairs, and I followed. By the time he reached the Intershop, he was out of breath. He stopped, furious, and mimicked the tone the official had taken. "'We will provide you with an occupation that allows for reflection and self-examination.'"

A man in a brown leather jacket emerged from the Intershop. He had the arrogant look of West Germans who just came to the GDR to throw their weight around.

"'If it's so important to you to be an individual, then you will also be granted individual treatment!'" Andreas screamed. "And you wanna know what this reminds me of? All that reformatory bullshit!"

"It isn't my fault! My grandpa's cracked!"

The West German guy tore open a pack of Marlboros.

"My dad's gonna kill me. He'll kick me out. I'm serious."

"Grandpa just has to tell them the truth. There's no other way."

Andreas's eyes widened. "Are you mental? Who's gonna believe that? Besides, I already told them it wasn't me, that Franz Klein did it."

I looked at him incredulously.

"What, do you think I'm an idiot? D'you think I'm just gonna take it? Why would he do something like this? And you know what? No one believed me! They said it came as no surprise because I'd been on their radar in the past. And that I should be ashamed of myself for throwing a confused old man under the bus like that!"

The West German guy made a sound with his nose that could have been a laugh.

Andreas turned around. "What the hell are you looking at?"

The guy smugly ran a hand through his black hair. The leather jacket creaked.

"Get out of my face!" Andreas snarled.

"Get out yourself." He scraped a match across the package, but it didn't ignite. "That is, if you can!" He grinned.

We scowled at him.

"What would you do for the chance, hm?" the guy asked, looking at us with the cigarette in the corner of his mouth. It was finally lit. "For a ride to Dortmund. In the trunk of my car."

He exhaled smoke.

Andreas's face flushed. I grabbed and pulled him away. "We need to think of something. I'll make Grandpa go to your office and explain everything."

All of a sudden, a coin rolled across the pavement and stopped at our feet. Five West German marks. It started to rain. The guy opened his umbrella and watched us expectantly.

"What the hell?" I yelled at him. "We don't want your dirty money."

But Andreas leaned over and whispered, "I'm gonna show him, just watch!"

He sank down to the wet pavement and threw his hands

above his head. "Oh, thank you, noble sir, thank you!"

He picked up the coin and screwed up his eyes as he studied it from all angles. Then he threw it away. The coin rolled across the ground and clinked as it fell into the storm drain.

The man looked back and forth between the drain and Andreas.

Andreas stood up. His knees were wet. "The sewer rats will be thrilled to receive a gift from one of their own."

The West German guy turned red, and his umbrella began to shake, he was so pissed.

"It's a great story for me to share with our beloved People's Police. The offer of a ride to Dortmund in your trunk!"

I crossed my arms. "You know, sir, assisting in an escape could get you a few years in an East German prison!"

The guy blinked nervously for a few seconds, then turned on his heel and left.

"And to think, Saxony Jensie lives with these jackasses now. No thanks!"

I crouched down and tried to spot the coin in the storm drain. An unsavory smell floated up. "Bummer about all the Raider bars we could've bought. If Saxony Jensie were here, he'd know exactly how many we could afford."

"Pick a hand."

I looked up at Andreas. "Huh?"

His hands were behind his back. "Come on, pick a hand."

"Left. What's going on?"

He opened his left hand. It was empty.

"Okay, fine, the right," I said, annoyed.

There was the coin. Five West German marks.

"Old magic trick. I'm not an idiot."

"Then what's down there?"

Andreas smiled. "I never would have thought our aluminum coins made so much noise."

A week later, I was expelled, barred from taking the *Abitur*. Mom cried every single day.

Andreas moved out because his dad completely lost his shit.

Andreas now lived in a condemned building on Patriotischer Weg.

There is a bird
that sailors have crowned their king of the sky.
He circles the world,
from South Pole to North Pole;
there's nothing too far.
The albatross knows no borders.

This song has been stuck in my head for ages.

Andreas's song.

I'm dizzy; I feel drunk. Maybe the pill was a bad idea.

Just swim. Ulrich's right there by the pool.

One stroke, then another and another.

He isn't mad at me for being so slow. Every time I reach the end of the pool for the flip turn, he squats down and reassures me.

You're doing everything right, he says.

Just don't stop. Simple as that.

I'll stay here with you, even after the other swimmers leave the pool.

Ulrich will be there for me. Like he always was.

They wanted to kick you out of the club, but I intervened. I wanted you to keep training because you're good. No one should give up like that.

Man, if they'd ever found out what I was training for. But you didn't snitch. You understood. I hope I didn't get you into any trouble.

He looks down at me and smiles, shakes his head. No, of course not.

Clouds, then sunshine. It's blinding.

Late afternoon.

Been in the water for almost twenty hours. Or is it eighteen? I can't do math anymore. What day is today?

Doesn't matter, Ulrich says, pointing out the direction from the side of the pool.

I know which way is west, even without his help. Just gotta keep following the sun.

I inhale water when I breathe. The swell is stronger on the right.

Where's your snorkel? Ulrich asks.

Lost in the storm.

And why are you dragging a meter of string behind you in the water? Take it off!

Can't. That string belongs to Andreas. When he gets back, we'll tie ourselves to each other.

Ulrich looks at me skeptically but doesn't say anything.

I can't swallow any more water, or it'll make me puke again.

If I could breathe on the left, it wouldn't be an issue. You tried to teach me, but I wouldn't listen.

Ulrich crouches down. Little tip. When you turn your head and there's a wave coming, just hold your breath.

He's looking out for me, isn't screaming his head off the way he used to.

Try to relax.

Relax.

Let yourself fall. It'll be fine.

I won't sense a thing. Won't be afraid anymore.

Peace and quiet, at last.

Nonsense, Ulrich barks. That's not what I mean! Keep swimming!

As long as he's there beside the pool, I can't let myself fall. He'd be disappointed.

Can't let that happen.

Can't let him down.

Plus, I have to find Andreas. If only I could fly!

I would soar into the sky, and from there, I could spot him.

You're not a bird, you're a fish, Ulrich says. Keep

swimming so you don't get cold. Move your arms. Right arm, left arm, right arm, left arm. If you can't keep up the pace, at least make sure to follow through. Everything else is just a waste of energy. You need to move to keep warm. You hear me!

I'm not even cold anymore. Deep down inside, my body is really warm. I've stopped shivering. I've gotten used to the cold.

But I'm so tired.

I want to fall into a bed that cradles me gently. Want to close my eyes. Someone reads me a bedtime story, maybe Mom. I close my eyes and listen. Warm and dry. I'm wrapped in a blanket. The sheets smell like lemon. Everything around me is clean and soft. I can sleep as long as I want. I pull the blanket over my head and drift off, floating through the clouds. No one will wake me.

Strange.

Something's wrong. My throat is freezing cold.

I can barely breathe. I throw back the blanket and sit up.

Not my bed.

Wetness.

Cold water. It seeps into my mouth, down my throat.

I gag.

Not my room.

The Baltic Sea. Fell asleep.

How could that happen?

Lie on your back, Ulrich tells me. Take a deep breath in, then out.

279

How could I not notice that happening?

It happens, Ulrich explains. The body can continue performing certain actions, even when not fully conscious. This occasionally occurs during long-distance training. Don't stress about it.

Is that what dying is like? Like falling asleep? A gradual drift over to infinity.

You're not drifting anywhere. Calm down. And take off your weight belt already. You haven't needed that for a while now.

He's right. Why am I still schlepping this thing around with me?

But it's his belt.

It will sink to the bottom of the Baltic Sea.

That's okay, Ulrich says and smiles. Now I'll always know where it is.

I undo the buckle with my numb fingers and remove the belt. I feel it slip from my hand.

Lighter. I'm suddenly much lighter.

Inhale and fill your lungs with air, as if they were two balloons. They will hold you up. You can't sink.

I take a deep breath and hold it.

It's true. I float on the surface.

I slowly exhale. Make little swimming movements, he says. They'll keep you up and don't require much strength.

I inhale again. And exhale. It's true, I really can't go under.

And now keep swimming. All you gotta do is move, and you won't sink. Believe me, just swim.

One, two, one, two, inhale, right arm, exhale, left arm, inhale, right arm, exhale, left arm.

I can barely get them out of the water. I'm not doing real strokes anymore, just slowly moving my legs, wiggling through the water.

Every inch counts. Think of it in stages, one foot, then another. Breathe.

Water hits me in the face and obscures my vision.

You closed your eyes. Open them up, or you'll lose your balance.

Inhale, right arm, exhale, left arm, inhale, right arm, exhale, left arm.

Leaving your body, losing your sense of what's a dream and what's reality.

See, they come,—and come flooding, those waters all!

Forget Schiller, Ulrich interjects. He's got no business here. You have to keep going. In, arm, out, arm, in, arm, out, arm.

I feel nothing, can't think.

Thoughts fly quick as birds, like albatrosses.

There's that melody again, stuck in my head.

It's still there, though Andreas isn't.

Majestically he sails,
he wanders the breeze as if he were a god.
He follows their ships

o'er high seas and past cliffs,
the thrill of the flight.
He finds them their way
o'er the sea.

I turn onto my back.

The sky.

Deep blue, white clouds.

If it's easier to swim on your back, do it.

Ulrich again.

Careful you don't choke on water. You gotta swim evenly; otherwise you'll stray off course.

Backstroke kick, one, two, one, two.

I look at the sun, and the drops of water on my goggles intensify the dazzling light.

You gotta try not to let your knees bend too much, so the energy goes into your body and propels you forward.

No backstroke flags hung above me, five meters from the end of the lane, marking the approaching pool wall. The signal to flip turn.

This lane has no end.

Move the legs, keep the body engaged. Intense pain in the muscles. They're hard and cold.

In the pool, I would be afraid of ramming my head into the wall.

Keep it up, Ulrich shouts. One, two, one, two.

My feet hurt so much.

One, two, one, two.

I know, I shriek. How 'bout you try swimming this far, then you'll know what it's like.

He didn't hear me. He really should try it himself, instead of just yelling *one, two* all the time.

Clouds drift apart, flow together, form mountains of water vapor.

How beautiful that looks.

Everything's made of water.

The jellyfish, the clouds—it's all water.

One, two, one, two.

I'm made of water too.

Clouds pile up in the blue sky. When they cover the sun, the color of the water changes.

You're falling asleep again. Turn onto your belly and do the crawl.

But I want to see the sky. It's so pretty up there, much prettier than down here.

You'll have time for that later, but right now you have to crawl.

You have to keep going.

Perform your strokes. Swim properly. Concentrate!

Left arm, inhale, right arm, exhale.

Sitting in his room that day, we had no clue.

Left arm, inhale, right arm, exhale.

Talked about it, as if it were easy.

Left arm, inhale, right arm, exhale.

Laughed it off, as if it were child's play.

Left arm, inhale, right arm, exhale.

283

Who's laughing now?

Left arm, inhale, right arm, exhale.

Andreas was acting really weird at the factory that day, distractedly wolfing down his eggs in mustard sauce and looking straight past me, while the sound of clattering dishes surrounded us. Lately, we'd been meeting up at lunchtime. None of Andreas's coworkers wanted to eat with him, and I didn't want to sit with any of mine either. At least we had each other.

"What's Heinz been up to?"

That's what Andreas called the guy who grabbed my butt whenever I walked by.

"Same as always. I turn away, but it doesn't help."

"Smack him, why don't you."

"They'd kick me out."

Andreas arched his eyebrows. "There are worse things that could happen. You could file a complaint."

I peered around the dining hall. The faces weren't friendly. It seemed unlikely anyone would take our side. I shook my head. "No way. Nothing to report here, real stand-up guy, thanks."

Andreas shrugged irritably. "What do I know."

The mustard sauce tasted like Duosan glue, and the potatoes were mushy. The egg yolks had a bluish tint.

"What sucks is that he follows me home every day.

Sometimes I just take off and lose him, but I don't always feel like sprinting. The other day, he walked right next to me and stared at my face the entire way there. He even came into my building but then stayed downstairs when I went up."

"Idiot. But there might soon be an end to all of this."

"What?" I asked with my mouth full. "What do you mean?"

He looked up from his plate. "Come over to my place later. There's something I have to talk to you about."

"What is it?"

He leaned forward and whispered, "Not here."

We cleared our dirty plates and returned to the factory floor. After work, I went to Andreas's apartment on Patriotischer Weg. His place was cold as always.

"It's already March, but you still freeze your ass off in here," I said by way of greeting.

"The coal stove doesn't work, but at least the water doesn't freeze in the pipes anymore. Besides, I'm armed against the cold." Andreas held up a bottle of vodka.

"Are you insane? Not that hard stuff!"

"Only today, 'cause it's Friday. No more, starting Monday. Promise."

Andreas had started drinking quite a lot in recent weeks. Everything seemed pointless to him. It did to me too, but I didn't like alcohol.

I walked across the creaky floor and plopped down onto the battered sofa, which was older than Grandpa. Andreas had picked all of his furniture from the trash, and

285

some of the stuff was still in pretty good shape. It was actually illegal to live in his building. It had been condemned and cordoned off by inspectors. The stairs to the second floor were busted, two broken all the way through, so you could see the cellar steps from above. In order to get upstairs, you had to hold on to the wooden banister and take a huge step over the hole. The building did, however, still have electricity and cold running water. To bathe, Andreas heated up water on an old cooking stove. The bathroom was half a flight up and communal, shared with the other squatters in the building.

Andreas was just happy to get away from his father. That, and he wasn't looking to get married, which was the only way to be allotted an apartment in Rostock.

Andreas opened the bottle and sat down in a wicker chair. He poured vodka into two egg cups and set them on the small wooden table between us.

I sprawled out on the couch and glanced at the guitar leaning against the wall. After Andreas lost his apprenticeship, he became obsessed with learning to play. A copy of *1984*, by George Orwell, lay on the floor beside it.

Andreas lit the white candle on the table.

"You shouldn't leave that book out in the open, or you'll wind up in jail."

"That's what I wanted to discuss with you."

He nudged the cup in my direction. The couch smelled musty, so I sat back up.

"What, jail?"

Andreas shot the vodka back easily. "It's where I'm headed, sooner or later. That much is clear."

"There's nothing clear about that. You just have to behave."

"Yeah, but I can't do that, and you know it."

"Hm." It was no use. Andreas really was bullheaded.

"And I don't want to just wait around for it to happen again. It was bad enough the first time."

"So what does that mean, you want to join the party now, so they'll leave you alone?"

"Ha!" Andreas snorted. "I'm sure my old man would love that." He leaned forward and lowered his voice. "I have a better idea. I'm gonna make a run for it."

I recoiled. "What?"

He gazed at the floor and fell silent for a few seconds. "Yeah," he finally said, lifting his eyes to meet mine.

"How? When?"

"Through the Baltic."

"Have you lost your mind!?"

"No, I haven't."

"What, in a boat?"

"No, swimming."

"You? But you've never trained. How the hell do you expect to pull that off?"

"Monday's my first day of training. No more booze, no more smokes. I'll go to the Neptune Pool after work, or the wave pool. Once it warms up, I'll swim in the Baltic.

I've already asked my relatives in the West to send a wet suit."

I sank back in the sofa and stared at him. "I don't believe it!"

"Plenty of people have done it."

"Yeah, but lots of them have died. My grandpa told me."

"You and your grandpa. What does he know? I'm surprised you think it's so strange. If I swam as well as you, I'd've grabbed my flippers and headed for Gedser ages ago. You'd make it to the other side, easy."

"You wouldn't even have to swim that far," I murmured. "Only till you reached international waters. There are plenty of ships there that could pick you up. Grandpa told me that too."

Andreas nodded. "He's right, for once." He downed another shot and was now good and buzzed.

I shook my head, over and over. "It's really dangerous!"

"No duh, I'm not an idiot."

"Why do you want to do it?"

"Why? You really don't know? Because I'll never have the career I want. I'll never be allowed to say what I think. I'll always have to lie. And I'll always rub them the wrong way. No one ever explains anything here. Just follow orders, that's it. Any idiot can do that. Herr Kuschwitz, you have to do it this way! Not like that! And no back talk!"

He looked at the floor.

"Why are you like this? Other people figure out how to make it work. Other people aren't constantly getting into trouble!"

"How the hell should I know? But I don't even care! It's just the way I am!"

"So you just don't care," I repeated irritably.

Somewhere, someone opened a window, and we heard music. Karat, "King of the World."

Suddenly Andreas leaned forward and laid his left arm on the table.

"What are you doing?" I asked, confused.

He turned his arm so I could see the inside of his wrist. A long scar. I'd never noticed it before, probably because he always wore a leather cuff. But not today.

I looked up and met his eyes. "Was that you?"

He nodded.

I couldn't believe it.

"At the reformatory. They found me soon after I did it. I went to the hospital and was sent straight back to work a couple days later. It was this huge deal, and I was constantly called in to the director's office. How could I shirk my responsibilities like that, he wanted to know, and a good citizen wouldn't do that, it was a cowardly thing to do, blah blah." His tone became scornful. "Dude can't even kill himself in peace here."

I felt a surge of rage and leaped up. "Of course not! What do you think? What would've happened to us, to Saxony Jensie and me?"

289

He snorted. "You'd figure it out."

"No," I screamed, "I wouldn't! I'm not allowed to study biology now either, or did that slip your mind? My dad's a mental patient, my mother's never around, my grandpa is unhinged, and that old perv at work wants to get into my pants! And now you want to leave me too!"

I burst into tears, although I didn't want to, and fell back onto the sofa. Andreas looked at me in shock. He'd never seen me like that before, but I didn't care. I just kept crying.

He leaned back in his wicker chair. It creaked quietly. "Shit." He reached for his leather cuff on the shelf next to his chair. He slowly wrapped it around his wrist.

"Straightforward logic," he murmured. "Before I go and kill myself, I can at least try to escape."

I pulled out my handkerchief and blew my nose. "Great. So when's this all happening?"

"Late summer, when the water's warm enough."

"It's never warm. It's the Baltic, not Lake Balaton!"

"Sometime in August."

I took a drink from the cup. The stuff was harsh and burned my throat, but after a few seconds, I started to feel warm, and my stomach settled.

"Where do you plan to start from, Warnemünde?"

"I dunno yet—still need to gather information. It's not exactly easy."

"Of course not; otherwise any moron could do it."

Andreas laughed darkly. "Exactly."

"Grandpa knows where the army is stationed along the coast. He pays close attention to stuff like that—it's an old habit from the war. I could ask him about it."

"You would do that?"

"He also keeps a bunch of maps of the coast in his bedroom. They're from 1935, but it's not like much has changed geographically."

Andreas nodded.

I had a lump in my throat. I was desperate for fresh air and alone time. "If you want, I can go see him right now. I'm sure he's home."

Andreas looked out the window. "Okay, why not. Should I come?"

I got up. "No."

"Bring 'im a bottle of Goldbrand." Andreas grinned. "A little firewater will loosen his tongue. And ask general questions. I don't want him getting suspicious and letting something slip or making another poster."

I swallowed with difficulty.

It was Grandpa's fault we were in this mess, there were no two ways about it. If he hadn't pulled that stunt, Andreas would still be apprenticing, and I'd be preparing for the *Abi*.

"Better not mention my name either."

"No, of course not."

I stood there uncertainly. Things felt fuzzy from the vodka. "I hope they don't ID me at the store."

"I'll ask Torsten if he'll go there with you."

Andreas and I vaulted over the hole in the stairs on our way to the ground floor. Andreas knocked.

Torsten opened the door. "I have an exam tomorrow," he said sullenly. Andreas explained what we wanted, then went back upstairs. Torsten grabbed his parka from the hook.

"Thanks," I said on the way to the store.

"No problem," he muttered, lost in thought.

"What're you majoring in?"

"Ag water management."

"Do you like it?"

"What can I say? Didn't make the cut to study medicine."

At the store on Doberaner Strasse, I gave him money and he bought the liquor, like it was no big deal. He must have been used to doing it for Andreas.

"Don't drink it all at once," he said with a wink as he left.

I set out for Grandpa's. I decided to walk all the way to clear my head. Doberaner Platz, Schröderplatz with its enormous digital clock, Augusten Strasse, Paul Strasse.

Grandpa was at home but headed straight back to the TV after letting me in. He was watching *Willi Schwabe's Attic*, one of his favorite shows.

I put the cut brandy on the table, right next to another bottle that was almost empty. He didn't react as I sat next to him on the sofa.

I looked at the TV. Marika Rökk was bounding across the screen.

"This lady here is singing that she doesn't need millions. Well, neither do I. I'd be happy with two pounds of coffee. None of those coffee substitute blends. The other day, I had to wait in line for a package of Rondo, can you believe that? Even though it tastes like goat dung."

"Grandpa, I wanted to ask you something. About the Baltic Sea."

"She doesn't need anything but music, music, music. What a joke! Fantastic propaganda. Preparing the people for tough times ahead. Everyone's dead, the country's been reduced to rubble, but that doesn't matter. I stroll down the burning streets, whistling a pretty tune. I don't need millions. What would I use it for, anyway? There's nothing left now but marching songs and Goebbels screaming."

"Why does this show always put you in such a bad mood?"

"And what do they even mean by music? There hasn't been any decent music since Herbert Roth died. Can you name a better song than 'In the Hills of Oberhofen' or 'The Hiker's Hymn'? Are there any?"

"'People Are People,' by Depeche Mode, for one."

He absentmindedly opened the Goldbrand and filled his empty glass.

I gathered up my courage. "Grandpa, I'm training in the Baltic this summer, and I'll need that old map you keep in your wardrobe. Can I take it home with me?"

He looked at me, his eyes bleary. "What for?"

"I have to figure out my starting points and measure the distances I'm going to swim. Like, from Nienhagen to Stoltera or Kühlungsborn to Heiligendamm. If I use a stopwatch, I can calculate my speed. That's important."

He waved a hand. "Sure, sure, fine. You know where it is."

That was easy. I went to his bedroom, which smelled like hard soap.

"What are you training for?" Grandpa called from the living room.

"A kind of marathon," I yelled back, opening the massive oak wardrobe.

"But why? You were kicked off the team and out of school. Rejected on every front imaginable. You're part of the working class now. Good luck with that!"

"I just like swimming."

"Maybe the frogmen would take you if you joined the party."

"No way. I swim because it's good for me."

"Bah!" Grandpa scoffed.

The map was tucked under a brown wool blanket. It was yellowed and stained. I pulled it out, went into the hallway, and looked through the door, which I had left ajar.

I watched as Grandpa raised his glass. "This right here is good for you! Cheers!"

I stuffed the map into my bag on the hallway floor. Outta sight, outta mind.

I returned to the living room. Heinz Rühmann was now on screen.

"My dear gents, I declare, on this you can swear," Grandpa sang along, then looked at me in surprise. He had clearly forgotten I was visiting.

I poured him more brandy. "Hey, Grandpa, where are the border towers along the Baltic coast again? You told me once, when I was young, but now I forget."

"What? Why do you want to know that?"

"It's a puzzle question in the latest issue of *Troll*, but I didn't bring it along."

"That's the kind of thing they're asking these days? My word! Times are changing, it would appear." He burped. "Incredible."

"Do you remember where the towers are?"

"Well," he said, stretching his back, "I'm sure I could recall a few. From east to west or west to east?"

I frowned at him in confusion, but then it clicked. We didn't want to go to Poland. "From Warnemünde toward Lübeck."

"I see." He rubbed his head. "So. Warnemünde, Stoltera, lots of NVA. Börgerende, east and west Kühlungsborn, lots of NVA there too. Meschendorf, Am Salzhaff, Gollwitz, Poel Island, Boltenhagen. From there things get tricky. You can't come ashore without attracting attention."

I nodded and made a mental note of the spots. Andreas would have to check things out for himself when he was there.

"Now I know what they're up to!" Grandpa exclaimed suddenly. "Whatever you do, don't answer the question in *Troll*—it's a trap! Anyone who can answer it will be deemed counterrevolutionary!"

"Just like you?"

He chuckled stupidly. "I tried to be one, but they didn't take me."

He was slurring by now. It was time to go.

I left the apartment with the map in my bag. It had been dark for a while now, and it was raining. Every third streetlight was busted. *The Name of the Rose* was playing at the Theater of Peace, and a few people stood in line for tickets. I had already seen that movie with Andreas.

My life would be unbearable without him. Unthinkable, that he'd soon be gone.

Suddenly I noticed Frau Kröger. She was walking down the street in front of me. Her head was down, and she was struggling with her umbrella, which whipped around in the wind. We hadn't seen each other since graduation.

Should I go up to her and say hi?

But what would I tell her, that I'd been culled? That I worked at the plant now?

I was so embarrassed. No more school, no more majoring in biology. Instead, it was can openers and ship propellers, day in, day out.

I thought of the book she had subtly advised against all those years ago.

How the Steel Was Tempered.

Now it was me being tempered, like they'd tried with Andreas for years. I could have burst into tears right there on the street, like a little kid. Frau Kröger hadn't been able to help him back then either.

I couldn't tell her I'd failed. Whether it was my fault or not was beside the point. And I was sure she'd be sad to hear that poetry bored me now, since it wasn't like it could do anything to improve my life.

I followed Frau Kröger for a short distance. When she slowed down, I hung back. Suddenly she stopped, shook her umbrella, and looked around. I jumped quickly into a recessed doorway.

I waited a few seconds and watched the rain. The drops pelted the street loudly, and wind buffeted the houses, so I didn't hear her footsteps.

"Hanna?"

Frau Kröger stood right in front of me.

The wind had damaged her umbrella, now crumpled on one side.

I wished the ground would swallow me up. I looked at her but couldn't speak.

"Since when do you hide from me?"

"Hello," I stammered, searching for words. "I didn't see you there."

She eyed me attentively but not as sternly as back in school.

"I had to take shelter, it's raining so hard."

She gestured with her umbrella. "Care to walk a ways

together?" She sighed with a glance at her busted umbrella. "I know it's not much of an offer. Where are you headed?"

"To see a friend on Patriotischer Weg."

"Come on, then, I'll take you there."

I slipped under the umbrella and jammed my hands into my jacket pockets so she knew I wasn't about to link arms with her or anything.

"So, how are things at your new school?"

Water streamed down the broken side of the umbrella, onto my shoulder. "Pretty hard, but otherwise okay."

I saw her smile. "You'll do just fine. You're a hard worker, and smart."

I walked beside her and tried not to bump into her, which wasn't easy, because we were dodging puddles.

"We have to wear red clothes in PE. Did you know that? I had to buy all new stuff."

She laughed. "There are worse things than athletes in red. I hope everything is going well otherwise."

I took a deep breath. What should I say? That Andreas, my best friend, was planning to flee?

I couldn't give him away.

"We have another strict party secretary there too. She can really make life hard for a person."

Frau Kröger stepped on a big cobblestone. It was loose, and water shot out from underneath, straight into her shoes. She cursed loudly.

"Just remember your plan to major in biology," she eventually replied. "Keep your goal in mind, and you'll get through whatever mess crops up." She glanced at me. "I'm hoping your grades are still good enough to secure your spot?"

I started to sweat and nodded mutely. If she only knew.

She confidently strode over a big puddle. "Nice that there are some things you can still count on."

We reached Andreas's building.

"Here we are."

She stopped and surveyed the crumbling exterior wall. "Are people even allowed to live here anymore?"

I shrugged. I didn't know what else to do.

"I hope *you're* not living here."

I shook my head. "No, just a friend of mine."

I didn't want to tell her it was Andreas, or she'd insist on coming upstairs with me.

She studied me, her gaze somewhat skeptical. "Stop by sometime, after you take the *Abi*. Twenty-two Margareten Strasse. I'll be interested to see what comes next for you."

"Sure, I'll do that."

She smiled and shook my hand. "Take care."

"Thanks. See you soon."

Then I dashed into the building and slammed the door behind me.

I burst into tears for the second time that day. I could barely contain myself.

I took a deep breath, in and out.

This is all so pointless, I thought, as I climbed the rotted staircase. If I couldn't even talk to Frau Kröger, who else was there?

I knocked. There was no doorbell.

Andreas opened the door. He appeared startled but let me in.

"Didn't expect to see me again."

"You're right, not this late." He eyed me. "Were you crying?"

I didn't respond but opened my bag and handed him the map. "Hide it carefully. If anyone finds this here, you're screwed."

"I know. Thank you."

I told him where the border towers were, according to Grandpa.

"If you want, I can pump him for more details. He goes bowling every month with comrade Johnson from the Coastal Border Brigade, which would be firsthand information."

"That would be great," Andreas said quietly. "I'm going out to Kühlungsborn on Sunday to check things out."

I suddenly felt desperately sad again and shook my head repeatedly. He'd clearly made up his mind.

"Come with me."

I freaked out. "And then? What then? Run away together, leave everything behind, just like that?"

Andreas lowered his eyes. "I meant to Kühlungsborn. On Sunday." He spoke very quietly. "It'll look less suspicious if we're wandering around there together."

He was probably right.

"Okay," I finally agreed. "Field trip for two."

I stormed out of the apartment without saying goodbye.

"Eight o'clock at the train station," he called after me.

I sobbed all the way home.

How did he expect to pull this off? He wasn't a real athlete, let alone a swimmer. No one could get in shape that quickly, especially not for a stunt like this.

I could rat on him. He would just go to jail, then, instead of drowning.

I froze in the middle of the street, absolutely appalled.

"Never, ever think that again," I said out loud to myself. "Never. You'd do better just to join him."

Left, in, right, out, left, in, right, out.

Left, in, right, out, left, in, right, out.

Left, in, right, out.

Have to

Left, in, right, out.

breathe evenly.

Left, in, right, out.

Warm

Left, in, right, out.

water.

Left, in, right, out.

One lane

Left, in, right, out.

after another.
Left, in, right, out.
Life buoy.
Left, in, right, out.
Big clock.
Left, in, right, out.
Shallow end.
Left, in, right, out.
Deep end.
Left, in.
Flip turn coming up.
Right.
Glide.
Tuck in.
Somersault.
Feet on the wall.
Push off.
Rotate.
Arms forward.
Strong kick.
Out.
Glide toward the surface.
Left, in.
So hard.
Right, out.
Something dark.
Left, in.
Look again.

Right, out.
Something there.
Left, in.
Stripe on the horizon.
Right, out.
Now it's gone.
Left, in.
Look again.
Right, out.
Maybe clouds.
Left, in.
It's land.
Right, out.
Gotta be land.
Left, in.
So many hours.
Right, out.
Going north.
Left, in.
Then west,
Right, out.
where the sun sets.
Left, in.
Don't swim in circles.
Right, out.
Could be land.
Left, in.
Maybe Fehmarn,

Right, out.
the pirate island.
Left, in.
Or Denmark.
Right, out.
Island of Rügen.
Left, in.
Drifted east.
Right, out.
Dots on the water.
Left, in.
Everything glitters.
Right, out.
Maybe boats.
Left, in.
The coast
Right, out.
maybe.
Left, in.
Ice cream stands.
Right, out.
Screeching gulls.
Left, in.
Kids feeding them.
Right, out.
Commotion in the air.
Left, in.
Andreas is there,

Right, out.
eating ice cream,
Left, in.
waiting for me.
Right, out.
What the hell happened?
Left, in.
Why did you disappear like that?
Right, out.
The string broke.
Left, in.
Swam on alone
Right, out.
to shore.
Left, in.
Knew you'd come.
Right, out.
You're the athlete, you know.
Left, in.
Better swimmer than I am.
Right, out.
If either of us made it,
Left, in.
it'd be you.
Right, out.
I'm waiting on the pier
Left, in.
like in Warnemünde.

Right, out.
Sun's in my face.
Left, in.
That's west.
Right, out.
Gonna set soon.
Left, in.
Better hurry.
Right, out.
He waves,
Left, in.
gulls above him.
Right, out.
The comic book is chafing.
Left, in.
Hopefully it's dry.
Right, out.
Legs are so heavy.
Left, in.
Arms too.
Right, out.
Can't move them.
Left, in.
Out.
In.
Out.
In.
Almost there.

Out.
How much
In.
longer?
Out.
I fly to the pier
In.
in my mind.
Out.
The mind is free.
In.
To Andreas.
Out.
It's important to have
In.
a goal,
Out.
says Ulrich.
In.
Out.
In.
Out.
You can do it.
In.
Yes.
Out.
In.
Didn't coach you for nothing.

Out.
No.
In.
Sunlight
Out
on the water
In
Pretty
Out
Warmth
In
Shoulda known
Out
he'd come in first
In
Always wanted to come in first
Out
Was even the first sent to the principal's office
In
So rude
Out
Principal Schneider
In
Andreas the Wiseass
out
you couldn't
in
win against him

out

in

out

in

"Enter!"

"Tee-hee-hee," Andreas whispered in my ear. "I've been here before."

The office reeked of Ata powder cleanser. Principal Schneider sat at his desk, his fat belly spilling over his gray slacks. He was writing something in pencil in a grid-lined notebook and didn't look up. We dropped our schoolbags and stood before his desk.

"Five minutes till recess," Andreas whispered, pointing at his new Ruhla watch. Max and Moritz were pictured on the watch face, and Moritz's eyes moved back and forth in time.

Principal Schneider looked at us. "Why did your math teacher send you to see me?"

Andreas nudged me. He wanted me to answer.

"Because we laughed during the moment of silence," I murmured. "By accident."

Principal Schneider nodded. "And for whom was this moment of silence observed?"

"We honestly didn't mean any harm," Andreas explained hastily.

"That's not the point. Tell me, for whom was this moment of silence observed?"

"For Leonid Ilyich Brezhnev."

"I see. And why were you instructed to observe a moment of silence for Leonid Ilyich Brezhnev?"

"Because he died."

"Precisely!" Principal Schneider stood up and hobbled to the window. "I'm sure you are aware of Leonid Ilyich Brezhnev's many accomplishments."

"Yes."

He cleared his throat. "And of Lenin's?"

"Yes."

Principal Schneider gave a little cough. "And of Honecker's?"

"Yes."

"And do we laugh at these people's deaths?"

"No."

"Honecker's still alive," Andreas whispered in my ear, then snickered.

"What are you whispering about?"

We stared at the floor and didn't move. Principal Schneider sat back down at his desk. The rubber soles of his shoes squeaked on the linoleum.

"Homework planners!"

We opened our bags and handed him the notebooks. Mine had a Smurf sticker on the cover. Principal Schneider studied it, then opened the planner and scribbled with his red pen. He did the same for Andreas.

310

The bell rang for recess. Principal Schneider gave us back our homework planners, and we ran into the hallway, where we bumped into Torsten, Martina, and Manuela. They all had red clown noses on. Andreas dug into the pockets of his jeans and pulled out a clown nose too. With his blond hair, he really looked the part. We all laughed.

"Read it," Andreas yelled.

I opened my planner and immediately spotted the new entry. "'Hanna behaved dishonorably with regard to the passing of Leonid Ilyich Brezhnev by failing to demonstrate the appropriate level of respect during the moment of silence.'"

Manuela giggled. "What about you?"

Andreas's voice sounded totally different with the nose on. "'Andreas behaved dishonorably with regard to the passing of Leonid Ilyich Brezhnev'—it's exactly the same. That's boring."

"Oh no," Martina suddenly said, looking down the hallway. Frau Thiel was approaching.

"What's going on here?" she demanded. She paused after each word. Her blue skirt billowed around her. "Take off those noses!"

I smelled lavender.

"But today's Carnival," Andreas responded exuberantly. "11/11!"

"No!" She took a breath. "Herr Brezhnev died yesterday. That means no Carnival today. You should be ashamed of yourselves! Take off those noses!"

Manuela whispered something to Martina.

"And it certainly means no telling secrets! The entire country is mourning the death of the leader of the Soviet Union and secretary general of the Communist Party. You should all be very ashamed!"

We obediently took off the noses and went outside for recess.

We were both in a bad mood on our way home, especially Andreas. He knew his dad would beat him as soon as he got home from work and read the disciplinary note in Andreas's homework planner.

Then Andreas had an idea.

"Wanna go to the wave pool? I'll run and grab my stuff. I'm gonna get in trouble later anyway, so it doesn't matter."

"Sure, sounds good."

I waited outside his building. He was back in five minutes. We swung by my house. Mom was at work, and Dad was luckily sleeping so deeply that he didn't hear me rummaging around. We ran to the train station with our swim stuff and rode to Warnemünde.

The wave pool wasn't as busy that day as usual. A couple of grannies clung to the side of the pool, chatting. They squawked gleefully whenever a wave splashed up in their faces. They all wore the same red swim cap.

"Everyone else is at home drinking vodka, 'cause of Brezhnev," Andreas commented.

We chased each other around the pool. He tried to

dunk me, and his goggles broke. Mine didn't hold a seal either. Our eyes burned, but we kept swimming back and forth, then warmed up in the wading pool and waited for the next wave cycle. We had never had this much room to swim. There was just one other person swimming, a guy with a hairy back, who moved swiftly through the water. We followed and tried to do the crawl, like him. I was terrible at it, and Andreas almost sank too. The man got pissed, because we were in his way, and shooed us into the nonswimmers' area. Andreas walked his feet along the bottom and moved his upper body, as though he were doing the crawl. I practically died laughing, it looked so stupid.

Back outside later, we almost froze. As always, we passed by the Hotel Neptun restaurant. The Broiler Grill House was packed, guests squeezed in around all the tables. We pressed our noses against the windowpane and watched the people inside. Whenever the door opened, we caught a delicious whiff of rotisserie chicken.

"It'll be a cold liverwurst sandwich for me tonight," Andreas remarked.

We walked back to the train station. In the park behind the casino, we slid down the white stone slide and got really creeped out. We were all alone in the dark.

Suspended in the water. Not sinking. Don't need to fight anymore. It holds me up, just like you said. Warm and bright. The sun, a reddish ball, enormous in front of me. Is it really there? Am I really here?

Keep swimming!

Is there a heaven?

Keep swimming!

A gull, far above.

Steady breathing!

Is it real?

Breathe!

There's another one.

You must swim!

It's looking down at me.

Land is nearby!

It circles above me, calling.

Concentrate! You must keep going!

The wind pitches it back and forth.

Turn onto your stomach!

I don't wanna.

You have to! Andreas is waiting for you!

That's right, on the pier. That's where I have to go. To the pier.

A boat, right there in front of me. Is it real?

It's a boat! Swim to it!

Just a mirage.

No! It's real!

I'll keep swimming till I reach land.

Swim to the boat!

Gotta dive. Can't let them see me.

Stay up!

No. Back to peace and quiet, back to darkness.

Rumbling underwater.

Can't dive deep enough. Return to surface.

A white wall in front of me.

A loud voice.

I touch it.

The wall is real, solid, doesn't give way, doesn't budge.

I hit it. It stays.

Something solid in the water.

The black felucca.

You're crazy.

Something grabs me.

I dive down, can't breathe, come back up.

"Closer! We have to get closer!"

Is someone yelling?

Again something grabs me, clasps my shoulders.

Can't fight back, wish I could disappear, find peace and quiet.

"Up, pull him up!"

Something slams into my back.

I fall onto something hard.

I feel sick. Everything is spinning. Like a merry-go-round.

I try to open my eyes but can't.

Bright flashes underneath my lids.

Several voices.

"He's a complete wreck."

Roaring in my ears.

Take a look.

Where am I?

"It's a she, not a he."

Gotta keep swimming.

Move your arms. Left, in, right, out.

I smack something solid.

"What's she doing? Is she crazy?"

I touch it. Solid.

No gliding. No water. No yielding.

Something solid. Underneath me too.

A floor.

Don't need to swim.

Where am I?

I open my eyes.

Two. Red and blue. Shirts. People.

Both blond. They move their lips, but I can't hear them.

Still that roaring, the wash of the waves.

Up and down, up and down.

A boat. I'm on a boat.

Up and down, up and down.

What country?

Where's the flag?

They lean over me.

". . . you doing . . ."

". . . you from . . ."

". . . are you . . ."

Stare at me.

What do they want.

It hurts to keep my eyes open.

The blue one squats beside me. "Where are you from?"

I turn. Can't give myself away.

Or Andreas.

"Are you from the East?" the blue one asks.

I don't respond.

"Crap," the red one says. "What do we do now?"

"Grab something to drink," the blue one says.

I try to sit up. Need to know where I am.

"Where?"

Up and down, I feel sick.

"Am I?"

The blue one scratches his chin. "Fehmarn."

We did it. I fall back onto the floor.

Fehmarn. Our destination.

We're here. I have to tell him.

I push myself up again. "Is he here?"

"What? Who?"

I try to lift my arm. It doesn't budge, not an inch.

"On the pier?"

He looks out across the sea and shakes his head.

The red one returns.

"She needs something to drink. She's hallucinating. And then we need to go straight back to port." The blue one takes the bottle and holds it to my lips.

I'm so thirsty.

Juice.

I take a careful sip.

Orange.

One sip, then another, then another. The sugar burns my tongue. Then the bottle's empty.

The blue one gets up. "Let's go. Back to port!"

"Those flippers need to come off," the red one says.

"Absolutely not," the blue one counters.

"But her feet look terrible!"

"Exactly. That's why we're leaving it for a doctor."

I turn away and look at the sky.

"She's from over there, isn't she?"

The gull, up above.

"Appears that way."

Is it always the same one? Probably not.

"They land here every so often. She came close to dying—we rescued her in the nick of time. Maybe we'll get a medal."

"We have to call an ambulance. And the police."

"She wouldn't have made it all the way to shore."

"Come on, let's go. We can talk about it later."

They fire up the engine.

I can't hear them anymore. I don't care what they're saying anyway. I want to see Andreas.

There's wind in my face, soft and warm.

I'll be on land soon.

We move across the water in the evening sunlight.

Innumerable stars sparkle on the sea.

On the horizon, I can see a bridge with a soaring arch.

The tips of my fingers hurt, like the times I was out sledding for too long. When I warmed them up on the radiator, it felt like they were being pinched.

That's how my feet feel too. The pain travels into my calves and spreads through my entire body.

I can barely breathe.

Don't flag now. You did it.

Andreas too?

Yes, Andreas too. Don't worry. You can rest soon.

We did it. Andreas will be standing on the pier, waving. Like back in Warnemünde. He'll be wearing his blue-and-white checkered shirt and be amazed at how I wound up on this boat.

He'll be singing his favorite song, his voice loud and joyful.

And should storms batter
with unfettered force
the oceans below him,
infinitely vast,
then propelled with fire, he climbs ever higher
to the freedom of the seas.

He'll probably give me a hard time because I didn't swim all the way to the end. I cheated by taking a boat, just like he did that time during the cross-country race at the ramparts. He hung back at the start and hid in the bushes. When we all came running by again, he popped out of the thicket behind us and hoofed it. He won the grand prize, a Heiko fountain pen.

Andreas can tease me all he wants. I'm just happy we made it. We can relax now, dry off, and eat something, like maybe a bratwurst or some potatoes.

Then we'll have an ice cream down on the beach. The first West German ice cream of our lives.

When we're feeling a bit stronger, we'll go to Hamburg to find Saxony Jensie. He'll lose his mind, he'll be so happy. Maybe he's not even there anymore, though. Maybe he's chilling with his new buddies in Berlin. What a champ.

Andreas and I will know where to find him.

The next time we see Saxony Jensie, it'll be on Kurfürstendamm and he'll still have that stupid preppy haircut. And his BMW will be old and junky, but he won't care. Neither will we. We'll all be insanely happy and so incredibly proud of one another.

Acknowledgments

This book grew over the course of many years, and many wonderful people accompanied me along the way. My most heartfelt thanks to my family and friends—you have enriched, inspired, and supported me. I wish to thank Lisa-Marie Dickreiter for her dramaturgical skills and impressive dedication—it's thanks to you that I found a publisher for the manuscript. And thanks to Bert for always being by my side—you're the coolest little brother in the world.

Glossary

Abitur, or *Abi*: Comprehensive examinations administered the final year of secondary school that serve as both a graduation qualification and a university entrance exam.

The **ADN** (**Allgemeiner Deutscher Nachrichtendienst**, or the General German News Service): The single authorized news and photo agency in the GDR besides Panorama GDR.

Application for permission to travel: In order to receive government approval to travel outside the Eastern Bloc or to relocate permanently outside the GDR—that is, to emigrate—East German citizens were required to submit an official request. Anyone caught leaving the GDR without permission was prosecuted for the crime of fleeing the republic.

The **Comecon** (**Council for Mutual Economic Assistance**, or **CMEA**): An international organization of Soviet states under the leadership of the Soviet Union. It was formed in 1949 as the socialist counterpart to both the Marshall Plan and the Organisation for European Economic Co-operation (OEEC). It was dissolved in 1991.

Delikat: Type of store in the GDR that sold "upscale" groceries—that is, expensive fancy food and drinks, or "delicacies." The products were mostly produced in the GDR, but imported goods could also be bought there.

The **Dieselmotorenwerk Rostock** (**DMR**, or the diesel engine plant): Founded in 1949, the DMR was a publicly owned enterprise (**Volkseigener Betrieb**, or **VEB**) that provided many parts for the East German shipbuilding industry. The government required many VEBs around the country to produce consumer goods in addition to their primary output to offset deficits in supply. Like the brown coal *Kombinat* that built coffee makers or the power plant that made Christmas tree stands, the DMR was responsible for manufacturing can openers.

The **FDGB** (**Freie Deutsche Gewerkschaftsbund**, or the Free German Trade Union Federation): The umbrella organization for the approximately fifteen individual trade unions in the GDR. As an instrument of the government, its primary goal was to promote East German economic policies. In addition, the FDGB was the biggest provider of vacation packages in the GDR and ran several of its own holiday resorts and vacation homes.

The **FDJ** (**Freie Deutsche Jugend**, or **Free German Youth**): The one youth organization officially recognized and sponsored by the East German government. Although participation in the FDJ was technically voluntary, nonmembers faced significant professional disadvantages later on.

Forum check: In the GDR, Forum checks were a form of hard currency administered by a company called Forum Außenhandelsgesellschaft m.b.H. Forum checks could be used at Intershops. One Forum check mark was worth one deutsche mark, the West German currency.

Glasnost (Russian for "openness") and **Perestroika** (Russian for "restructuring"): These designate the movement of Soviet political reform introduced by Mikhail Gorbachev in the mid-1980s. Glasnost is primarily associated with a new-found freedom of speech and the press, as censorship came to an end. Perestroika signifies the restructuring of social, political, and economic systems aimed at improving economic efficiency.

Intershop: The retail store chain sold Western products that could only be purchased with convertible currency (and later with Forum checks) but not with the East German mark.

Jugendfreund/Jugendfreundin (m/f): Member of Free German Youth.

The *Jugendweihe*: An initiation ceremony that took place at age fourteen and marked young people's transition into adulthood.

The **KGB** (Russian for the **Committee for State Security**): The Soviet Union's domestic and foreign intelligence service from 1954 to 1991. Its functions included international espionage and the surveillance of political dissidents within the Soviet Union.

Kombinat: Companies with similar production profiles, but that managed different stages of production (raw materials, semifinished products, finished products), were organizationally combined in what was known as a *Kombinat*.

Military defense training: Starting in 1978, a required course in ninth and tenth grade in polytechnic secondary schools. In addition to theory taught in the classroom, students also received practical training at army or civil defense camps.

Ministerium für Staatssicherheit (**MfS** or **Stasi**, or the **Ministry for State Security**): As the GDR's domestic and foreign intelligence service, the Stasi monitored all of East German society, from the working class to its highest echelons, and also operated as the investigating authority for "political crimes." Domestically, it primarily served the Socialist Unity Party of Germany, or Sozialistische Einheitspartei Deutschlands (SED), as an instrument of oppression and surveillance of everyday citizens, helping to cement the party's power.

The **NVA** (**Nationale Volksarmee**, or National People's Army): The East German army from 1956 to 1990.

Pioneers: Until joining the FDJ, nearly all children—from first through seventh grade—were **Young Pioneers** in the **Ernst Thälmann Pioneer Organization**. At first glance, this political organization appears similar to other scouting groups with social activities, but in fact it served to shape children according to socialist ideals.

Reformatories (*Jugendwerkhof*): Part of a system of special homes run by Youth Welfare Services in the GDR. Reformatories were used to reeducate youths between the ages of fourteen and eighteen who were considered "at risk" within the context of East German education or who failed to meet state standards for ideal socialist personality traits.

RIAS (Radio in the American Sector): Established following the Second World War by the US military administration. It was located in the West Berlin neighborhood of Schöneberg. It broadcast two radio stations and later added a TV station.

SERO (Sekundär-Rohstofferfassung, literally "secondary raw material collection"): A *Kombinat* in the GDR. It ran recycling drop-off centers and redistributed reusable goods.

Stasi: See *Ministerium für Staatssicherheit*

The **Trabant** (known colloquially as the **Trabbi**): A small personal vehicle produced in fairly high quantities. The car served to motorize the GDR, but the assembly process was very slow, which led to long waiting lists for the vehicle. The Trabbi now enjoys cult status.

Vopo/VoPo (A slang term for **Volkspolizei,** or **People's Police**): East German law enforcement.

Young Pioneers: See *Pioneers*.